UNCHAINED

EMBERS

UNCHAINED

EMBERS

Krystal Zoppa

Unchained Embers

Krystal Zoppa

ISBN paperback: 978-1-7371236-0-6

ISBN E-book: 978-1-7371236-1-3

Cover design by Bianca Bordianu Design

To my husband: Thank you for your support as I scrambled to get this story out of my head and onto paper. I wouldn't be able to do the things I enjoy doing without you cheering me on and encouraging me to dive in and go for it. I love you!

To my kids: You are weirdos but you're my weirdos and I love you. Now go bug your father.

Prologue

Sometimes, a flame can be utterly extinguished. Sometimes, a flame can shrink and waver, but sometimes a flame refuses to go out. It flares up from the faintest ember to illuminate the darkness, to burn in spite of overwhelming odds.
~Karen Hesse

Alira's heels sunk into the rain-softened dirt of the lot as she stepped out of the jeep. She smoothed the wrinkles from her skirt and looked around bewildered. Where the hell were they? She could barely remember her date's name and her cell phone was hovering on the edge of that signal-no-signal line. It looked like they were in the middle of nowhere, but she could see the glow of the city lights over the trees surrounding the hell hole he had driven them to. She knew she should have taken her own car. After apologizing half-heartedly for needing to take a detour before dinner, her date claimed he had a business matter come up that couldn't wait. She had agreed to go along instead of rescheduling. Once again, she realized too late that she may have made a mistake.

He smiled as he came around to the passenger side. He offered his arm, but she declined. He shrugged and started for the entrance without her. Stepping out of his car, she shivered as she looked up at the neon lights following the line of rain gutters. A large brightly lit sign sat on the roof illuminating the row of motorcycles parked along the front of the building.

Riggs Bar and Tavern.

Great. A biker bar. She would stick out like a sore thumb in a place like this wearing her short strappy summer dress with its red roses over white. So much for being able to blend into the background. There was no chance of that happening in a place like this. She really hoped what's his face was done with his business emergency quickly. At that point, all she wanted to do was go home and cuddle on the couch under a blanket with a glass of red wine in her hand, and a rom-com on the TV until she fell asleep on the couch.

With a sigh, Alira followed her date into the bar.

An uncomfortable silence descended upon the bar as the door closed loudly behind her. All eyes shifted to look her way. Some of the men let out low whistles while she saw others lick their lips in a way that left nothing to the imagination as to their thoughts. Their intense attention made her skin crawl. She clutched her purse adjusting the strap crossways over her body as she steeled her spine. With a deep breath and a determined stride, she made her way to the bar to sit on one of the stools. Alira made sure to sit with her back to the wall so she could see anyone that may approach. It was a force of habit.

"What can I get you?" the bartender asked, startling her with his appearance seemingly from thin air.

"Oh, umm, I'll take a soda if you have it," she requested. Her voice was just barely loud enough to be heard. The bartender winked and grabbed a can of coke from the fridge behind the bar.

"Thank you," she said as she popped the top on the can.

Suddenly her date appeared next to her smelling strongly of booze, already swaying on his feet. Alira leaned back against the wall automatically trying to get some distance from him. How could he possibly be drunk already? There was a hint of white powder under his nose and she knew it wasn't just liquor that had quickly gone to his head. They hadn't even been there a full fifteen minutes yet! He leaned closer until she could feel his breath on her skin. She froze and her blood ran cold. When he placed his hand on her knee and started to slide it up to her thigh, she slapped at it, trying to deter him.

"Come on baby! Your brother said you were up for a good time! So, let's have a good time!" he sneered as he tried moving his hand up her thigh once more. She attempted to shove him away this time. Instead of backing up, he somehow shifted closer and pressed his lips against her neck. Alira squealed in angry surprise and shoved at him again. He barely moved.

"Hey buddy, you need to back off. She doesn't seem real interested," the bartender ordered in a low voice. Her date laughed against her neck before pulling away. He didn't go far as he tilted his head and glared at the bartender. His breath smelled strongly of beer and something else she couldn't name but it made her want to gag. She choked down the bile that rose up in her throat.

"I paid for a good time. I'm going to get it," he slurred before turning his attention back to her neck. She cringed and squeezed her eyes closed wishing to be anywhere else but there at that moment. Shoving him away hadn't worked. He was determined and she was not physically strong enough to fend him off. Then, in the blink of an eye, he was suddenly gone.

With a surprised yelp, he was thrown away from her. He landed on the floor with a hard thud several feet away. Standing between her and the heap of creep on the floor was a giant of a man. His broad shoulders blocked most of her view as she tried to process what had just happened. The giant watched the man on the floor for a couple seconds before turning around to face her. His hard expression as he looked her over was terrifying. She shrunk back under his gaze. This entire night was nothing but one giant fiasco and now this monster of a man was staring at her so intently it made her heart race faster than she was sure it ever had before.

"Marcus, tone it down. She's already freaked out and your glare isn't helping!" a dark-haired beauty ordered forcefully as she shoved him away. She faced off against the giant without so much as a sign that she was intimidated by him. Alira watched their exchange with wide eyes until the heap on the floor stirred and struggled to its feet. Her date spun around almost falling over and squinted at her in the dim lighting of the tavern.

"Are you ready to go or what?" he snapped at her as he grabbed a shot off a nearby table, downing it. He swayed a little bit on his feet. Alira started to shake her head, but the giant stepped between her and the loser she'd shown up with once more, effectively blocking his view of her. She almost breathed a sigh of relief. Almost. Her skin crawled as she remembered his hot garbage-scented breath on her neck.

"She won't be going anywhere with you," the giant growled in response. She watched as he flexed his fingers but never made a fist. He stood tall, seemingly relaxed as he stared down her date who stupidly didn't get the message.

"I paid for her company. Her brother promised me it would be an easy lay!" the creep yelled angrily. It was clear he didn't realize that he might be in danger if he provoked the giant before him.

He tried to move around the giant only to have his advance blocked by two more similarly sized men as they moved out of the shadows. The creep stumbled back at their sudden appearance in front of him as though he hadn't noticed them standing off to the side. Heck, she hadn't really noticed them until they moved. Her focus had been on the scene happening before her eyes.

The young dark-haired woman stood just in front of her watching as the giant and the two slightly smaller giants handled the jerk her brother had clearly sent her way as a cruel joke in a long line of cruel jokes. Some things never changed.

Alira narrowed her eyes and slid off her stool. She started to ask the bartender if he could call her a cab when there was a sudden flash out of the corner of her eye and the giants moved as one. With a mixture of shock and amusement, she watched as they grabbed her slime ball date to escort him out in a less than kind way. He squealed like an angry pig as she watched them toss him unceremoniously outside closing the door behind him.

"I'm so sorry you had to deal with that jerk! Are you okay? By the way, I'm Karma!" the young woman introduced herself quickly as she turned to face Alira. She held out her hand with a smile. Alira shook it with a soft smile in return. She was still unsure about the turn of events that had just taken place, but she was grateful someone had stepped in to help. Even if it were in the form of an intimidating male with a scowl that could scare the polar icecaps into melting instantly.

"Alira. And thank you. Do you know of a cab company that will come out this way? I'd really like to go home now. It's been a bad night and I'd love to curl up with a big glass of wine to help me forget it ever happened at all," Alira stated hopefully.

Karma shook her head. Alira's shoulders slumped. How in the hell was she getting home? Maybe they could point her in the right direction. She could walk home. It couldn't be that far, could it?

"No cab companies but I can take you home if you're okay with it!" Karma volunteered happily. Alira nodded. She didn't really have much of a choice if she wanted to get home any time soon. To be completely honest, Alira wasn't thrilled with the prospect of walking either. Karma was being so nice to her and Alira didn't want to impose upon her any more than she already had. She had to admit that she was more than eager to get home and hide behind locked doors for a while.

"I'd appreciate it. If it's not too much trouble," Alira replied with a thankful smile.

"It's no trouble at all. I'd like to make sure you get home safe and that creep leaves you alone," a deep voice said making Alira jump. She clutched her purse tightly to her chest instinctively like a shield. The giant walked over slowly as if he were approaching a scared animal. He towered over them with a stern look on his surprisingly handsome face.

Alira caught herself staring. She hoped nobody noticed as a blush rose up to color her cheeks.

Karma smacked him on the arm.

"Lighten up. Can't you see you're making her nervous? Go bother Austin or Kenny you big ox!" Karma ordered forcefully as she pushed at him to go. He didn't budge. He didn't even adjust his balance. Alira clutched her purse even tighter trying to channel her nervous energy onto something tangible.

Alira must have a kick me sign on her somewhere that everyone else could see. Her brother had made a fool of her again and again. She hated that she never saw it until it was too late. Alira told herself that she really should stop attempting to date. It never went well. It almost always ended up with her in some sort of mess thinking she had finally met a decent guy only to learn it was another goon sent her way. Sometimes she figured it out quickly and other times, like tonight, she'd been too late to see it. At least tonight it hadn't gone too much further. She shuddered to think what would have happened if Karma and her giants hadn't come to her rescue.

Karma patted her arm gently and nodded to the door with an easy smile. Alira took a deep breath and forced herself to loosen her grip on her purse. Together they moved across the bar, heading for the door. Was he still outside? Was he waiting for her?

Please, please be gone!

The door opened and she breathed a sigh of relief. The ugly jeep was gone. There was no sign of her loser date.

"Marcus, you get to fold yourself into the backseat. No complaining," Karma told him happily as she skipped down the steps to the lot toward a little blue Nissan sedan.

"Whatever you say, baby sis," the giant grumbled but followed along behind them like an angry bodyguard.

"He's your brother?" Alira squeaked out in surprise stopping to stare between them. She almost fell over when her heel sank into the soft dirt. Marcus caught her before she could fall on her butt. He held her steady for several seconds before he glanced at her footwear and raised an eyebrow. Marcus lifted her into his arms to carry the rest of the way. Alira threw her arms around his neck in a panic. She clung to him before she could stop herself and accidentally smacked him in the face with her purse as she flailed. She started to apologize only to clamp her mouth shut. Alira stilled in his arms as she met his hard stare with wide scared eyes. Karma stood with the passenger door open, giggling at them.

"It's nice to meet you too," he growled before placing her gently in the front seat. The tickle of his breath against her skin sent sparks through her body. That was a new feeling. No man had ever had that affect on her.

Alira gave Karma her address as Marcus stuffed his large body into the small backseat. Within minutes, they were off.

Chapter 1

"Karma, come on! I just don't understand why you think I need to date anyone! I'm perfectly happy on my own," Alira whined as she reached for her coffee on the counter. She stuffed a few dollars into the tip jar and smiled her thanks at the barista. The chocolatey scent of her mocha coffee teased her nose, enticing her to take a sip. Karma gave her a knowing look as the flavor exploded in her mouth. Alira's eyes lit up. How had she never had a mocha coffee before? This was amazing! She very well may have a new addiction. That and chocolate-covered almonds. Which reminded her that she needed to do some grocery shopping and get some more while she was at the store. Her kitchen was practically bare and she had been eating out way too often the last few weeks.

Together, they headed for the patio winding their way around the other customers who were still waiting for their drinks. Alira scanned their surroundings, watching people as they walked along the sidewalk or carried on conversations with friends at other tables. She couldn't remember a time when she didn't check her surroundings. Growing up in her family had always felt less than safe, especially with her brother and his sketchy behaviors. Her only saving grace in the house had been her older sister, Mara. That was until her parents had sent Mara away at fifteen to attend a boarding school in France. Alira had seen Mara a total of five times since she was nine. Mara was happy so Alira never wanted to bother her with her problems. She didn't need the worry.

Karma waved her hand in Alira's face to get her attention. Alira blinked and refocused with a smile. Her thoughts had drifted again. They were doing that a lot lately.

"Sorry," she offered before taking another sip and sighing in pleasure.

"What are you worried about?" Karma asked. Her voice was laced heavily with concern as she spoke.

Alira had told her all about her family in the year they had known one another since meeting at Riggs Bar and Tavern. At that point, Karma probably knew Alira better than anyone ever had in her life. The Duvall's had welcomed Alira into their family with open arms, no questions asked. It was still a foreign concept to know there were families out there who didn't lie, scheme, and abuse but actually cared about one another. Despite their warm welcome of her, she still felt like an outsider. It was a difficult role to break away from when that was all a person had known growing up. She had never been a welcome addition in her family and had known it from a young age.

"I can't shake this feeling that I'm being watched. It's been a few months since my brother tried to send another shark my way. I guess I'm just feeling a little uneasy, you know, waiting for the other shoe to drop," Alira explained as an involuntary shiver raced down her spine. She jumped when a passing car backfired.

Karma frowned. She didn't know how to help Alira relax. She had seen firsthand the trouble Alira's brother insisted on causing for her. The only thing she could do was be there for her friend.

Alira didn't have photos of her family in her apartment. She just had an old photo of her sister and that was it. No current ones. Alira did have photos that Karma had given her from barbeques with the Duvall's. Photos where she was laughing and having a good time. Photos that looked like she had always been there.

"You know, I can give Austin a call. He can put one of his guys on watch for you. He's been threatening to do it anyway since the last incident," Karma suggested gently.

So far Alira had been heavily resistant to the idea of a personal bodyguard. She didn't feel right accepting the offer. It didn't help that Austin had been adamant that he would not accept her money for the service. Alira was set for several lifetimes from a trust her grandfather had set up for her before he passed away when she was seventeen. Though Austin didn't know she had the money to pay for his assistance. None of the Duvall's knew. None except Karma but she wasn't telling a soul. Alira had been adamant she didn't want anyone looking at her differently. She missed her grandfather. He and Mara had been the only ones who had cared about her growing up. She was who she was because of her grandfather and his support.

Alira shook her head, once more denying the offer to engage Austin's services in providing some elite bodyguard to follow her night and day. She simply couldn't do it. It already felt like she was being followed. Having someone paid to follow her and watch over her; the very thought made her feel helpless. She was not helpless! Not to mention being followed by someone that was paid to do it for her safety worried her. It didn't matter if they knew the risks and accepted them. She didn't want anyone to get hurt because of someone else trying to get to her. It wasn't worth the risk to them. She wasn't someone famous. She wasn't special. She was just Alira Hervowe. A nobody.

"Alira, you're glaring again," Karma told her in an amused tone. Alira spent a lot of time glaring unknowingly when she slipped into her head. Karma had just grown used to it. She had taken to telling Alira she was glaring to pull her back from her self-destructive thoughts or the memories that would send her spiraling if she dwelled too long.

"Marcus? Hey Duvall!"

Marcus lifted his head from the table to glare at his brother. Kenny stood tapping his pencil against the clipboard he was holding and glared back.

"Can I help you, Kenneth?" Marcus asked not bothering to hide his annoyance.

The plans rolled out on the table in front of him were wrong. His new assistant was clearly an idiot who was incapable of reading. He had delivered the wrong plans to the worksite. Again. The building plan laid out before him was for the project across town that had been put on hold due to the company's inability to pay Duvall and Sons Construction on time. His company and the guys didn't work for free. Where the hell were the plans for this project? He should be looking at the plans for a new Trinity Bank branch. Instead, he had a strong desire to yell and fire Kenneth's newest hire for incompetence. This simple mishap delayed them by a full day at least or for however long it would take to locate the correct blueprints. He still had to pay his crew for the hours on site but would also have to send them home. No sense in having them sit on their asses at the site without work to do.

Slamming his hands down on the table, he pushed away and strode past his brother. With a whistle, he got his crew's attention. Marcus explained the situation while trying to keep his own anger under control. The men grumbled and some threw hands up in frustration. This had happened twice in one week. It was two too many. Behind him, he could hear Kenny talking to someone. When Marcus turned around to tell him to shut his trap, his focus zeroed in on the new assistant. He narrowed his eyes and watched as the younger man shifted nervously under Marcus's hard stare. Good. He should be nervous.

"You have delayed two big projects for this company. I can't have that level of incompetence here. A simple mistake can result in a serious injury. I refuse to allow that to happen. These are good, hard-working men with families to take care of and I absolutely will not have them pay for your inability to handle even the most basic of tasks!" Marcus told him angrily. He was struggling to control his anger. He was failing. He needed a break but more importantly, he just needed someone capable. Was that really too much to ask?

He missed Carmen. He had lost track of the number of assistants he had gone through in the last four years and judging by the grimace on his brother's face, so had he.

"You're fired," Marcus said coolly. He felt anything but calm.

Without another word, Marcus turned on his heel and walked over to the trailer used as the foreman's office. He heard Kenny mutter something just before he slammed the door behind him hard enough to rattle the windows. Once inside, Marcus paced back and forth in the small space before finally settling in the chair behind the desk and leaning back. He stared at the ceiling while taking deep breaths in an attempt to calm his anger. Anger at so many things; at so many people. He closed his eyes only for his peace to be interrupted by the trailer door opening and Kenny stepping heavily inside. Kenny pulled the door closed firmly behind him. The windows didn't rattle this time.

"You left these on the table outside," Kenny said as he smoothly dropped the roll on the desk in front of Marcus. Marcus pinched the bridge of his nose between his thumb and forefinger. It was better to just keep his mouth shut at that moment. Maybe if he managed that, his brother wouldn't scold him for firing another useless assistant.

"Karma, I have so much work to get done and all I want to do is take a nap. I think I'm going to need more coffee," Alira whined as she stared up at her apartment building from the passenger seat of Karma's little sedan.

Alira had little desire to leave the vehicle and she had even less desire to climb the stairs to the building. Thank goodness for the elevators inside. Living on the fifth floor and having to climb all those stairs would have been enough to convince her that it would be completely acceptable to just curl up in Karma's backseat and take a nap there instead. Alas, her bed was calling to her.

Work could be done later. After she had a chance to sleep. The stress was getting to her which probably wasn't helping with the feeling of being watched. For all she knew, she was just being paranoid due to exhaustion. She felt wiped out since she had started this planning project for the annual charity gala the mayor's office hosted. There were three weeks to go before the event. She could afford a nap before diving back in for final preparations. With a wave goodbye to Karma, Alira hopped out of the car and practically ran up the stairs into the building.

The elevator ride up to her apartment was uneventful as she sipped at her coffee while the floors ticked by with a ding. A yawn escaped her as the doors slid open on the fifth floor and she stumbled out into the hallway. Alira tripped at the threshold and watched in horror as her coffee flew out of her hand. Glancing around to make sure nobody was in the hall to see her fumble, Alira breathed a sigh of relief. The last thing she needed was her elderly neighbor, Mrs. Cooper, fussing over her. The older woman was incredibly kind but Alira didn't have the mental stamina to deal with her today. Mrs. Cooper could rival a five-year-old with endless questions and conversation. If there was an award for talking someone's ears off, Mrs. Cooper would be the reigning champion. Alira had become a professional at dodging her, usually claiming she forgot something in her car or just remembered she had an appointment. There had been instances where she had heard her speaking to someone as the elevator doors opened and Alira had quickly hit the button for another floor to avoid her. She wasn't proud of that fact, but it was better than being stuck in the hallway for an hour with a persistent chatterbox when one was in a hurry or just wanted to go to bed.

"Great," she grumbled as she leaned down to pick up the now empty paper cup and lid. At least the hallway would smell good for a little while. Too bad though. She had really been looking forward to finishing that coffee. She could always go back to the coffee shop later. With that in mind, Alira fumbled with her keys to unlock the door. After several muttered curses, she was finally inside her apartment. Dumping her purse and keys on the counter, Alira made sure to lock the door behind her. She tossed the cup into the trashcan, kicked off her shoes, and headed to bed. Her plush pillowtop mattress was calling to her, beckoning her to snuggle into its softness and drift away to sweet sleep.

Screw changing clothes. She was too tired to care. Not that it mattered anyway. Her fitted jeans and sapphire blue sweater were comfortable so sleeping in them was no hardship. Not when she was as exhausted as she was. After plugging her phone into the charger, she flopped down on the bed face first and closed her eyes. Just a quick nap and she would be good to go.

"Marcus, you can't keep burning through assistants. This is ridiculous. He made a simple mistake that anyone could have made. You didn't need to fire him over it," Kenneth explained harshly.

There it was. That scolding he had hoped in vain to avoid. Marcus's mood darkened further. Kenny didn't get it. He never understood that simple mistakes elsewhere were big mistakes in their business. He didn't see the numbers when projects were delayed over mistakes that could easily have been avoided. It cost them money. A lot of money. Not that they were hurting but delays were costly, and it infuriated him when things didn't run smoothly. Marcus had always prided himself on efficiency and finishing projects ahead of schedule. So had his father when he had started the company. It had contributed to their success in an incredibly competitive field.

Of course, now their father was retired and had handed the business over to him and his brothers despite the fact the only ones truly interested in managing it were Kenneth and himself. Austin had signed over his share in the company and started the Duvall Protection Group which provided personal security to anyone who needed it. He had completely washed his hands of construction and branched out on his own. His other brothers, the twins, Adam and Aiden, managed the crews on other projects contracted to Duvall and Sons Construction. Their assistants weren't idiots so why did he have such bad luck with his own assistants?

"Kenny, do you even look at the numbers anymore? Do you see how expensive an incompetent assistant winds up being when they are incapable of doing something as simple as delivering the right plans to the correct worksite? I gave the twerp a chance and even picking up the adjusted plans from the office was too much for him to handle! I can't have people working for me that don't show at least some common sense in verifying they have the right pieces for the task before running out of the main office to screw up my day!" Marcus explained angrily, his voice louder than intended. He ran his fingers through his hair in frustration.

Kenny just shrugged. He didn't have the energy to argue with his brother over this. Besides, as much as he hated to admit it, he had a right to be angry. This latest assistant had been clueless despite best efforts to teach him. Hell, he'd already forgotten the kids' name himself so what was the point in denying that Marcus's anger wasn't justified? He knew nobody would ever compare to Carmen and he knew his brother knew that, but they couldn't keep burning through assistants like a kid burning through Halloween candy when their parents weren't watching. It wouldn't end well if they developed a reputation for not keeping assistants around for very long. Well, a worse reputation for it. As it was, they were going to have to resort to utilizing employment agencies to widen the pool of available options if this kept up. Marcus could be kind of a beast to work for at times.

"I'll find someone," Marcus growled as Kenny turned to leave. One more thing on his growing list of things to get done. He needed a vacation.

"Fine. You do that," Kenny told him with a roll of his eyes. Marcus knew he would believe it when he saw it. He was way too busy with the end of the year paperwork and meeting deadlines. This time of year, he had no time whatsoever to interview for a new assistant so it would have to wait until the new year and things slowed down some. He also wasn't going to ask Kenny for help because he didn't want to put that stress on anyone else even if he wouldn't admit it out loud.

Alira opened her eyes, stretching as she did so. She blinked in the darkness and stared at the window surprised to see the sun had set. As she was reaching for her phone to check the time, her stomach rumbled angrily. She hit a button to light up the screen.

9:30pm.

Great. Too late to go grocery shopping. The store closed in thirty minutes and was twenty minutes away on the other side of town thanks to all the streetlights. Looked like she was grabbing take-out. Again.

With a groan, she rolled out of bed not bothering to fix the mussed covers as she made her way to the bathroom. She had to at least brush out her hair before appearing outside of her apartment. Alira had no desire to look like she had been thrown in front of a high-speed wind fan. The matted look was not a style she was comfortable going with.

After taming the frizz, she vowed to set aside time to deep condition her dark tresses and possibly get a trim done. She was well overdue for some self-care. A massage sounded like heaven too. Yup, she would schedule that first thing in the morning. It would be her reward for a job well done on the gala. Perfect! Something to look forward to after all the work was done!

After checking the locks on the windows and slipping on her shoes, Alira grabbed her keys and purse. Checking the time on her phone once more, she headed out into the hallway for the elevator. She locked the door, double-checking she locked the bolt. It was still strange to how quiet the building became after dark. At first, it had been unnerving but now it was just oddly reassuring that she rarely heard other tenants as she walked through the hallways.

Her car was parked in the garage. It made her wonder if Harold was on duty yet. He was on an odd schedule this week, so she didn't know for sure. Harold was always willing to walk with her to her car. It would give her a chance to ask how his daughter had done on her winter finals. Alira knew Cammie had been worried about her math final for the semester but Alira had graciously stepped in to tutor her. She was positive that Cammie had aced it, but she wanted to ask Harold for confirmation. She smiled as she pressed the button for the first floor and the elevator doors slid closed.

"Good evening, Harold!" Alira called as she entered the security office with a smile. Her smile brightened further as Harold grinned and stood up from his chair in front of the security monitors.

"Miss Hervowe! How are you this evening?" he asked leaning in for a hug. Alira adored him and Cammie. They were both such warm, happy people. It was hard not to like them. Harold had been one of the first people she had met when she moved into the building shortly after her eighteenth birthday. He and Cammie lived in an apartment on the second floor, so he didn't have a commute for work. He was always available in an emergency. Not to mention it was nice having a friend so close by.

"Harold, how many times do I have to tell you to please call me Alira?"

A blush crept to his face as he smiled.

"My apologies. Force of habit," he explained as he took a step back giving her a once over. He always did this. It was one of the ways he checked on her. Cammie had told her he did that to anyone he cared about. It was just how he was. Harold never hesitated to make sure that she was okay. Several times he had reminded her it was going to be chilly and she should have a coat with her. He would also remind her to wear sunscreen during the summer. He was one of the few men that didn't make her nervous even though he was an impressive six foot two. He had a genuinely warm smile that always met his eyes. His salt and peppered hair always looked a little disheveled. His reasoning was because he would just mess it up when he had to wear his hat while patrolling the building. Alira thought it made him more relatable. He wasn't the typical security guard robot while on duty. He was friendly and social while still being serious about his job.

"I was wondering if you would be kind enough to escort me to my car?" Alira asked him. She knew full and well that she never really had to ask but always did anyway as a courtesy.

Alira greatly admired Harold. He had been raising Cammie all on his own since she was a year old. Cammie's mother had just walked out on them both without a word. Alira knew that with Harold's caring nature, it had broken his heart into pieces, but he never allowed much to get him down and he had really stepped up as a dad for Cammie. Alira couldn't think of many men that would take on raising a daughter all on their own.

Alira smiled as she thought of Cammie. Cammie was a good kid with goals to attend Yale and pursue a law degree after high school. Her math grade was making her high school career a bit of a challenge. Alira had no doubts that Cammie would conquer the troublesome math mountain.

Harold walked with her to the garage happily. As they entered the garage, a strong gust of cold air made her shiver and wish she had grabbed her jacket on the way out of her apartment. Her sweater had been fine earlier, but another layer would have been a benefit in the much cooler temperature now. She clenched her jaw to prevent her teeth from chattering.

The lighting in the garage was dim. It always made her feel a little uneasy, especially when she was alone. One never could tell if someone was lurking in the shadows. Alira eyed a darker corner of the garage warily as they reached her car. She used the remote to unlock the door. Harold politely waited until she was seated comfortably in the driver's seat before he closed the door but not before reminding her to wear her seatbelt. She smiled her thanks and pulled the belt across her body. It clicked into place as her other hand went for the button to lock the doors. Harold waited until she had backed out of the space before heading back into the main building. She waved as she pulled away. He waved back with a smile and disappeared inside.

Alira turned right as she exited the garage. Still unsure of what she wanted to eat, she figured she would just drive until she saw something that sounded good. The benefit of where she lived was that it wasn't exactly city-level living, but they weren't a hole-in-the-wall town either. It did still mean she would have to drive the dark stretch of road to the other side of town for dinner though. She could cut right through town, but it would take longer with the stoplights.

For the most part, it was a very relaxed area that not many outsiders really knew about. In fact, Alira had found it purely on accident and fallen in love with the town. Little did she know that it would become her home or that she would become the go-to party planner there and in neighboring towns. Planning events wasn't about the money for her. It was about the fun of it, the joy. The thrill in watching weeks of hard work come together to culminate in an event enjoyed by all in attendance. People came from all over to attend the charity events Cedar Pleasant hosted yearly.

Cedar Pleasant was tucked into the upper part of Nebraska where the state line met with the Iowa and South Dakota state lines. It was easy enough to drive into the more populated areas for shopping and such but what Cedar Pleasant offered was usually enough to keep residents busy. Cedar Pleasant had a total active population of about forty-five hundred residents. The area was primarily a vacation point a couple times a year; usually the summer and fall to early winter. In the summer, people would come in for hiking and camping. For Thanksgiving and Christmas, the town would go all out with holiday events. They always drew a huge crowd with the Thanksgiving Turkey Trot which was a 5k run that went through downtown. The city always held a fundraiser dinner the following evening to raise money for the Cedar Pleasant Children's Cancer Research Center. The center provided cancer treatment for children as well as helped cover expenses for families while undergoing treatment in one of their hospitals. The event always brought in a great deal of money and families never had to worry about a bill for treatment. Christmas was a whole other monster of events with the Christmas Gala being the biggest event on the calendar. The very monster Alira oversaw. All proceeds from events from early October to the Christmas Gala on Christmas Eve went to the cancer center. Alira was more than happy to put in the time to make it a spectacular evening as a result. If her behind-the-scenes planning could help families have a little less stress in their lives, she was thrilled.

As Alira drove along the quiet highway, she turned her radio down. She could hear strange sounds she hadn't heard before. Was that coming from her car? There was a clinking sound immediately followed by a loud pop as the steering wheel jerked hard to the left. It sent her car careening into oncoming traffic and straight toward a semi-truck. Headlights blinded her as she yanked the wheel to the right trying to pull the car back into the correct lane. The car veered off to the right narrowly avoiding the collision as horns blared, only to go racing across the shoulder and speed straight for the thick brush of trees that lined that stretch of road.

Alira slammed her foot down on the brake pedal, eyes growing wider the closer the car got to the trees. Why wasn't the car slowing down? She tried the brake again but there was no response from the vehicle. The resistance that was normally there was nonexistent.

Oh God, this is going to hurt.

Alira closed her eyes seconds before the car came to a violent shuddering stop. She felt the impact as the car hit the trees and the back end bucked up before settling back down roughly. The seatbelt hugged her tightly as her body slammed against its hold while the airbag deployed on impact. Glass shattered around her.

Chapter 2

Karma's phone lit up on the desk as it started vibrating against the wood.

Perfect.

She must have forgotten it when she was in the office earlier picking up some files. Marcus reached for the phone prepared to answer and tell whoever was calling that his sister was not available but froze when he read the screen.

SOS – impact detected.

Shit. Without a second thought, Marcus grabbed his keys out of the top drawer while simultaneously opening the GPS on his cell phone. After quickly plugging in the coordinates shown in the alert, he sent a quick text to his brother, Austin. He knew Austin would be at their parent's house by now for their weekly family dinner which meant Karma would already be there too.

"Karma left her phone on my desk at the main office. SOS alert came on. Heading to coordinates now. Let Karma know it sounds like Alira was in an accident. Will update."

Seconds after hitting send, a message pinged back. Marcus didn't bother opening it as he jogged to his truck, hitting the remote start button as he moved across the parking lot. The engine purred loudly to life. Sliding in behind the wheel, Marcus didn't waste a second throwing the truck in gear and peeling out of the lot following the directions the GPS gave him.

Alira opened her eyes and leaned back against the seat with a groan. Her whole body hurt. There was a trail of something wet and sticky making its way down the side of her face. What was that? Lifting her hand and pressing it to her temple, she pulled her hand away. Great. Just great.

She was bleeding. Judging by the amount of blood on her hand, it was a lot too. She tried to control the panic bubbling up in her chest.

Where was her phone? Looking around the car, squinting in the dark, she spotted the silvery color of her purse with its contents spilling out on the floorboard. Her phone was sitting just underneath it flashing brightly and lighting up the material.

SOS Alert Sent to Karma Duvall.

The message would flash until someone turned off the alert. At least the app program worked. This was definitely not how she had wanted to find out though. In fact, Alira had hoped she would never find out if it worked but she was thankful at the moment that Karma had talked her into downloading it. Alira's thoughts were foggy as she tried to focus on the next steps of what she needed to do but her conversation with Karma kept pushing forward from her memory.

"Alira, this app is great and may come in handy in the future," Karma said excitedly and showed her the app information on her phone.

"It won't do any good. I don't have anyone that would care or want to be my emergency contact," Alira said shaking her head already. She didn't really have anybody. She couldn't bother her sister with it and with her living happily half a world away, it wouldn't do any good anyway.

"Well, you have me."

"Karma, I'm so glad we're friends but I couldn't ask you to do that," Alira told her as she chewed worriedly on her lip.

"You're not asking me. I'm volunteering. There is a difference. I'm in your corner," Karma told her seriously. Alira couldn't help but smile. Perhaps Karma was right. Alira hadn't really considered that she wasn't completely alone since befriending her.

"Well, if you're okay with it, let's do it. Thank you."

Marcus slowed as the GPS on his phone showed he was close to the coordinates. He flipped a switch on the dash and floodlights on the roof of the truck lit up the area ahead of him forcing the darkness to retreat away from their reach. He scanned the roadside searching for Alira's car. Tire marks going left caught his attention before they veered sharply back to the right side of the road. He traced their path across the shoulder lane and into the grass heading straight for the tree line. He spotted the glint of metal tucked tightly between two massive trees.

⊠

Turning the wheel quickly, he guided the truck to a stop on the shoulder and turned on his hazards. Quickly, Marcus dialed Austin's number as he hopped out of the truck.

"Austin, I'm going to need an ambulance and a tow truck out here. I found her car," Marcus said grimly. He spoke quickly into the phone.

"No, I don't know how bad it is yet. I just pulled up, but it doesn't look good. The car is sandwiched between two trees and it looks like the front end is completely crumpled in. I have to go. Just get them out here now."

Marcus hung up and shoved the phone into his back pocket. He moved quickly as he made his way down the hill toward the trees and Alira's car. The closer he got, the worse it looked. A sinking feeling formed in the pit of his stomach. He was afraid of what he would find.

Please be alive.

As he reached what was left of her vehicle, he could hear the sirens of emergency vehicles screaming in the distance. Austin worked fast. He had to give his brother credit for that.

"Is someone there?" Alira's panicked voice called from inside the car. Marcus released the breath he had been holding. She was awake. That was a good sign. He didn't know what he would have done if she was unconscious or worse.

"Alira!"

"Marcus?" she called back shakily. She sounded confused. Quieter than normal too. Scared.

He looked around for an easy access point to get to her, but the car was tucked so tightly between the trees that he wouldn't have been able to squeeze between them and the car. He also didn't see a break in either direction that might provide an accessible option. The only choice appeared to be to go up and over the car.

"Hang on Alira. I'm going to have to climb over. There's an ambulance on the way," Marcus called out to her. She didn't respond.

Worry crashed into him like a hurricane making landfall. Quickly he jumped onto the trunk and crawled carefully over the roof toward the front of the car. The whole front end of the vehicle was a crumpled mess of tangled metal wrapped around a tree that still stood firmly rooted and unmoving in place. The windshield was gone. Jagged pieces of glass stuck up here and there but for the most part, there was nothing left. The driver-side mirror hung precariously by a wire for the defroster system. As Marcus carefully dropped to the ground beside her window, he noted the broken glass scattered around crunching under his feet. He realized the driver-side window had also shattered in the impact, probably from the side mirror slamming into it as her car went between the trees that were now holding it solidly in place. They were unwavering in their hold on the vehicle.

Alira couldn't comprehend what was happening. Why was Marcus there? How was he there? It was her imagination playing tricks on her. She had hit her head pretty hard on the steering wheel. Why hadn't her airbags deployed? He had come to her rescue once before in the bar. Flowers. She still needed to finalize the centerpiece arrangements. The collision alert went to Karma's phone. Why was she in her car? Right, dinner.

Her head hurt something fierce! The roof creaked and buckled overhead startling her. Why would someone climb over her car? They could just walk up to the side as any normal person should! Alira groaned as she pressed her hand to her head again and held it there.

Focus Alira! Focus!

The drumming in her head seemed to be growing louder. She couldn't seem to straighten out her thoughts. They were a jumbled mess in her mind. It was like someone had dropped a file sending papers scattering every which way and they were all out of order now. The pages of the book had been ripped out and stuffed back in the wrong place. Alira tried so hard to focus on that moment but as soon as it was within reach, it danced away.

"Alira? Sweetheart, can you talk to me? Tell me what hurts?" a voice asked next to her startling her. She jumped against the seatbelt and yelped in pain.

"Everything. Everything hurts," she said through clenched teeth as she leaned her head back against the seat with her eyes closed tightly. She attempted to take several deep calming breaths. It didn't help. It hurt to breathe. Alira could feel the panic welling up inside her threatening to boil over. She was trapped in her car. Marcus was there. He seemed concerned about her. He wasn't concerned about anything. Least of all her. The drumming in her head intensified scattering her thoughts once again.

God, why won't this pounding stop?

Flashing lights shone through the interior of the car as the ambulance pulled up to a quick stop behind Marcus's truck on the road. A firetruck was not far behind them. Marcus watched as they parked the truck crossways to block the road against any traffic. He was sure there was an officer further down the way already detouring anyone that may come their direction. Two-lane highways were always an event when

⁂

21

there was an accident. The whole road would be blocked in both directions until the accident had been cleared. That would make it easier to get Alira out safely.

Alira sat with her eyes closed and the palm of her hand pressed firmly over the still bleeding gash. All she could focus on was the increased pounding in her head. It felt like there was a marching band, complete with cymbals, banging around in her skull. The sirens from the emergency vehicles didn't help. Not even a little bit. She could feel Marcus looking at her but for the first time in the year she had known him, his presence didn't make her nervous. On the contrary, it helped prevent her from having a full-on panic attack right there. Maybe it was the situation. It outweighed the nervousness she usually felt around him. He was still a giant of a man with a larger-than-life presence you couldn't miss if you wanted to and he was so gruff all of the time. She had avoided being alone in a room with him and his brothers but mostly him. The air was always so charged when she was close to him.

Charged like lightning was about to strike. Damn it! Focus Alira!

A massive, deeply ingrained fear of hers - being alone with a man. And now here she was, alone with Marcus. Men scared her. Dates scared her. Dates had always been difficult for her on the rare occasion she even bothered trying to go on one. It didn't help that she had never had a second date with any of the men that she had gone out with. Half of them had some connection to her brother and the other half only wanted to get into her bed. There hadn't been a single one that wanted a genuine connection with her. Since she obviously had the time, if she was being completely honest with herself, she never wanted that second date because she was truly terrified of the other shoe dropping. This was just another drop in the Alira Bucket of Screwed Up Shit.

"She's awake but she's unfocused. Her name is Alira Hervowe."

"Alright, we need to get you out of there before we can get to her," a man's voice spoke out over the car. Alira was startled from her scattered thoughts on dating and Marcus. Who was that?

"No, I'm not moving until the car is out. You won't be able to get to her without moving the car anyway. It's wedged in here pretty good."

Marcus's voice was firm as he spoke to someone behind her. All Alira could see was Marcus's stomach as he leaned on the car. His t-shirt hugged him tightly. Alira had the sudden desire to reach out and trace the faint lines of muscle she could see through the material. She almost followed through on the desire until another voice spoke, giving her pause.

The other voice was muffled and Alira couldn't quite make out what they were saying. She could tell by Marcus's tone that he was not backing down as white lights bobbed around her. She assumed they were flashlights. More muffled voices followed. Marcus snapped out something she couldn't understand either just as a wave of nausea hit her, distracting her from following through on previous thoughts.

Alira was so focused on controlling her breathing and trying to stave off a panic attack that when the car shifted, her attempts to stay calm failed. Her hands flew out and she gripped the steering wheel tightly. The plastic feel of the deflated airbag felt strange under her touch.

So, it had deployed. Why didn't she remember that?

She focused on it. The slight texture of it; how it moved when she flexed her fingers. Even how it smelled. Then, she began to shiver. It was like her body finally caught up with the chill in the air. Or maybe she was in shock. Both explanations seemed plausible, but she didn't know which was true. Everything in her head was moving so fast and so slow all at once as her thoughts were dancing all around her again just out of reach.

"Alira, the firefighters are checking over the car making sure it's safe to move it. They're going to have to pull it out from between the trees before we can get you out of there," Marcus explained as he leaned in to look at her. She barely heard him but nodded.

Alira shut her eyes tightly as she squeezed the steering wheel tighter. She could hear the blood rushing loudly in her ears over the pounding in her head. The trickle of blood from her temple had slowed and she could feel it drying on her skin. Could they stop being so loud? Her head felt like it was going to explode. Each creak of the trees; the firefighters hooking the chains to her car – it was all so stinking loud! She wanted to scream. She didn't realize she was crying until a large warm hand covered hers on the steering wheel and gave a gentle but obvious squeeze. The hand was gone as quickly as it had come but seconds later, a warm heavy material was being placed over her. She could smell the leather and a faint scent of peppermint. Alira opened her eyes to see Marcus's leather jacket draped over her. The warmth of it seeping in and taking away some of the chill she was feeling.

"Alright, they're going to pull the car now."

Alira nodded, acknowledging she had heard him. Her eyes snapped shut once more. She inhaled sharply as the car jerked back roughly. She wanted out. She needed out now. She reached for her seatbelt fumbling with the buckle.

"NO! Stop! Stop the wench!"

The backward movement of the car stopped instantly. Marcus's face appeared in the window; concern clearly etched his features as he reached in to stop her.

"You have to keep the seatbelt on until the paramedics can determine it's safe to take it off," he told her as he waited for her to stop struggling.

Her eyes popped open and moved to meet his. She felt the breath leave her body. His normally hard features had taken on a softer edge as he looked in at her.

"I've got you," he said to her honestly.

Alira began breathing again and nodded. She could do this. When Marcus stood up and motioned for them to continue, his hand stayed on the door frame. Even that simple gesture helped her immensely in regaining some control over her panicked state of mind. Closing her eyes tightly once more until it hurt, she pressed her hands over her ears and tried to block out the noise. She tried to focus on the smell of the leather of Marcus's jacket, the weight of it. Alira didn't know how much more she could take. Could a headache make your head explode or just make you wish that it would?

Austin and Karma arrived at the scene. Austin rolled his SUV to a stop just behind the firetruck as Karma stared in horror from the passenger seat. Alira's car was totaled. There was no doubt about that. It was destined for the junkyard. From what they could see before they even stepped out of the vehicle, it was enough to freeze hearts in fear. The whole front side of the car was an absolute mess. It was clear the car had taken on a tree and lost the fight. Karma watched in surprise as the trees hugging Alira's car shook violently while the vehicle was ripped from their grasp. Austin sat next to her matching her expression. They watched as Alira's car was pulled free of the trees and their brother strode out after it like it was the most normal thing in the world. The trees swayed back and forth angrily.

"He didn't..." Karma said in disbelief.

"It appears he did," Austin answered in response. Marcus had put himself in an incredibly dangerous position. He could have been hurt if anything had happened while the emergency crews extracted the vehicle. They exchanged a knowing look before getting out of the truck. A fireman stopped them from advancing any further.

"That's our brother and my best friend. I'm her emergency contact!" Karma all but yelled as she tensed in preparation to bolt past him. Austin put a hand on her arm and pulled her back. She glared at him before yanking her arm out of his grasp. He shook his head to dissuade her. He knew what she had planned.

"Miss, can you tell me where it hurts? Any loss of feeling anywhere?"

Alira just shook her head. That was the problem. She could feel everything, and it hurt like hell. She groaned as the paramedic checked her over as best as he could without removing her from the vehicle. He had taken Marcus's jacket off of her and handed it over to him. When the paramedic gave a thumbs up to his partner, Alira watched as Marcus stepped back to allow them to bring the backboard over without hindrance from him. Alira cried out when the first paramedic reached in to unclip her seatbelt. He had barely touched her, but it hurt more than words could describe. He guided the belt away from her body as gently as he could, but the movement still caused a great deal of pain. She wondered why he didn't just cut the belt but realized it wouldn't have mattered. It would have hurt regardless and the buckle itself hadn't been jammed so there was no real point in cutting the belt itself. It would have taken twice as long to get her out and she wanted out. She wanted out of there now. She didn't care how much it hurt to move; she would get herself out if they didn't hurry up.

Marcus stood back as far out of the way as he could be while still keeping Alira in his view at all times. He stood clenching his teeth together. He needed to know what could have happened that would have caused her to careen off the road and unable to stop before her car slammed into the trees. She was lucky to be alive, but they also didn't know if there were any internal injuries yet. Looking at what was left of her car – Marcus was amazed she had even been conscious when he arrived. The speed limit for this stretch of road was marked at forty-five miles per hour. Judging by the look of her car, she had been doing at least that, if not more, when she hit the trees.

"Oh my God! Are you okay? What can I do?" Karma fired off her questions as she met the paramedics at the ambulance. Alira winced. The light shining from the back of the ambulance was blinding and painful. She raised her hand to cover her eyes unable to think of anything else.

"Is anyone riding with her?" one of the paramedics asked as they placed Alira on the stretcher and anchored her down before lifting her into the back of the ambulance. Karma opened her mouth to say she would be riding with Alira, but Marcus had already climbed in the back. Karma stared after him in surprise.

"Her phone and purse are still in the car. Get them. We'll meet you at the hospital," he told her as he tossed her his keys. The look on his face and the tone of his voice told Karma that arguing would do absolutely nothing to change his mind. The result would be the same. Marcus was riding in the ambulance to the hospital with her best friend and nobody was going to stop him. Since time was of the essence, Karma clamped her mouth shut and nodded. The medic climbed in and pulled the doors closed behind him. With blaring sirens and flashing lights, the ambulance took off quickly heading toward Cedar Pleasant Hospital and leaving Karma staring after them in complete shock. What the hell had gotten into her brother? Was he finally coming around?

Austin retrieved Alira's personal items from her mangled car and walked over to Marcus's truck. Karma stalked over to him fumbling with Marcus's keys as the ambulance faded into the distance. Austin tossed Alira's bag through the open passenger window. It landed on the seat with a soft thud.

"I can't drive this beast of a truck. Switch with me," she ordered and tossed Austin the keys. He laughed lightly as he caught them mid-air.

Karma hated driving bigger vehicles. She was actually bad at it. If you wanted someone to clear a road of traffic cones, then Karma driving a truck would get the job done! Her Nissan was the perfect size for her needs and that was what she was comfortable with. Marcus's truck was massive. It was definitely a work truck, but she knew he would kill her if she so much as sneezed on it. If she somehow managed to scratch the paint, he would never let her live it down. Hell hath no fury like a man that loved his truck. Nope, Austin could take that blame if anything happened. For now, they needed to get to the hospital. Karma was fairly certain the rest of her family was either already there waiting or on their way. As soon as Marcus had texted Austin about the SOS Alert, they had been waiting anxiously for any updates. Dinner had been postponed.

The ambulance wailed down the highway speeding toward Cedar Pleasant Hospital. Marcus did his best to stay crammed in the corner seat out of the way as the paramedic finished attaching various cords to Alira. Her hands were fisted at her sides and her eyes clenched tightly closed as the heart rate monitor beeped. The safety straps crossing her body held her securely in place, but the pain was evident with each bump in the road jarring her. Her face showed the tension as tears streamed freely down her cheeks as she tried keeping her whimpers to herself. Marcus watched silently, clenching his jacket in his hands, unsure of how to help or if he even could. This helpless feeling gnawing at him made him angry. Why hadn't he just let Karma ride with her? Karma would know how to help. She always knew what someone needed. The family always joked that it was her superpower. Marcus didn't have any superpowers. He was just a construction company owner that fired one assistant after another. If he had a superpower, it was scaring people and not much else.

The ambulance rolled to a stop under the awning for the emergency department. The rear doors opened almost immediately to show a crew ready to take over. Marcus watched as they expertly rolled the stretcher out while the paramedic listed everything from the scene and what had been assessed on the way. Marcus hopped out after Alira and tried following. A nurse stopped him with a firm hand to his chest.

"There is a waiting room down the hall that way. Someone will come to get you when we know more," she told him sternly as she pointed in the direction he was supposed to go. When his glare failed to intimidate her, he grumbled and tossed his jacket over his shoulder before starting down the hallway in the direction she had indicated.

Just before reaching the waiting area, his phone pinged. Marcus pulled it out of his pocket as he continued walking. It was Karma asking where he was. He typed out a quick reply before stuffing the phone back in his pocket. Looking around the waiting room, thankful it was mostly empty, he made his way to a chair in the corner. Marcus ignored the wide-eyed stares of those he passed. He was used to it. He knew he made people nervous but that wasn't his problem. If they wanted to be intimidated by his presence, he wasn't going to go out of his way to change their view of him.

Marcus sat with his head resting against the wall, with eyes closed, when a rustle of activity sounded from down the hall in the direction he had just come from moments before. He was on his feet moving before he realized what he was doing. Karma rounded the corner quickly. She almost slammed into him followed by his parents and four brothers, who all slid to a stop to avoid smacking into one another.

Somehow, he wasn't as surprised to see the entire family there as he probably should have been. Alira had been welcomed as one of their own quickly; almost the instant Karma had first brought her to dinner. Alira's story had not been a secret thanks to Karma filling them in so they wouldn't overwhelm her. It hadn't stopped his mother from fawning over Alira. If anything, she was very motherly toward her. At times more so than she had been to her own children, which was saying a lot because there had been no lack of nurturing and love while they were growing up.

Their mother was an incredibly wonderful woman always taking in strays who could use a little extra care. Not that Alira was a stray.

Alira laid as still as she could while the MRI machine clicked and boomed around her. She hated confined spaces. One of the many punishments, while she had been growing up, involved being locked in a dark closet for hours on end until someone remembered to let her out. The longest she had been locked away was three days before they came to unlock the door. They kept a bucket and a jug of water inside the closet for her. No food. It had also been used as a torture method by her brother.

An involuntary shiver ran down her spine at the memories. To distract herself, Alira tried to remember the smell of leather from Marcus's jacket. She tried to focus on the warmth of it. Anything to push back the increasing claustrophobic panic threatening to overtake her. She could feel her heart beating in her chest with increasing speed.

"How you doing in there?" the female voice sounded over the speaker.

"My head is killing me and I feel like I am going to be sick," Alira replied over the noise. She felt like things were moving in slow motion. Her head felt heavy and fuzzy even as the drummer inside pounded away on his drum like he was an angry rocker at a concert. Finally, the machine went quiet.

Alira breathed a sigh of relief. She closed her eyes and waited. She was half a second away from begging them for her freedom when a kind nurse appeared and pulled her free from the machine. Alira imagined that it was what a party platter would feel like when it was pulled out of the fridge. That was if party platters had feelings. She giggled to herself as her thoughts ran away with her. A second nurse appeared to help ease her back onto the gurney. Once the safety rails clicked into place, they were off to the next area. She no longer cared where or what the next test would be. All Alira wanted to do was close her eyes and sleep for a week. Getting some pain relief would be nice too. Her adrenaline spike was coming down and all this moving about was not helping. The small amount of morphine the ER doctor had given her through her I.V. line hadn't done much to ease the pain she was in. She really just wanted to sleep and not move until all the aches and pains disappeared.

Karma paced the waiting area anxiously. Was Alira alright? When would they know anything? Where in the hell was the damned doctor? Austin and Kenny had tried in vain to convince her to just sit down and wait patiently but Karma had never been good with being patient. She was worried. She and Austin had waited for the tow truck to show up so they could find out where they would take Alira's car before rushing to the hospital. How long had they been waiting?

"Hervowe?" a voice called. Karma jumped in surprise and realized she had been glaring at the floor as she paced. Behind her, the whole Duvall family stood. All except for Marcus who stayed firmly planted in his seat appearing to be asleep. The doctor's eyes widened as he looked them over. Charlotte, the family's matriarch, stepped forward.

"I'm Charlotte Duvall. Alira is my daughter-in-law," Charlotte explained smoothly. Multiple sets of eyes went wide but nobody dared speak a word over the blatant lie. Mr. Duvall just smiled and nodded like he was in on the joke. Karma stared at her mother suspiciously. Charlotte ignored her. The doctor nodded and glanced at the clipboard he held in his hands. The man was completely oblivious to what had just happened in the waiting room.

"Is her husband here or on his way?" he asked looking around once more trying to determine who to direct patient updates to.

"Oh yes! Marcus, dear…"

Marcus's eyes snapped open.

What the hell?

What the actual hell?

He stared at his mother with narrowed eyes wondering what she was playing at. He had heard her lie smoothly about Alira being her daughter-in-law. He certainly didn't expect it to be him that would get volunteered as her husband though. The expression on her face told him he would need a miracle to save him if he argued. No one went against mom. The woman was downright devious when she wanted to be. So, with no fuss, he lifted himself out of the chair gaining his feet and crossing his arms. With two easy steps forward, Marcus stood next to his mother. She smacked at him to uncross his arms, but he ignored her. Instead, he stared pointedly at the doctor and cocked his head maintaining a neutral expression on his face. He could feel his siblings staring holes into the back of his head. He ignored them too. His mother was up to something. What that something was remained to be seen but she was definitely up to something.

⁂

"The good news," the doctor said and then cleared his throat. "Your wife does not have any internal bleeding. The bad news is she has a concussion. She also had severe bruising from her seatbelt as well as a laceration at her hairline that required closure. Once we got that cleaned up and got a good look at it, we were able to get a couple small stitches in there. She has some bruising on her ribs that will make breathing fairly uncomfortable for a little while. Your wife is going to be pretty sore for some time. We have her on an I.V. drip for now and she's been given morphine for pain. You can see her if you'd like."

Marcus nodded. The Duvall's moved to gather their coats before following the doctor through the maze of hallways to Alira's room. A nurse approached the group and whispered something to the doctor as she eyed the family wearily. Karma nudged Marcus with her elbow. He followed her stare to see a man dressed in a suit standing at the nurse's station with a jacket tucked over his arm.

"That's Alira's brother. I met him once and will never forget that piece of human-shaped garbage," she hissed low so only Marcus would hear.

Marcus stiffened beside her. His mood took a dangerous turn as he strode forward. Karma quickly diverted him by shoving him towards Alira's room. She had that look on her face that their mother would get when the boys were about to find themselves in some serious trouble. Austin and Kenny weren't far behind him in case they needed to step in. Somehow, they knew when to become a barrier.

The rest of the family pulled up the rear as they entered the room. Karma was already bedside patting Alira's hand asking how she was feeling by the time Aiden closed the door behind him. Alira smiled sleepily and stammered out a response. Marcus stood off to the side with his brothers and father while the ladies fussed over Alira. Alira smiled. She slurred as she tried answering their questions and conversing. It was amusing listening to her try to speak but the words were slow to form. Marcus shook his head trying to hide his smile. She was higher than the clouds thanks to the morphine they had given her and it showed.

"Go away!" Alira yelled suddenly, her eyes focused hard on the door. Standing in the doorway was the man they had seen at the nurse's station. None of them had heard the door open.

The man was dressed in a dark double-breasted suit with a sky-blue button-up shirt underneath. His tie matched his suit color. His pocket square matched the color of the shirt. The slacks were perfectly creased while his shoes were so shiny that they could almost double as a mirror.

His brown hair was perfectly styled without a single hair out of place. Cold green eyes peered around the room assessing his new audience.

"Come now sister, you don't mean that. I came as soon as I heard you had had an accident," he said smoothly. There was a hint of malice in his voice. A smile appeared on his face though it never reached his eyes. Cold. Unfeeling. It radiated off of him in waves. This was a man with no heart, no morals, and no regard for others. It was clear he was one to keep an eye on.

"Leave, Grayson. You have no right to be here," Alira ordered with great effort as she fought to control the fear claiming her even through the morphine haze. She had managed to scoot further up in the bed as she tried to get more distance between Grayson and herself. Her words still slurring but it was obvious she was struggling to keep that hidden. She couldn't hide the fear in her eyes no matter how hard she tried. It looked like she was staring at the devil himself. Marcus stepped forward and clasped her hand firmly with his own. She gripped tightly without looking away from her brother. The move wasn't lost on Grayson as his cold assessing eyes shifted from Alira to Marcus, sizing him up.

"I'm Grayson Hervowe. Who might you be?"

Chapter 3

"I'm Alira's husband."

All eyes turned on him, including Alira's. Marcus kept his focus firmly on Grayson even as Alira's grip on his hand tightened. Only when Grayson blinked did Marcus turn his attention to Alira. His expression softened as he looked down at her petite form in the hospital bed. For the first time since he had met her, he saw no nervousness in her eyes as she stared back at him. It caught him off guard, but he hid his surprise. Instead, he smiled and leaned down over her. Her eyes drifted closed as he pressed a light kiss to her forehead while his free hand brushed lightly against her cheek. Marcus was careful not to touch the bruising that had begun to show there. Grayson's eyes narrowed as he watched the scene before him.

"Interesting," he remarked coolly and adjusted his already perfect tie. It was the only sign that he was getting annoyed with the situation. Alira jumped as if she had somehow forgotten her brother was in the room. Marcus watched the fear return to her eyes instantly, even as she winced in pain from the movement despite the morphine in her system. He gave a gentle reassuring squeeze to her hand before releasing it. When he straightened to his full height, the atmosphere in the room changed drastically. It became dangerous. Karma shifted her position subtly to shield Alira the best she could with her own small body. Austin moved with her while the rest of the brothers seemed to spread out around the room. They stood tall and steady with arms crossed.

The defensive move wasn't lost on Grayson. Charlotte and William stayed where they were but didn't appear the least bit surprised about the change in the room either. Marcus casually walked around the bed, effectively placing himself between Grayson and Alira. His eyes never left Grayson as he moved. Austin stepped to the side to allow his brother space.

Alira couldn't believe what was happening. She had just been in an accident. Her car was totaled but she hadn't seen just how bad it was in the dark. Her brother was there in her hospital room along with the entire Duvall family. Marcus Duvall had just announced that he was her husband and not a single person had said a word to contradict that statement. None of this made any sense!

This was a hallucination. It had to be. Her car had hit that tree pretty hard after all. It was a logical explanation. She could also feel the morphine dulling her senses but even that couldn't slow the fear that welled up from deep within her upon seeing her brother. It worried her wondering how he even knew she was there. She knew Karma would never have called him. She may have called Mara but even Mara wouldn't have called Grayson or their parents for that matter. Neither of them wanted anything to do with them so how did Grayson know exactly where to find her? A wave of nausea washed over her, but she choked it down.

"I think it's time you respect your sister's wishes and leave," William Duvall spoke as he stepped forward. His tone was cool but the threat was clear. Alira never would have expected to hear anything like it from William. The brothers, definitely, but their father? Nope. He was a mild-mannered kind soul. It was clear where the Duvall brothers got their impressive height from. William Duvall was a man who easily towered over most people.

Grayson's eye twitched. It was a sign that he was losing control of his usually calm façade. Alira flinched. That twitch had always been a defining clue that bad things were coming her way. She felt the panic creep closer to the surface. Felt it well up inside her until it exploded outward before she could get control of it. Alira fumbled with her I.V., trying desperately to take it out quickly. The damn medical tape was really sticky! She needed to get out of there.

Karma felt the bed shake suddenly. She turned just in time to see Alira struggling with her I.V. line. She reached out to stop her, but Marcus was already moving. How he had known what Alira was doing with his back turned to her, Karma could only guess but somehow, he just knew.

Marcus grabbed Alira's hands quickly as gently as he could without hurting her further. She had managed to get the I.V. out partway before he stopped her. The needle was held loosely in place by the tape, but it was clear the line would need to be redone. Marcus's grip was firm on her hands. He shifted to sit on the bed more easily so he could pull her into his arms while keeping his body between her and Grayson. Alira didn't have the strength to push him away. Instead, she leaned against him accepting the strength he offered. He suppressed a groan at his body's natural response to her and focused on trying to calm her instead. Even still, his heart rate sped up slightly as he wrapped his arms around her. Whoa. Questions for another time.

"I'll see you soon little sister," Grayson told her with a cruel chuckle as he turned to leave. Alira stiffened in Marcus's arms. He hugged her a little tighter. Marcus didn't want to hurt her but knew she needed it. Alira buried her face in her hands as she leaned into his chest. A deafening silence filled the room as they listened to Grayson's footsteps fade away down the hall. Charlotte whispered something to William that sent him quickly out of the room. Austin reached around Karma to press the call button for the nurse's station. William returned a second later with a nod to his wife.

Several minutes passed before a nurse appeared. Adam quietly explained that a new line needed to be placed though he didn't go into detail as to why or how it had come to need replacing. The nurse nodded and left to get the necessary supplies. If she had questions, she certainly didn't show it.

William cleared his throat loudly and tilted his head toward the hall. The Duvall family slowly filed out of the room, though, a bit unwillingly. Marcus eased Alira away and encouraged her to lay back on the bed. She refused. Instead, she sat up with difficulty and pulled her knees to her chest. Marcus felt a strong urge to pull her back into his arms and hold her until she felt safe again. He resisted. He had played the role his mother had thrown him into. It was done now. Besides, he had building plans that still needed to be drawn up back at the office. They would have already been close to finished if he hadn't rushed out to find his baby sister's best friend on the side of the damned highway. He wouldn't even be here now if Karma hadn't left her phone on his desk!

Agitated, Marcus paced the hallway while his family stood huddled together talking in hushed tones. He tuned them out. The more he thought about what he knew of Alira's family, especially her brother, the angrier he became. Grayson was a bastard. Alira's reaction to seeing him standing in the doorway to the room had just about broken his heart. She had been so relaxed, surrounded by the Duvall's, until Grayson had shown up. Alira's calm had vanished in the blink of an eye. Her fear had come on so fast and so strongly that even the morphine high couldn't keep her down. He had no doubt that she would have run if she had been able to. Alira damn near ripping her I.V. out was proof of that. He had never seen anyone with such an intense fear of another human being in his life. How he had kept his cool was beyond him. No, that was wrong.

He had stayed calm because Alira needed him to. She didn't need someone else to fear and if he had allowed his rage to overcome him, Marcus knew he would have seen that same fear in her eyes when she looked at him.

"Earth to Marcus," Adam said waving his hands at his brother. Marcus glared but Adam was unbothered. The man rarely smiled. Something other than the glare would have concerned him.

Adam was one of the twins. He stood just a few inches shorter than Marcus at an even six feet tall. Adam and Aiden shared the same light brown hair and dark eyes. They took after their mother with their lighter complexions. All of the Duvall men got their height from their father. Adam and Aiden were the shortest of the boys with Marcus being the tallest. They would be mirror images of one another except that Adam had a scar going through his left eyebrow near the outer edge from when Aiden snapped him with a tree branch when they were ten. It made it almost impossible for them to play their switch-up game with their teachers after that. It hadn't stopped them from trying anyway.

"Adam don't be rude. Marcus, we were just talking about who should stay with Alira tonight. Do you have any suggestions?" Charlotte asked him pointedly. Her question caught him off guard. Why would she think he would care as long as someone was with her that could handle Grayson if he came back?

"I don't know, mom. Maybe you should be talking to Austin about this. He's the one that handles protection details for celebrities and the like," Marcus snapped unable to hide his annoyance. His mother raised an eyebrow in response. Marcus looked at his father questioningly. William backed up with his hands raised and shook his head with a smile. Great. His father would be no help in this. Whatever his mother was up to, he already didn't like it and it was clear that he would get no assistance from the rest of his family. Even as he tried to gauge the situation, his siblings spoke in hushed tones amongst themselves. Karma had a sly smile on her face as she spoke to Kenny. Marcus tried to ignore it.

Marcus watched as his mother seemed to size him up before she nodded and turned to say something to Austin that he couldn't hear. Feeling his annoyance growing, Marcus ran a hand roughly through his hair. He had work to do. Building plans didn't draw themselves and checks didn't write themselves either. Aiden stepped up next to him offering his silent support. Of the six, Aiden was the quiet one. He had a habit of hanging back and observing things. Aiden saw things others ignored or never noticed. Bit of an old soul, as their grandmother used to say. He also wasn't going to give away what their mother had up her sleeve, so Marcus didn't bother asking.

"You know mom is up to something, right?" Aiden asked just loud enough that only Marcus would hear him. Marcus nodded with a scowl. He had started to get the feeling that he knew exactly what she was about, but it seemed they were all in on whatever her end goal was. All except for him. Bunch of traitors.

As he stood with crossed arms waiting for them to fill him in on what the hell was going on, the door reopened behind him and the nurse exited the room. She saw his family huddled together and smiled as if it was the sweetest thing she had ever seen. Marcus almost laughed. Aiden jabbed him with his elbow and gave an easy shove toward Alira's room. Sitting with Alira was far more preferable than standing around the hallway waiting for a decision to be made. He was sure it would be Austin staying with her. He had the training to handle any issues with ease anyway.

As Marcus entered the room, he moved cautiously so as not to startle Alira. He hated knowing that she might be afraid of him. Much to his surprise, she appeared to be sleeping. Her curled position facing the door seemed to be a defensive move. Given what had happened just fifteen minutes prior, he really couldn't blame her. Hell, Austin was always checking dark corners and watching people a little harder than most people would. Marcus just figured that was because of his job but thinking back on it, Austin had always been more cautiously aware of his surroundings. Similar behaviors he had observed in Alira. The difference was that Austin had no real reason to have those habits from an early age.

He felt the anger rise up as he made the connection between Alira's guarded behavior and what Karma had told them of her past. His hands curled into fists. With great effort, he resisted the urge to punch the wall. Marcus really needed to get back to the gym. It helped greatly with having an outlet for his anger and right now, he was furious. How anyone could hurt someone, especially someone as sweet and kind as Alira, was beyond him. Her family should have protected her. Instead, they had abused her in ways he could only guess at. She deserved better. She deserved a real family.

"Why are you so angry all of the time?"

The quiet question pulled him away from the dangerous path his thoughts were taking. Marcus took a breath and forced his hands to relax, fully extending his fingers and wiggling them. Alira watched him through half-closed eyes like she was unable to open them any more than that. He started to step forward but seemed to think better of it and stopped. Instead, he sidestepped to sit in the chair near the door.

"How do you feel?" he asked quietly needing to change the subject. She stared at the ceiling before looking back at him. The faintest glimpse of a smile pulled at the corners of her mouth before her tongue swept out to wet her lips. She looked thoughtful for several minutes before truly focusing back on him.

"That's a loaded question, isn't it?"

He smiled at her response. It was a smile that met his eyes. Her breath caught in her throat. Whoa. He was incredibly handsome when he smiled. Alira imagined that if she were to open up the dictionary to the definition of handsome, she was almost positive his picture would be there showing the example. She could only remember a handful of times where she had seen him really smile. He didn't tend to do it often. It was heart-stopping each time she saw it though. Alira could remember asking once why Marcus rarely smiled and Karma told her that he used to smile all the time. She never elaborated on why he didn't anymore. She had simply gone quiet and then quickly changed the subject. Alira never asked for details. It didn't feel right to ask for them. She had dropped it and forgotten about it until she opened her eyes to see him standing in the doorway watching her silently. Alira could only guess why that memory popped into her head at that moment.

Karma stood quietly outside the door listening to the exchange between her brother and her friend. Whatever their mother had up her sleeve appeared to already be in process. Karma barely caught the smile that tugged at the corner of Marcus's mouth when Alira had replied to his question with a question of her own. Her big brother didn't smile too much anymore. She could count on one hand the number of times she could remember him smiling since Carmen died and each one had been in Alira's presence. The surprise hit her like a ton of bricks. Dear God, her mother was right. The woman was a genius! Karma would never admit that out loud. It would go to Charlotte's head having one of her children admit that she was right. Nope, it simply couldn't be done but wow. How had she not seen it herself?

Alira smiled sleepily as Karma came into focus before fading out again. The morphine was doing funny things to her head. Her thoughts felt like they were swimming and things were moving in slow motion again. The relief it brought from the pain circulating through her body made her feel light and floaty. Karma spoke to Marcus before coming over to her to say goodbye. She said something that Alira didn't quite catch, but it was okay. Whatever it was, it was completely fine. Alira closed her eyes and allowed herself to finally drift off to sleep. She was safe for now. She wouldn't be alone.

Marcus followed his sister out into the hall, closing the door softly behind him. He had this feeling he might raise his voice a little bit and he didn't want to disturb Alira now that she was finally dozing off. Karma stood before him with an incredibly stupid smile plastered across her face. He knew that smile. It was the same smile every time she had a secret to tell that always turned out to be news he didn't want to hear.

"Out with it," Marcus ordered. Karma's smiled grew bigger. He didn't think it was possible but there it was. He was not amused. Not even a little bit.

"Well, if you really want to know, everyone has work tomorrow. Austin specifically has a really big client schedule tomorrow and the rest of the week, so he wasn't able to stay anyway. Mom didn't think you would mind staying with Alira tonight. Austin said he would try to put a detail on her tomorrow during the day, but nights would be difficult on such short notice. Kenny said to tell you not to worry and he would handle the site this week. Also, that he was heading home to draw up the plans you were supposed to be doing earlier," she explained practically chirping each word like a happy little bird at a feeder.

Marcus couldn't hide the mixture of emotions that played out across his face. Karma laughed. She was pretty pleased with herself skirting around the fact that everyone had just left without so much as a word to him. His baby sister was getting entirely too much joy from this. What were they thinking? Alira was like a skittish cat around him. He couldn't stay here with her! Karma should be the one staying. At least with Karma there, Alira would be able to truly rest. The doctor had wanted to keep Alira overnight and reassess in the morning how she was doing before they discharged her.

"I work a double tomorrow. I won't be off until after nine tomorrow night. You'll be fine!" she said happily and patted his arm in mock sympathy.

Before Marcus could respond, Karma turned and practically skipped away down the hall. Muttering to himself about the lack of loyalty, Marcus turned to go back into Alira's room since he had been assigned the role of babysitter. He pushed the door open quietly and stepped inside.

The door clicked closed softly behind him. Suddenly nervous, he just stood awkwardly next to the visitor's chair he had been sitting in earlier. Before his family had rudely thrown him under the bus. He wasn't sure what to do now. Obviously, now that he was thinking about it,

Karma staying wouldn't have helped anything because she was just as ill-prepared to handle keeping Alira safe as Alira presently was. No, it was best that one of the brothers stayed. Clearly, he was not getting out of this. After all, he had been assigned the role of her husband in this act. He sighed. *Here goes nothing.*

Alira opened her eyes, blinking quickly as she did. The dim lighting of the room was still painfully bright. She ached all over. Her head no longer felt like it was stuffed full of cotton and the marching band had dwindled down considerably to just a couple drummers instead of the entire band. Slowly, she glanced around the room. When her eyes landed on the sleeping form in the recliner tucked away in the corner, her heart skipped several beats. She hadn't expected anyone to stay with her, least of all him. She guessed he must have drawn the short straw because there was no way he would have volunteered to stay on his own.

Every gathering she had been to since meeting the Duvall's, every single one, Marcus had kept his distance. Not that she had been very open to being friends. The man was downright intimidating. From the full tribal tattoo that she knew covered his right arm from shoulder to wrist to the regular shadow of a beard that traced his strong jaw. He was impressively tall. Strong too. She doubted the man had an ounce of fat anywhere on him based on how nicely muscled he was. Not that she had been looking. He wasn't body builder bulky like some other men. Marcus was sleek like a muscular jungle cat. Every movement he made was fluid and graceful. His expressive brown eyes always reminded her of warm melted chocolate. They fluctuated from dark to light brown based on his mood.

Her fingers itched to trace the scruff along his jaw.

"Oh – hey. You doing okay?" Marcus asked sleepily as his eyes landed on her. He shook his head and rubbed his hands over his face in a scrubbing motion. His usually perfect hair was in disarray from the pillow he had been using while he slept.

Alira stiffened. She had been caught watching him sleep.

How embarrassing!

She quickly relaxed as she remembered how dimly lit the room was. There was no way he could have seen that she was – well that she had been checking him out. He couldn't know that she was remembering the feel of his arms wrapped around her earlier and how much she had liked it despite the situation. How truly safe she had felt for probably the first time in her life. There was also no way he could know that she wanted him to hold her again. No possible way. But what if, somehow, he did?

"I'm a little thirsty. I went from my head feeling like it was stuffed with cotton to my mouth feeling like it is instead," Alira answered softly as she met his eyes from across the room.

He felt a smile tug at his mouth and instead cleared his throat. He stood slowly, allowing himself a full extension stretch after sleeping in the chair. When he leaned back with his arms up over his head, his shirt rode up exposing his lower stomach offering her a glimpse of the washboard abs she knew he had. Alira's mouth dropped open before she could stop it. Then her eyes drifted to his hips. She traced his V-lines down to the waistband of his jeans and felt her heart start to beat faster. She caught sight of the happy trail going down...

The heart rate monitor picked up the change and beeped an alert. She stared in horror at the machine as her cheeks burned red with embarrassment. Marcus finished his stretch and looked at her with concern until he noticed her flushed face. It took all of the willpower he possessed to stifle his laugh. He had actually caught her staring and boy, was she flustered!

"I'll, uh, get you some water. Would you like ice?" he asked trying to hide his amusement. Her blush deepened at his question. Alira grabbed the pillow that had been propped under her hand with the I.V. and buried her face in it; mortified.

Marcus waited to see if she would come out of hiding. She peeked up over the top hoping he had left the room so she could try to smother her embarrassment without an audience but there he stood; watching her with a softly raised eyebrow and a lopsided grin. She groaned and hid behind the pillow again. His laughter caught her off guard. What surprised her more was the feel of his breath ruffling her hair just before he kissed the top of her head. He was gone with the door already closing behind him when she lifted her head. She never even heard him move. The man moved so silently it always surprised her given the sheer size of him.

Marcus left the room before either of them could question what had just happened. He wouldn't have been able to explain it no matter how much he tried. Something had just come over him making him move before he realized what he was doing. Oddly enough he didn't regret doing it. It felt right in the moment. It was like there was an invisible string pulling him closer to her.

"Did you need something?"

The nurse sat behind the desk not bothering to look up from her book as she spoke. Marcus had to admit that he would never have noticed her there if she hadn't said something. She held a pen in her free hand fidgeting with it. He narrowed his eyes. This was the person in charge of patient care? Really?

"Yes, the patient in room 210 is thirsty and they never brought the pitcher of water in that they promised. Also is your cafeteria still open? We're starving up here," he said allowing his annoyance to bleed heavily into his tone.

The nurse huffed and set her book down. Her annoyed mood changed the instant she looked up at him. It wasn't so much looking at him as it was undressing him with her eyes. It made his skin crawl. He didn't understand the attention. He never had. Now if it had been Austin standing here instead, he would have soaked it up. Austin would likely go home with her number and a date planned. His brother was the ladies' man extraordinaire. Marcus was not even on that level. He avoided that plane of existence like the plague. Being a man whore was not his idea of a good time. He had more important things to worry about.

"The cafeteria is closed but the kitchen is still running until midnight," she informed him and ran her tongue over her lips as she handed him a menu. "I can order whatever you'd like. They'll bring it right up."

Marcus ignored her attempts at flirting with him and reviewed the menu of available items. After telling her what he wanted to order, she phoned it down, eyeing him the whole time she spoke into the receiver. He looked around the hallway to avoid her stare. Once she hung up, he thanked her coolly and went back to Alira's room.

"Scoot over!" he told her urgently as he closed the door behind him. He strode over to the bed and motioned for her to move over. She stared in wide-eyed confusion.

"Just do it! I'll explain in a minute!"

Alira did as he ordered. She grimaced as a small jolt of pain shot through her ribcage. He climbed in next to her quickly, careful not to jostle her further. She stared at him curiously. Strange that she wasn't afraid of being this close to him. Normally she would be remembering where all the exits were but not now. What had changed? She realized that it didn't really matter. It wasn't until that moment, so close to him, that she noticed how chilly the room was. The warmth radiating from him called to her; enticing her to lean into him and soak it all up. An involuntary shiver ran through her.

As if reading her thoughts, his arm slid gently around her shoulders and hovered waiting for permission. Accepting his unspoken invitation, Alira snuggled up against his side with a sigh as she felt instantly warmer while his arm wrapped gently around her.

He smelled good. Really good. Good Lord, what was wrong with her?

Alira lay curled up against Marcus with her head resting on his shoulder perfectly when he reached for her hand automatically and placed it on his chest over his heart. She closed her eyes enjoying his touch and the heat he gave off. She didn't even open her eyes when the door opened and someone entered with a squeaky wheeled cart. Marcus shifted slightly getting more comfortable but his arm around her stayed firm holding her against him.

"If you need *anything* else, I'm just right outside at the desk," a female voice said. The hint in her words was undeniable. Marcus shook his head. Alira's fingers curled against his chest as though she was afraid that he would leave and take advantage of the nurse's blatant offer.

"I think my *wife* and I will be fine with our late dinner but thank you," Marcus told her firmly with a gentle squeeze to Alira's hand. Alira took his hint and bit her tongue over being called his wife. Again. Instead, she opened her eyes and gazed up at his face. He was smiling down at her with soft eyes. An exasperated sigh sounded from across the room before footsteps retreated to the hallway. The door closed softly behind them.

"You, sir, owe me an explanation but I'm staying right here because you're warm and I am freezing," Alira told him as she rested her head back on his shoulder and tapped her fingers on his chest. He liked the sassy tone he heard in her voice.

Marcus's arm tightened around her for a quick hug and he laughed. She could stay there as long as she wanted as long as she was comfortable. He was actually enjoying this. Alira felt good in his arms. She moved her head just enough to look up at him and waited for the story she knew he had to tell.

"I went out to ask about the water they never brought in and order food because I was starving. Figured you might be hungry too. As soon as that nurse looked at me, I got the distinct feeling that she wanted to pounce on me. She laid it on thick. I may have panicked a little," he explained sheepishly. Alira burst out laughing.

"Ouch!" she said between giggles. Marcus leaned to the side and raised an eyebrow in question. "So, I rescued you! My how the tables have turned!"

Marcus chuckled.

"Yeah, I guess you did," he said with a smile before reaching to pull the TV table closer so they could eat. He helped her sit up straighter so she could eat more easily. She only winced twice.

He turned the TV on with the remote and surfed through the available channels a couple times until finding a movie they could agree on. Together they settled into a comfortable silence as they ate their late dinner and laughed during funny moments in the movie.

Alira nibbled at bits of her meal knowing she needed to eat something but not feeling as hungry as she usually did. She didn't know if her lack of appetite was due to the stress over the last several hours starting with her accident or if it was because of how close she was to Marcus. It didn't really matter. Her appetite would come back soon enough. Maybe. Being hungry is what had landed her in the hospital for the night. Well, that and her lack of available time to do any grocery shopping.

She put the last bit of garlic bread back on the tray and pushed it away. She was shivering again. Alira was reasonably sure it was due to the I.V. pumping cool solution into her body but the room was still cold too. Gathering up some of the blanket, she pulled it up under her chin despite her body's protest at the movement. Her ribs throbbed painfully but she tried to ignore it by focusing on the show that was now playing. She had no idea what it was called or what it was about. She didn't even really know what was happening. The cops in the show were yelling at the suspect. Why there was a suspect at all was beyond her.

"Still cold?" Marcus asked. Alira nodded. He held out his arm for her once more in silent invitation. She shook her head suddenly feeling unsure as she pulled the blanket a little tighter against her body. Marcus made a sound that resembled a growl. This was the Marcus she was familiar with. The sweet cuddly Marcus confused her. He gripped her shoulder and pulled her gently back against him. She stiffened.

"You're cold. I'm warm. Relax," he told her gruffly. She could feel the heat from his body seeping into her own already.

He felt the tension slowly fade from her as she relaxed against him. Alira shifted trying to get comfortable but stilled instantly at Marcus's sharp intake of breath. She slowly lifted her hand away from the growing bulge in his jeans while blushing furiously.

"I'm so sorry! So sorry! I didn't mean..."

"It's fine. It was an accident," he said cutting her off even as his head fell back with his eyes closed. He took several deep breaths. Alira stared at him with wide eyes. She had just... her hand slipped. She didn't know how but it had. Oh no!

Slowly his eyes opened and shifted in her direction. She jerked back as if she had been struck. Her whole body tensed angrily. Tears welled up in her eyes as she attempted to breathe through the pain. This was horrible. She felt like she was more bruise than a person. When deep breaths failed because they hurt, she started taking short sharp breaths. That only made things worse. One tear slid down her cheek. Then another and another. She closed her eyes tightly trying to stop them. Marcus's arms were around her instantly pulling her against him.

"I've got you. Just breathe," he told her calmly as he used the pad of his thumb to wipe a tear from her cheek. His soothing tone broke through to her as his other hand rubbed lightly along her back. She settled back against his side and automatically rested her hand over his chest. Marcus moved his hand to rest on hers, entwining their fingers together. She focused on his steadying heartbeat under her hand. Marcus tucked the blanket around her as she cuddled closer. He knew she had fallen asleep when her shivering stopped and her breathing became slow; steady.

Chapter 4

Karma stood with her mother staring in surprise at the sight before them. They had arrived at the hospital at eight sharp for visiting hours. Alira was expected to be discharged at some point later that day and Charlotte had insisted on being there for her. Karma had happily agreed to go along but nothing would have prepared her for seeing her best friend snuggled up to her big brother sleeping soundly. Or that her brother would be just as relaxed as was evident by his snoring. His arm was firmly wrapped around Alira while her arm was draped across his waist. They both looked so content. It was both weird and adorable rolled into one.

Marcus heard whispering. He opened his eyes to find out who was in the room with them. Near the door stood his mother and sister with huge smiles on their faces. He looked to Alira quickly and back at them as he motioned for them to keep quiet with a finger to his lips. He knew Alira would be embarrassed to be seen in such a position. She didn't need the worry. Charlotte pursed her lips tightly though the excitement shone brightly in her eyes while Karma danced happily. He glared and pointed at the door. Their faces fell but they respected his silent order. Karma still somehow managed to dance her way out to the hallway. The door closed behind them.

Alira shifted but didn't wake up. Her sweet, contented sigh pulled at him. He took the opportunity to look at her more closely without worry that she would shy away. Judging by how she acted, she had no idea just how beautiful she was. Marcus touched her face with his fingertips. His fingers buzzed with electricity as he traced her jaw lightly. He scowled.

"Damnit," he growled at the ceiling.

Alira stirred. Her eyelids fluttered open. She stretched slowly before lifting her head to meet his eyes. What she saw made her rear back so fast she slammed into the rail. His expression was dark. It was the same dangerous look he had worn at the bar the night they met. It had terrified her then just as it did now. She felt the fear bubbling up inside her like sparks erupting into a wildfire. Her breath came faster and faster until she was gasping for it; hyperventilating as she tried to fight her body's deeply ingrained reaction to the fear that was trying to take over all sense she had. She clutched the blanket tightly to her, averting her gaze away from him.

Marcus stared at Alira genuinely shocked as to what he was witnessing. Her sudden flight response surprised the hell out of him. He was afraid to move for fear it would make things worse, but he had to do something. Slowly he reached over and touched her arm. She flinched away. Hard. He knew the sudden movement had to have hurt though she didn't make a single sound to show it. He pressed forward.

"Alira?"

She froze at the sound of her name before tucking her face into her blanket-wrapped hands. Marcus's mind raced on how he could fix this. He did the only thing he could think to do — he pulled her into his arms as he had done last night and simply held her. She fought against him for mere seconds, but it was enough for her to knock the TV tray over in her panic. The sound of the table crashing to the floor seemed to break her out of her panic attack. It also had the unfortunate result of drawing a crowd as three nurses, two doctors, and his mother rushed into the room looking for the emergency. He waved them back.

"Too many cooks in the kitchen, people," he said loudly directing his attention back on calming Alira since he was the screw-up that set her down the path to hopping on the panic bus. He didn't hear them slowly funnel out of the room. Although, he could feel his mother's stare drilling holes into his back. Alira stayed stiff in his arms for several long, painful minutes. He didn't know what else to do except wait until she was ready to let him back in. He had no idea how much time passed before she relaxed and curled into his side again. Marcus didn't care. He would hold her until the end of time if that was what she needed him to do.

"What did you do?" Karma yelled at him. Marcus rolled his eyes as his sister stormed into the room hollering. Alira was still wrapped tightly in his arms shaking. She had refused his requests to look at him; to talk to him. So, he waited. Then Karma had come barreling into the room like an angry lioness protecting a cub.

"Nothing. He did nothing. This was all me," Alira's muffled voice sounded from the blanket cocoon resting in his embrace. She moved. Marcus loosened his hold and Alira unwound herself from the blanket though she was careful to make sure his arms stayed around her.

Karma stood glaring at Marcus regardless. This was somehow entirely his fault and she was going to give him a piece of her mind as soon as she got the chance. She had gone along with their mother's plan last night because Alira was supposed to be safe with her brother. She had even been all smiles seeing them cuddled together that morning. That went out the window when she heard the nurses talking. Karma knew Marcus would never allow anything to happen to Alira if it was within his power to prevent it. What she hadn't counted on was that he would be the one causing harm! Karma was furious. Her stupid moose of a brother was a clueless oaf.

Marcus had disappeared as soon as the nurse brought Alira's discharge paperwork in. He said something about needing to get to the office. No goodbye. Nothing. He just muttered about plans at the office and disappeared through the door. Alira felt cold. She knew it was her fault that things were even more awkward between them than they had been before. Mrs. Duvall had insisted she and Karma drive Alira home despite her protests and insistence that she take a cab instead. Mrs. Duvall wouldn't hear of it. Alira blushed over Charlotte's mothering. It was something she had never had much of growing up, so this was something new for her; someone doing something for her without expecting anything in return.

Charlotte also insisted that she do some grocery shopping after seeing the meager offerings of Alira's kitchen. The older woman had come into the living room with a glass of water and point-blank asked when the last time Alira had been to the store was. Alira had stared like a deer caught in the headlights of an oncoming car. She didn't have an answer for her because she honestly couldn't remember the last time she had done a real grocery run. It had been a while. She had been eating out most days. It was easier to just grab something when she had been so busy with plans for the gala. Mrs. Duvall clicked her tongue in disapproval as Karma appeared with a blanket and pillows from Alira's bedroom.

"You don't have to do this. I can manage on my own. I can order pizza. I'll be fine. It'll last me a couple days and I have my laptop. Working remotely for a few days won't be a problem," Alira told them as she tried to stifle a yawn. Karma set the bedding down on the couch allowing Alira to make the decision if she wanted it or not. Alira smiled. Her best friend in the entire world always allowed her to make her own decisions even with the smallest things. Karma handed her the laptop from the table.

"I know you won't rest until you can get some work done. Mom and I will be back with some groceries. You know she isn't going to leave that one alone," Karma said grinning. Alira nodded as she opened her laptop and watched the screen come to life. Charlotte jiggled her keys at Karma. Karma

rolled her eyes but followed her out making sure to grab Alira's keys so she could lock the door behind them.

Alira breathed a sigh of relief when they were gone. So much had happened in the last twenty-four hours that she needed to process. She didn't know where to start. That would be a problem for another day. The quiet was nice. There was work that needed to get done if she wanted to take the weekend off and be lazy hanging around at home watching movies.

"I absolutely will not! I have work to do and can't be babysitting a grown woman who is safely ensconced at home!"

Mrs. Duvall marched forward until she was toe to toe glaring up at her eldest. Marcus scowled back. His mother was naturally unbothered by his refusal to budge. She was determined and he knew it was only a matter of time before he gave in. He would not give her the satisfaction so quickly. It was a rare opportunity to ruffle her feathers, so to speak, and he was going to enjoy it.

So, there he stood, firmly rooted in place as his fierce little mother tried to intimidate him into immediate compliance. He knew she was capable. She had given him life after all and knew everything there was to know about him. Well, almost everything anyway. There were just some things sons didn't share with their mothers. Charlotte would use whatever tactics she deemed necessary, but when it really came down to it, she knew her boys never wanted to disappoint her and would do whatever she asked of them in the end. He had already mentally agreed to do what his mother was asking of him, but she didn't need to know that. She could sweat for a bit. It would be good for her. With that thought, his scowl gave way to a grin. Charlotte eyed him suspiciously. Marcus took a step back to lean against his desk.

"Alright mother, why? I only ask because this has the distinct feel of you trying to play matchmaker," Marcus explained as he rested his hands on the edge of the desk and leaned forward. She frowned. He waited patiently for her to answer. The longer he waited, the more amused he became. He could practically see the wheels turning in her head as she considered her response.

"Your sister and I saw you this morning. You both looked pretty cozy. Why wouldn't I play matchmaker when I see the opportunity to do so? You were more relaxed than I have seen you in far too long."

Marcus didn't hide his surprise over her honesty. Truth be told, he had expected some classic dance-around maneuver meant to send him on the path she thought best but instead, she had laid it all out in a straight line for him. This was the first time his mother had not tried to make him think something had been his idea. As much as he didn't want to disappoint her, he knew that he would.

Charlotte watched the emotions that played out across her son's face. She knew why. She couldn't feel bad. She had watched her happy son fade to become a man who rarely smiled. He dove headfirst into running the construction company and didn't leave much room for anything else. It was well past time he did more for himself! She reached out and touched her hand to his cheek.

"Mom, you know why I can't," he whispered sadly.

"Sweetheart, it's been four years. You can. You need to move on. Carmen wouldn't want you to spend the rest of your life wallowing and holding yourself back," she replied softly. He shrugged. Marcus knew she was right, but he wasn't ready. He didn't think he ever would be. He hated that his mom was right though. He and Carmen had had endless conversations on hypothetical events. Marcus just never expected one of them to become reality. His shoulders slumped.

"I will take the groceries over and check in on Alira. I will even keep an eye on her until Austin can schedule someone full-time next week," he spoke firmly. Charlotte smiled. Perfect. She had already spoken with Austin and he was on board. Marcus simply didn't need to know that. In fact, Austin had been the one to suggest that Marcus take the groceries to Alira's apartment. If her eldest was going to be blind and stubborn, well, it was up to his family to point him in the right direction. Charlotte had no problem being the front runner for the push he so desperately needed. In the process, maybe Alira would be forced to admit her own feelings. They had all seen them looking at the other when they thought nobody else would see. That sweet young woman had been through hell and was understandably uncomfortable around men. She had also been welcomed into the family with open arms. Of course, it had taken several months of Karma dragging her to family dinners and weekend barbeques before Alira could even be near one of her boys without looking like prey cornered by a predator. She was still understandably nervous, but she was able to interact without shaking like a leaf in the breeze.

⏎

Marcus took a deep breath as he stood to his full height. He was done at the office for the day. They were heading into a long weekend and the office would be closed for the duration anyway. The crews needed the long break after all the work they had been putting in. He needed to shower and grab a change of clothes from his place, but then he would be ready to head to Alira's for the grocery drop-off after that. Meanwhile, his mother stood near the door impatiently.

"Alright. I'm going," Marcus huffed as he reached for his leather jacket and keys.

Alira closed the laptop and placed it on the side table. It was time for a break when her eyes started crossing while she was staring at the screen trying to read the same email and getting nowhere. This event was important. There was still so much left to do before the big day. She was exhausted; mentally and physically. Hungry too if the rumbling of her stomach was anything to go by. There should still be some chips in the pantry.

With a groan, Alira struggled painfully to her feet. Who knew a walking bruise could hurt so much? She still hadn't looked at herself in the mirror. She was afraid of what she would see when she finally did. The thought of a nice hot bath crossed her mind. It was enticing. Having decided to pass on the search for chips in favor of a soothing bath, Alira made her way down the hall to the bathroom to start running the water. After starting the water, she dug around under the sink for the lavender-scented bubble bath Mrs. Duvall had gotten her as a birthday gift months ago. She had told Alira that it was for a time that she needed to relax the most. This seemed like the perfect time to use it.

Alira was slow to remove her clothes. She gasped when she caught sight of herself in the mirror. There was a thick dark bruise running along where her seatbelt had crossed over her chest. A bruise had formed around the stitches at her hairline that extended down to her jaw. There was some minor bruising around her right eye. She assumed it was from when her hand had been blown into her face by the force of the airbag as it deployed on impact. It was all still a fuzzy memory, but it was there nonetheless. Her entire body looked like a roadmap of discomfort from the accident. No wonder she hurt so much. Walking bruise was a fairly accurate description of her present state of being.

Turning the water off, Alira carefully slid one foot into the tub followed by the other and eased herself down. The heat was already working its magic on her aches. The scent of lavender filled the bathroom soothing her senses. Closing her eyes, she allowed herself to sink in and soak in the warmth. She needed this. This was for her. At that moment, she vowed to take more baths because it felt fabulous. It helped that her tub was massive so she could easily sink down so just her head was above the water. She leaned her head back against the edge of the tub and enjoyed the soothing warmth as the scent of lavender wafted through the air enveloping her in a cloud of relaxation. It was almost heavenly.

Marcus pulled into the parking garage and parked in guest parking. He was still angry because somehow his mother had managed to sneak the groceries into his truck before ever even talking to him at the office. That woman was downright devious when she wanted to be. She also bought enough to feed a small army. He didn't even know if Alira had room in her kitchen for all of this having never been to her apartment. The closest he had gotten was when he and Karma had driven her home from Riggs Bar and Tavern last year. Karma had walked her up because Marcus had gotten the impression that he was most unwelcome. After the evening she had that night, he hadn't wanted to make things worse.

"Sir, which unit?"

"I'm sorry, what?" Marcus asked turning to see who was speaking. A man with salt and peppered hair wearing a security guard's uniform stood at the desk waiting for an answer.

"Oh umm, I'm heading up to the fifth floor. Apartment…" Marcus was drawing a blank. He didn't remember the unit number. He knew his mother had told him. Hadn't she? He pulled his phone out of his pocket to check his text messages. Nope. No apartment number. Just the building address. Great.

"What's the tenant's name?" the guard asked in an amused tone. This clearly happened a lot judging by the look on his face. Marcus, however, was not amused. He was annoyed. He had been wrangled into this and being questioned by the rent-a-cop only increased the annoyance he felt at the situation.

"Hervowe."

The guard's eyes narrowed.

"Is Miss Hervowe expecting you?" he asked suspiciously. Marcus tried to make sense of the guard's change in attitude at the mention of Alira's name. Marcus narrowed his eyes at the man.

"She should be. I have her groceries," Marcus growled and lifted the bags he was holding like the guard hadn't noticed them. The guard nodded.

"Well how about I take you up then? It's time for me to do another round anyway," the guard spoke firmly almost as if he was daring Marcus to argue with him. Marcus had to admit that he admired the man's commitment to his job. Marcus nodded in agreement only because he had grocery items that needed to get put in the fridge and he didn't have the time to play twenty questions with the man. He made a mental note to ask Alira about the security guard.

The elevator ride up to the fifth floor was quiet. Neither spoke. Marcus tried to ignore him while the guard seemed to be watching him from the corner of his eye for the entire ride up. The tension in the small space increased with each floor until the doors slid open. Marcus indicated the guard should step out first. He followed him out. The guard walked down the hallway until he stopped at Alira's apartment and knocked. Marcus rolled his eyes and set down the bags he was carrying. He fumbled in his pocket for the keys his mother had given him. After slipping the key into the lock, he pushed the door open. He could feel the guard's eyes boring into his back as he pocketed the keys before heading inside with the groceries.

"Alira?" Marcus called out. Splashing followed by a loud thud sounded from inside the apartment. He and the guard exchanged a worried look.

"Marcus?" a confused Alira called back.

"Yeah, it's me! Mom couldn't make it with the groceries. Are you okay?" he responded tentatively as another thud sounded from down the hallway. No response. Worry washed over him like a wave. He quickly set the bags on the small dining table just inside the door and strode down the hallway.

"I'm coming in," he called when he reached the partially open door.

A panicked squeal sounded followed by frantic splashing and another thud as water could be heard sloshing to the floor. He pushed the door open not sure what to expect. Soft light lit the bathroom. There was a robe folded over on the counter. He peered around the room. His gaze stopped on the tub where a blushing Alira sat with her knees pulled tightly to her chest staring at him with wide surprised eyes.

Marcus snatched the towel off the hook and held it out for her as he turned away. It was a mistake. A big mistake. He could see Alira's reflection in the mirror. She stretched out carefully as she moved to stand. Marcus felt the blood rushing to his groin making his jeans uncomfortably tight. Thankfully Alira didn't seem to notice. Marcus stared at the ceiling while she contemplated the best way to get out of the tub without exposing herself.

"Hey, is everything alright in there?"

Alira squeaked. She slipped in her hurry to reach for the towel, sloshing water out of the tub once more and onto the floor.

"Just a minute," she called out before slumping down. Marcus peeked over the towel at her.

"Marcus, can you help me?" she asked quietly. Her voice was so low he almost didn't hear her. Before she could ask again, thinking maybe he hadn't heard her, he had scooped her up soaking his shirt in the process. Alira flung her arms around his neck afraid she may slip out of his hold on her. It was a mistake they realized simultaneously. His breath tickled her bare breasts sending delicious shivers down her spine. He groaned and lifted his eyes to the ceiling.

"Marcus?"

"Yeah?" he responded, his voice taking on a rougher tone than normal. He was trying not to acknowledge the fact that she was naked in his arms or how nice she smelled. Or even how much he wanted to bury himself between her thighs until she was shaking from the sheer pleasure of it.

"You can put me down now," she whispered against his neck as her fingers unconsciously played with his hair. Her breath on his skin sent sparks coursing through him straight down to his groin. He groaned again. Taking a deep breath, Marcus eased her gently down to stand on her own. He turned his back and closed his eyes only once he was certain she had her balance.

She quickly wrapped the towel around herself and touched his arm. When he turned back to her, the look on his face stole her breath and sent her heart galloping wildly.

Marcus took her chin in his hand tilting her head back. Bright blue eyes met his. His thumb traced circles along her jaw as his other hand moved to her waist. Alira's hands slid up his chest and wound around his neck where her fingers tangled in his hair. He leaned down, a breath away from pressing his lips to hers. He stopped. Sensing his hesitation, Alira lifted up on her tiptoes meeting him. Their kiss was feather-light at first; just a whisper of touch between them. Her fingers tightened in his hair, nails teasing his scalp. Marcus pulled her roughly against him and deepened the kiss. She whimpered against his mouth as her nails raked down his back. The intensity built with each second.

⁇

"Alira? Everything okay in there?"

Marcus broke away first. She leaned against him for a second before stepping back. When she looked up at him, his usual hard expression had replaced the soft and gentle one she had seen seconds before. Without a word, he turned away from her and walked out of the bathroom. Marcus had kissed her. And she had kissed him back. Alira took several deep breaths before unwrapping the towel and drying herself off.

"Alira will be out in a few minutes. She slipped in the tub and after her accident, she's sore," she heard Marcus say. Shaking her head, she quickly pulled on her pajama shorts and an old T-shirt. Well, as quickly as she could anyway. Her body protested each and every movement leaving her gasping for breath as she waited for the intense shooting pain to subside enough that she could move again.

Marcus headed into the kitchen to begin putting the groceries away. He pulled things out of bags shaking his head. His mother sure knew how to stock a kitchen. He quickly put the cold items into the fridge and tried not to think about what had happened in the bathroom with Alira. He hadn't been thinking clearly. It had been so long since he had kissed anyone, had wanted to kiss anyone and she had been there. It was convenient. It was out of his system now and it wouldn't happen again. It *couldn't* happen again.

"Harold! How are you?" Alira asked happily as she moved slowly down the hallway. Marcus looked up when he heard her voice. He couldn't help it. She smiled a brilliant smile that lit up the room. He watched as she hugged the security guard without any sign of worry or stress. He couldn't help but smile as he watched how relaxed she was as she conversed with the guard. Harold. She had said his name when she greeted him. Marcus shook his head and continued putting the groceries away. He had just put the bread into the breadbox on the counter when he heard his name. He froze mid-task and listened. He knew he shouldn't eavesdrop, but he couldn't help himself.

"So, who's the delivery boy?" Harold asked jokingly as he inclined his head toward the kitchen.

"That's Marcus. He's, umm, he's Karma's older brother. He's only here to help out after my accident. He drew the short stick on babysitting me. He wouldn't be anywhere near this building otherwise. He doesn't like me much," Alira explained with a shrug. A cabinet slammed in the kitchen startling her. Harold looked between the kitchen and Alira with an amused smile on his face.

"I really don't think that's the case," Harold said with a wink. Alira shook her head. No, Marcus couldn't stand her. He saw her as his sister's friend and nothing more. Despite the fact her lips still tingled from his kiss, she knew it hadn't meant anything to him. Marcus had no interest in her. She was fairly certain he had no interest in anyone. He was a workaholic who didn't have time for anything else. Marcus was always gruff and closed off, even at his family dinners. He was there because of family obligations otherwise she was positive he would just live at his office and nobody would see him.

So why had he kissed her?

"How did Cammie do on her finals?"

"She wanted to tell you herself, so you didn't hear it from me, but she aced them!" Harold bragged. Judging by how proud he sounded, Marcus assumed they were speaking of his daughter. Only a parent would be that excited and proud of their kid.

"I know nothing!" Alira promised while she pretended to zip her lips closed. She conversed some more with Harold, joking and laughing as old friends would.

Marcus had finished putting the groceries away and moved toward the living room. He stood leaning against the wall watching how light and carefree Alira was with Harold. He had to admit that he was surprised to see her like that. Her melodic voice washed over him as he listened to their continued exchange. For some reason, he couldn't take his eyes off of her. He didn't think he had seen her so comfortable. Even when she was talking to Karma. He and his brothers were usually around then too. Maybe she was the same way with Karma that she was with Harold at that moment when it was just the two of them. That thought made his heart squeeze painfully in his chest. She was afraid of him and his brothers and it was why she was always tense at dinners. Damnit! She didn't need to be afraid of them. Didn't she know that by now?

"Well, I had better go do my job," Harold said seriously as he edged closer to the door. "You take good care of our girl here. She's something special."

With a nod, Harold hugged Alira and left, closing the door behind him. Alira moved to the door and leaned against it as she turned the bolt to lock it. She rested her forehead against the door for several long minutes. She didn't feel good. She really should have sat down while she talked to Harold, but she hadn't wanted to appear impolite. Her body hurt and she was running low on energy. The exertion it took to even lean against the door the way she was – it was a lot, and she was fading fast. With a deep breath, she turned toward the couch as she willed her energy to hold out just long enough for her to get there. Marcus stood offering his hand. She didn't meet his eyes as she tried to wave him off. Then her knees buckled as her strength gave out. Marcus was there in an instant to catch her.

"I've got you," he told her softly as he lifted her into his arms and carried her to the couch. She tried not to lean into him. Alira definitely also tried not to notice his sculpted chest beneath the fitted tee he wore or how his muscular arms held her with ease. She also tried to ignore how he smelled. The scent of fresh-cut grass with a hint of peppermint teased at her nose. There was something else there that she couldn't pinpoint but it was intoxicating!

Marcus set her down and reached for the blanket draped over the back of the couch. Carefully, he tucked it around her before moving to the opposite side to sit. They settled into an uncomfortable silence as neither knew really what to say. Alira reached for the remote but put it back down on the table before reaching for it again. She needed something to disrupt the awkwardness between them. The TV clicked on to reveal a couple kissing at the end of a movie. Alira changed the channel quickly. Her stomach growled angrily. She remembered she had planned to order a pizza after her bath. That was until Marcus had shown up and thrown the entire plan into chaos with his concern and kisses. She shivered as heat pooled low in her belly at the thought of kissing him again.

Alira tossed the blanket off. It took some effort to get off the couch and stand but she did it. Giving a wide berth around Marcus, she made her way to the kitchen. She was curious what groceries he had brought over. Her cupboards were full. She made a mental note to thank Charlotte for restocking her kitchen. This was really too much, but she was grateful for it. Tears sprang to her eyes though she brushed them away. She still had no idea how to process that anyone would care about her. It was a very foreign feeling, but the Duvall's were doing their best to teach her that not all families were horrible. It was heartwarming.

"Do you want me to make you something?" Marcus asked from the living room. Alira stood leaning against the counter while she stared at the cupboards. She wasn't so sure she trusted his cooking skills. Did he even know how to cook? Not a chance she was willing to take. She still had pain meds to take and she didn't need food poisoning on top of everything.

"I was just going to order pizza," she called back. Alira scanned the counter for her phone but didn't see it. It had to be there somewhere. Marcus appeared as if he had heard her thoughts and handed her the phone. She snatched it out of his hand and tried to wave him off again. Instead of leaving, he leaned against the wall with his arms crossed over his chest, watching her with an expression she didn't understand. She wanted to tell herself that he made her uncomfortable, but it would be a lie. More than anything, she wanted to feel his arms around her once more.

"You can leave, Marcus. I don't need a babysitter," she informed him roughly and tried to push past him. He shifted to block her exit instead. Before she could ask him to move, his mouth was crashing down on hers. She melted against him instantly. His tongue teased at her lower lip. Her lips parted and she opened up to him. His tongue slipped in to meet hers, tasting and teasing. She moaned into his mouth while gripping his shirt tightly. His strong arms wrapped around her as he deepened the kiss. It was a searing kiss that made her mind go blank and curled her toes. Just as quickly as it had started, it was over. Alira was left clinging to him, breathless and shaking in his arms, positive that she would fall to the floor if he let her go. He pressed a kiss to the top of her head as he held her. She was sure he could feel her trembling.

"I'll order the pizza. Extra pepperoni?"

She nodded against his chest. All at once, there were so many thoughts in her head, and she was afraid to move. Something about being in his arms felt right. It was like she was meant to be there. That feeling terrified her.

Chapter 5

Alira just about jumped out of her skin when there was a knock at the door. She had been so focused on the movie they were watching that she had forgotten they had ordered pizza. The movie was your typical holiday movie where the girl goes home for Christmas, meets the boy, they fall in love but then there is some misunderstanding that pushes them apart until the end where it all comes together for the happily ever after. It was the same story time and again with different actors, but it always got to her. She envied those characters. The endings always made her a little emotional.

She started to get up to answer the door, but Marcus shook his head at her. Fine. She didn't like answering the door anyway even if there was a magic human on the other side bringing her food. If he wanted to get up, who was she to say no? Besides, she would get to watch him walk away. Her eyes widened at the direction of her thoughts. Good lord, two kisses with the man and her thoughts were running away with her.

"You alright there?" Marcus asked noticing her blush. She shook her head.

Yup, completely fine if you count wanting to kiss you again as 'alright'.

"Just hungry," she admitted quickly trying to change the subject. The look on his face said he wasn't buying it. Marcus raised an eyebrow at her but didn't press. He grabbed his wallet off the counter and went to answer the door. She watched him walk away, biting her lip as her imagination started to run wild. Alira shook her head trying to shake the thoughts away while he paid the delivery driver.

Alira tried to focus on the new movie that started playing but got distracted by the bulge of his biceps as he set the pizza down on the coffee table. The way his shirt hugged his torso in all the right places made her bite her lip again. How the hell was he so fucking hot? She had tried not to notice that she had an attraction to him because she wasn't looking for anything, with anyone, ever. He was her best friend's brother which usually meant he would be off-limits anyway, but the man was total eye candy. Anyone with eyes would agree. It didn't matter that most men as a whole scared the crap out of her. She still knew an attractive man when she saw one. She would have to be blind not to notice Marcus.

Stop! Stop thinking right now! God, even your thoughts are rambling! Just eat the damn pizza and watch the movie!

"You must really like pizza," Marcus said with a knowing smile as he pulled paper plates, crushed red peppers, and parmesan cheese out of the bag the pizza place sent with all deliveries. Alira watched as he put a slice of pizza on a plate with some crushed pepper and parmesan before handing it over to her. She stared at the plate in her hands not bothering to hide her surprise.

"Is that alright? Did I get it wrong?" he asked concerned as he started to take the plate back. She shook her head and refused to give it back twisting away from him.

"No. No, I'm just... you know how I like my pizza?" she stammered out. She stared down at the pizza slice with its extra pepperoni and sprinkled red peppers and parmesan cheese. Marcus shrugged like it wasn't a big deal. Alira didn't quite know what to make of it or of him. One minute he was this closed-off gruff male and the next he was melting her into a puddle with his kiss or fixing her pizza exactly how she liked it.

Marcus grabbed a couple slices out of the box and sprinkled the crushed pepper and parmesan on them. He moved to sit on the floor in front of her. It was an intentional move on his part. If he sat on the couch with her, he knew he would forget all about eating and kiss her again. He couldn't do that. The way she melted in his arms made him want more but he couldn't do that to her. She deserved everything and he had nothing to give her.

Alira sat watching their fourth movie of the evening. Marcus watched as her head bobbed sleepily before she would jerk back and cringe. She had insisted she didn't need any of the pain medication she had been prescribed but it was obvious that she was hurting. Every breath she took was slow and agonizing. She was clearly uncomfortable in the position she was sitting in, but she refused to move for fear it would cause more pain.

Marcus couldn't sit there any longer watching her suffer. He used the couch as leverage to stand. He took their empty plates into the kitchen, depositing them in the trash bin, before returning to claim the pizza box. He located storage containers for the remaining slices so that he didn't need to play a puzzle game trying to get the box into her full fridge.

Marcus cleaned up their leftovers with ease while Alira leaned back on the couch. She was exhausted but determined to watch as many movies as she could since she had the weekend to hang around without needing to work. It was great knowing she was caught up despite her car accident. Alira had been adamant about not taking any pain medication because she didn't really hurt that badly. She had lied. She had lied hard. Her body protested even the slightest movement and it felt like she was continually holding back tears. Marcus must have noticed because he appeared before her with a glass of water and a Percocet.

"Take it. You've been sitting stiffly and trying not to cry for over an hour now. There is no reason to torment yourself. Rest and heal so you can resume life," he ordered shoving them at her. She frowned.

Marcus didn't move. She was going to take that pill and drink the water even if he had to sit on her until she did. When Alira held out her hand, he knew he had won. He watched triumphantly as she swallowed the pill and drank the contents of the glass.

Alira grumbled as she handed the empty glass back to him but deep down, she was grateful. The truth was, she'd been avoiding getting the pain pill herself because she dreaded how uncomfortable the task would be. She also had no interest in asking Marcus to help her. She was still embarrassed about the tub incident even if it had led to something completely unexpected and surprisingly welcome.

When Marcus returned from the kitchen, he sat down next to her sliding his arm along the back of the couch as he got comfortable. She watched him thoughtfully as he stared at the TV.

He could feel her eyes on him. He tried to appear relaxed as he stared at the television not really watching what was playing. He was too aware of her. Too aware of how close she was to him. Marcus tucked his fingers between the cushions and flexed them into the material hoping it would distract him. It didn't. It somehow made things worse.

"Marcus, why did you kiss me earlier?"

The question was out before she could stop it. She had been thinking it but had no intention of giving it a voice. Too late now. She hid under her blanket, horrified that her mouth had betrayed her. Alira could feel the heat rise in her cheeks which made it all that much worse. Why couldn't her head and mouth just work together for once in her life! Alira cringed when she felt the cushion beside her shift. Slowly the blanket shielding her slid away revealing Marcus's intense brown eyes staring right into her soul.

"Alira…"

His rich deep voice washed over her sending warmth coursing through her. When he reached up to touch her cheek, she leaned into his hand automatically. His touch made her forget all about her embarrassment. The pad of his thumb stroked gentle circles along her jaw sending tiny sparks out like fireworks. Alira wasn't sure what was happening between them but could admit that she wanted to find out.

Marcus didn't have an answer for her. He wished that he did. What he had been feeling since picking up Karma's phone and seeing that SOS alert – something had shifted in him when he thought he might lose someone else he cared about. And he did care about her. He cared more than he had realized. He could admit that much. When he had seen what was left of her car at the scene, he had been so afraid of what he would find when he got closer. Finding her awake and relatively intact… His heart had started beating again.

"Marcus?" Alira asked tentatively. He hadn't noticed her hand move to cover his over her cheek. Her fingers curled around his for several seconds before pulling his hand away. She shifted away but held his hand in her lap.

Alira's fingers itched to trace along his jaw; to be tickled by the stubble there but she resisted the urge. What she saw written on his handsome face made her feel unsteady. In the year she had known him, she had never really been this close to him, but she had also never seen him so vulnerable either. He was always so unreadable; serious and unchanging but something had changed. What that happened to be was anyone's guess.

When Alira pulled her hand from his and stood, all he could do was watch as she walked down the hall. He didn't know what to say or how to answer her question. It gnawed away at him. Alira deserved an answer.

Alira splashed water on her face and stared at herself in the mirror. The bruising had darkened considerably. She looked like an MMA fighter who had her butt handed to her and then some. Felt like one too but the Percocet was kicking in and she could feel herself getting drowsy as the pain she had been feeling ebbed slightly. As if on cue, she yawned. It was time to sleep. She wouldn't last much longer no matter how much she wanted to watch another movie. Reaching for her brush, she struggled to run it through her long tresses. Some knots gave her more trouble than others, but she managed and was soon running the brush through with ease. She brushed her teeth before returning to the living room.

Marcus had fluffed her pillow and set her blanket up for easy use upon her return. He didn't take his eyes off the TV when she entered. She shivered and checked the thermostat. Sixty-five degrees. Her thermostat was set for seventy degrees with the heater on. She dreaded calling maintenance. Having a working heater in November was necessary for their location regardless of the fact the weather had been unseasonably warm. The forecast showed that was going to change over the weekend. They were expecting the first real snowfall of the season. The heater would be a problem for the morning. It was too late to put in a service request anyway.

Alira settled into her spot on the couch and pulled her blanket snuggly around herself. Marcus shook his head at her. She glared. Her glare immediately turned to concern as she eyed the door realizing it wasn't locked. Angrily she attempted tossing her blanket off so she could lock the door. Marcus stopped her.

"I'll get it," he told her as he stood. It would allow him to take his boots off anyway. He could feel the chill in her apartment as he moved toward the door. He flipped the locks and removed his boots, leaving them next to her shoes by the dining table.

When Marcus turned around, Alira had wrapped a second blanket around herself and buried her nose. He laughed and moved to sit next to her. He settled in and held his arms open. She contemplated saying no and keeping her spot. Before she could question it further, she moved to his side pulling her blankets with her. Marcus pulled the blanket over his lap as she snuggled against him. Alira rested her head against his shoulder as his arm curled around her drawing her even closer. He leaned back so that he was almost laying down and pulled her with him. She was tucked nicely between him and the couch when suddenly her head shot up and she stared at him.

"You know you don't have to stay," she said quickly though quietly. He smiled softly and pressed a kiss to her forehead.

"Sorry, you're stuck with me for the weekend. Austin can't get anyone posted until the end of next week," he told her. She nodded and rested her head on his chest once more.

He was staying. For the weekend. She tried not to think about it. Instead, Alira settled more comfortably against him still in awe of the fact that she felt no fear or desire to put distance between them. His heartbeat steadily against her ear lulling her to sleep. As she drifted off, he hugged her to him, careful not to squeeze too hard so as not to hurt her.

Marcus held her close as she slept on his chest. She shifted so her hand rested across his stomach as she settled into her dreams letting out a contented sigh. He traced soft lines up and down her arm while he surfed through the channels on her TV. When he was unsuccessful in finding something to keep his attention, he went back to the movie they had been watching despite having no clue what it was about or what was happening. Marcus turned the volume down just enough for it to be a whisper in the background and wrapped his arms around her holding her close. He couldn't stop himself from inhaling deeply enjoying the scent of her hair. She smelled faintly of lavender from her bath mixed with her strawberries and vanilla-scented shampoo. It was a heady combination.

Marcus woke with a start not recognizing where he was at first. Alira groaned. Marcus glanced at his watch and realized she was due for another dose of pain meds, but he didn't want to wake her. She quickly settled back in, which he assumed meant that she was okay for the time being. He took the opportunity to pull the blanket back over her.

Gently brushing the hair from her face, he lightly touched the bruise at her temple and traced it down to her jaw. It had been a whirlwind over the last thirty-six hours, and this was the second night he slept with her in his arms. He couldn't say he didn't like it because he sure as hell did. Only a complete fool would try to deny it. He just wouldn't admit it out loud. It wasn't as if things would go anywhere so it didn't make sense to get anyone's hopes up. His family had been trying to set him up for over a year now. Needless to say, their attempts so far had been unsuccessful. Hadn't they? Gazing down at her beautiful face as she slept soundly on his chest, he wasn't so sure anymore.

Alira jolted painfully awake and looked around her dimly lit living room. Marcus lay snoring with his arm lazily wrapped around her. She was tucked comfortably between him and the back of the couch with her leg slung over his hip. While her heart settled back into a normal rhythm, she rested her head back down on his chest. As she was closing her eyes allowing his heartbeat to lull her back to sleep, she heard it. Someone was messing with the lock at her door. She sat up quickly ignoring the sharp pain rocketing through her body. Marcus was awake in an instant. He didn't waste any time gaining his feet. She glanced at the clock hanging in the kitchen. Four in the morning.

"Who is it?" Marcus called loudly as he marched toward the door. Alira stood anxiously as he smoothly unlocked her door and swung it open ready to confront whoever was on the other side. She heard the door to the stairwell slam shut as Marcus leaned down to pick something up off the floor. Alira pulled her blanket tightly around her shoulders.

"Have a secret admirer?" he asked quizzically as he closed the door behind him.

In his hand was a single red rose. Alira stared in horror. Before he realized what was happening, Alira dropped the blanket and ran down the hallway to her bedroom. Suddenly confused, Marcus followed her. By the time he reached her room, she had tossed her pajama shorts on the bed and was tugging on a pair of sweatpants as quickly as she could. She hippity-hopped past him as she struggled to get her socks on her feet. She slipped her feet into her shoes, grabbed her keys and phone from the kitchen counter, and was out the door before Marcus could stop her. Marcus didn't bother with his boots. He slammed the door behind him as he ran after her. She hit the stairwell and was already down to the third-floor access before he had cleared the access for the fourth floor.

"Alira! Wait!" he called after her but she either didn't hear him or she ignored him.

Alira had to move quickly. Her body screamed at her to slow down or stop but she couldn't. If he was back, she needed to know. Her life depended on it.

"Harold, I need to see security footage from all access points to my apartment, including stairwell access!" she explained quickly as she slid to a stop in front of the desk in the security office. Harold didn't even bat an eye as he pulled up the footage. Marcus appeared seconds later as Alira leaned over Harold's shoulder scanning the screens. She pointed at the upper right corner screen. With a couple keystrokes, the footage was shifted to the large screen in front of him.

"Alira, what's going on?"

She ignored him again and kept watching the screen intently. Marcus watched as she checked the monitors closely. He knew the minute she saw what she had been looking for. Her entire body tensed up. She exchanged a look with Harold. Slowly she turned to face him.

"Marcus, I need you to close the door," she told him seriously. He didn't like what he heard in her voice, but he closed the door quietly. She took a deep breath and when she looked back at him, all he saw was fear. Not fear of him but it hurt regardless. Harold patted her hand before turning back to the screens. He pulled a flash drive out of the desk drawer and started transferring footage files to it. Alira leaned back against the desk. She looked like she was trying to get her thoughts in order before speaking.

"I need you to call Austin. I need you to call him now," she spoke quietly as she stared at the floor. Marcus started forward but she put her hand up to stop him.

"Please, just do it. I promise I'll explain why but I need... I need to hire his company first."

Marcus nodded and moved to use the phone on the desk. He dialed Austin's cell quickly and waited for him to answer. When he didn't pick up, Marcus dialed again.

"Whoever this is that is stupid enough to be calling me at four in the damn morning had better have a good reason or a death wish," an angry Austin growled into the phone as he answered.

"Austin, it's me. I need you to meet me at Alira's apartment building now," Marcus told him never taking his eyes off of Alira. "No, the security office on the main floor."

He rattled off her address and hung up.

"He's on his way."

Alira nodded and turned back to the monitors. Harold handed her the flash drive. She gripped it tightly. He was back. Her heart raced so fast it was like she had a herd of stampeding horses in her chest. It couldn't be a coincidence that he had shown up shortly after her accident. There were no accidents when he was around. Heaven help her. Alira spoke quietly to Harold who nodded in response before pushing away from the desk and standing. Marcus stepped out of his way as he opened the door to leave the office.

"Alira, what the hell is going on?"

"I'll explain when Austin gets here. We can head back to the apartment until he does. Harold is calling in Zeke to come in early and he's going to meet us upstairs," she explained quickly. That had not been the response he was expecting but he accepted it. Whoever had left that rose had her scared. Not scared like she had been when her brother had shown up at the hospital but still scared. Scared enough to bolt out of her apartment practically on the heels of whoever it had been.

Austin was annoyed at being woken up before the sun had even considered rising but as soon as Marcus spoke, he had been up and moving. Marcus wouldn't have called unless it was serious. He threw on a pair of jeans and an old t-shirt. He texted Marcus that he would be at the building in fifteen minutes before he slipped on his boots and ran out of the house.

A knock sounded at the door making Alira jump. She had taken another dose of medication at Marcus's insistence when they had returned to the apartment. Marcus stood as Harold opened the door. Austin entered. He was clearly not pleased. Alira visibly flinched as he stepped into her apartment. Marcus caught her reaction from the corner of his eye and easily shifted his position on the couch to shield her. He knew her reaction was automatic but that didn't mean he wanted her to feel like she should shy away.

"Why the hell am I here at almost five in the morning guys?" Austin asked stopping short as he watched his brother move to shield Alira from him. Alira sat furthest from the door that she could get in her living room while Marcus and the building security guard were between her and the door. It was obvious their positioning was intentional. Alira touched Marcus's arm. He leaned back against the couch and waited. Austin grabbed a dining chair from the table and spun it so he could sit straddling the seat. Harold closed the door, blocking it with his body. Alira nodded and stood. Her ribs protested the movement.

"First of all, Austin I know I said I didn't want to hire your company but now I need to. I don't have a choice anymore. The reason I need to hire your company is that I used to be engaged. I broke it off. I was seventeen and he was my brother's best friend. Only he seemed like he wasn't like Grayson. Around me, he was sweet and kind. I should have known better because anyone who associates with my brother is never a good person. He fooled me," she told them and started pacing. Marcus and Austin stared at her not really understanding where this was going. She grew increasingly agitated as she tried to get to the point.

"When I turned eighteen, I broke it off and moved away. I had only agreed to say yes when he asked me partly because I thought he really cared about me and partly because Grayson threatened to hurt my older sister if I said no," she explained. "She was safe where she was at school, but I didn't know that at the time. When I turned eighteen, I received access to a trust fund my grandfather had set up for me. I left as soon as I knew my sister was safe and they couldn't touch her."

"What Alira means to say is she has a stalker and a restraining order in place," Harold said before she could stress herself out further trying to explain the situation. Austin leaned relaxed against the back of the chair with his chin resting on his arms. He sighed deeply and pulled his phone out of his back pocket. Marcus rose to his feet. He ran his hand through his hair. The more he learned about her past the more surprised he was that she was so...normal. Austin stood and put the chair back at the table.

"I will get a couple guys scheduled to start on Tuesday. Unfortunately, that's the earliest I can do. This is our busiest time of the year and I'm stretched thin as is," Austin told them. "And I am not charging you a thing. You have bigger fish to fry by the sounds of it."

Alira shook her head. She would not accept the detail unless she could pay for the service. It was coming up on the holidays and he had employees who shouldn't work pro bono simply because she was a friend of the family. She loved the Duvall's, but she paid for services, no matter who provided them because you respected a person's place of business.

"Austin, Tuesday is acceptable, but I insist on paying whatever your fee is. If you will not accept that, then I will not be able to utilize your company's services and would have to call someone else," she told him firmly. Both Marcus and Austin stared in surprise. Her voice never wavered, and she didn't avert her gaze when she spoke. She stood tall and stared him down. Harold choked on a laugh from where he stood by the door.

"If it's a matter of thinking that I can't afford it, don't. I can afford it," Alira said quietly.

They knew she had a trust fund. They didn't need to know how much was in it. She hated bringing up her money no matter what the reasoning was. Austin started to protest but Harold stopped him with a raised hand.

"Boys, she owns the building," he told them with a smirk.

Chapter 6

She owned the building. She owned the building?! Marcus raised an eyebrow while Austin stared at Harold in disbelief. Alira shrugged. The way they were staring made her want to hide under a rock. Not even Karma knew she owned the building. There had been no reason to tell anyone. The only ones who knew were Harold and Cammie. Not even her maintenance staff knew she was their boss. She had a property manager that handled everything. Alira didn't have to worry about the building. She could do the things she really enjoyed instead. Until that point, nobody had needed to know but apparently, Harold thought it was important information regarding the situation. He was probably right.

Alira swayed on her feet. The adrenaline had started to wear off and the latest dose of pain relief was making her sleepy. Marcus patted the couch next to him. She didn't argue. She sat and pulled her legs up to her chest, leaning over on the pillow resting on the arm of the couch. Harold motioned for Marcus and Austin to follow him into the kitchen. There were so many thoughts racing through her mind, so much worry. Her eyes shuttered closed against her will.

"Well, that was unexpected," Austin said as he leaned back against the counter.

"No kidding but that's not the point. We need someone here 24/7. After meeting her brother at the hospital, I can only imagine what his friends are like," Marcus told him seriously. His voice was low as he spoke. He had questions. The first and most important one – was her accident really an accident? Austin scowled.

"I'll have her car looked over," Austin said angrily. Marcus nodded. They had clearly had the same thought. As the men spoke and made decisions for her wellbeing, Alira slept on the couch. She had struggled to keep her eyes open when Marcus had stood. She had attempted to listen to their conversation, but sleep had claimed her quickly, pulling her down into its depths.

Alira shifted restlessly on the couch. Marcus walked over to sit with her. He rubbed her arm gently. She settled almost immediately at his touch. Austin cocked his head curiously as he watched his brother who was solely focused on Alira. He had seemingly moved without realizing it, but he never missed a beat in their conversation.

It was decided that all building guests would need to check-in and check out at the main desk in the lobby for the foreseeable future using a valid ID. Non-residents would have to check-in at the desk even when with a resident. Nightguards would increase to three with one in the security office at all times, one patrolling the building doing security checks and the third would sit at the main desk. Marcus would be staying nights at Alira's apartment and one of Austin's guys would be with her at all times during the day when Marcus or Austin couldn't be there. They agreed to other precautions, but it was decided that Marcus would be the primary guard with her. After telling Grayson that he was her husband, they had appearances to maintain until her ex-fiancé and her brother were dealt with.

"Austin, if you wouldn't mind staying with her... I have to make a jewelry run," Marcus said with an exasperated sigh. Austin agreed, not bothering to hide his smile.

"Get some rest, Harold. We've got her covered," Marcus told the security guard. Harold checked his watch and nodded. He should get going anyway. He had to line up the extra shifts and do one final check of the building before handing the shift over.

Austin was sitting on the floor dozing with his back against the couch when Marcus returned. His heart skipped a beat when he looked up to see Alira still passed out on the couch behind his brother. She hadn't moved an inch since he had left a couple hours ago. She probably wouldn't have allowed Austin so close to her otherwise. Let alone slept so peacefully there.

The sun shone brightly through the open blinds falling over her like a blanket of light. Her long dark hair took on a blue-black hue as the sunlight kissed the strands. The bruising on her skin was a dark angry-looking purple but he could already see that it was fading some. Unable to help himself he kneeled on the floor next to her sleeping form. He brushed a loose strand of hair away from her face before delicately trailing his fingers down her cheek to trace along her jaw. She was so peaceful as she slept; not a care in the world despite the glimpse he had gotten into her world recently. The Alira he had seen last night was not the skittish young woman afraid of her own shadow. The woman he had seen last night didn't let her fear control her actions. As soon as she had seen that rose in his hand, she had moved. She hadn't stood frozen in place. She had genuinely surprised him.

Austin watched silently as his brother kneeled beside Alira. He watched how he caressed her face; careful to avoid the more tender spots. He had to wonder when Marcus would admit it to himself because the rest of the family had already seen how he felt about her. It was obvious in how carefully he kept his distance but still watched her. It was obvious in how he cared for her now when he thought Austin was asleep and wouldn't see. It had been a long time since he had seen his brother so openly. He couldn't remember him being that open with Carmen. Carmen had been Marcus's great love before their future had shattered into a million pieces. Marcus had shut out the world after that.

Watching him now - the way he was with Alira – it was as if she were his whole world. He hadn't ever been that focused on Carmen. Marcus had insisted they keep up the charade that he was Alira's husband, and he would be the primary person with her at all times. They had then needed to explain to the security guard how that story came about. Harold had chuckled and said something about how mothers could be incredibly sneaky beings.

"I know you're awake, Austin," Marcus said quietly as he continued to watch Alira sleep. Her hand rested on the pillow just under her chin. He resisted the urge to lace his fingers with hers. Instead, he shifted so he was sitting with his back pressed against the couch.

"I should get going. Scheduling to do and a brother to leave to figure out his feelings for the woman he has adamantly denied having feelings for," Austin said jokingly as he rose to his feet. Marcus shook his head.

"Thanks," he replied sarcastically. Damnit, even his brother couldn't seem to keep his mouth shut. He had clearly been talking to their mother too much. Marcus scowled.

Alira woke slowly. She stretched and rolled. Her muscles protested the movement, as did her ribs, but the stretch was worth it. It was one of those stretches that made a person shudder as the warmth seeped in to wake sleepy muscles. Despite her whole body reminding her that she had to take it easy, she felt well-rested. The mouthwatering scent of sizzling bacon cut through the air and slashed through her sleepy morning haze. Slowly she stood, moving cautiously, and followed her nose to the kitchen.

Marcus stood in front of the stove flipping pancakes while bacon sizzled in the pan. Alira took the opportunity to appreciate the view. His soft hair was ruffled in a way that made her think he had just rolled out of bed and started cooking breakfast. His shoulders were strong and broad. The man didn't seem to have an ounce of fat on him as her eyes skimmed down his back to his incredibly sexy ass. His fitted tee didn't leave much to the imagination and the way his jeans fit, hugging him in all the right places – her heart skipped a beat. She wanted to touch every muscular plane of his body; wanted those sculpted arms of his around her every chance she could get. She tried to imagine what he would look like without the clothing because if how he looked in the clothes was any indication...

"You keep biting that lip and I may be forced to bite it for you instead," he said in a low husky tone. Alira jumped.

When had he turned around?!

A blush rose to her face at having been caught in a less than appropriate daydream about running her tongue over his toned abs. She couldn't help the heat that pooled low in her belly. Alira could admit that she wanted him. She had never wanted anyone or anything so much in her life.

She wanted his lips on hers again.

Alira moved before she could talk herself out of it. Marcus dropped the spatula he was holding and met her in the middle. His mouth crashed down roughly on hers as he gathered her tightly against him. Her arms slid around his neck pulling him closer as her fingers wove into his hair. He nipped at her lower lip making her groan. Alira pressed against him feeling his growing erection against her stomach.

Marcus growled and gripped her perfect ass in his hands. He lifted her effortlessly. She wrapped her legs around his waist while running her tongue along his lower lip, enticing him. He broke the kiss long enough to turn off the stove before he carried her from the kitchen. Upon reaching the couch, Marcus laid her down gently, following her. Alira loved how his body felt as it covered her own. He pressed teasing kisses along her jaw, making sure to nibble at the sensitive skin just below her ear. She arched against him wanting more.

"Marcus," she moaned softly. He froze. Then just as quickly, he moved away from her.

Alira had no idea what had happened. One minute they were getting hot and heavy and the next, Marcus had moved as if she had burned him. Without a word, he headed back into the kitchen. She sat up as confusion slammed into her like a rogue wave and with it came a heavy dose of self-doubt. She replayed the last few minutes in her mind trying to see where it went wrong. She had said his name. That was it. She couldn't think how that had been bad. With a groan, she shoved away from the couch and headed down the hallway to her bedroom. Once in the room, she gathered up some clothes for the day and prepared to go shower. She slammed the bathroom door, unintentionally, but it sure felt good.

Marcus heard the water start running in the shower and tried not to imagine the water cascading over her voluptuous body. He had messed up. Boy, oh boy had he messed up. He ran his hand roughly through his hair and angrily flipped the large pancake in the pan. Muttering to himself, Marcus pulled out two plates to put pancakes and bacon slices on both. He opened the fridge looking for the butter and syrup.

"Hope she's hungry," he muttered as he carried the plates to the small dining table.

Alira finished her shower. She wrapped her towel securely around her body as she stepped out of the stall and reached for her comb. As she combed through her hair, she settled on a braid for the day since it would make it easier to deal with. At least with it braided, it would stay out of her face and Marcus wouldn't be able to brush wayward strands away. What was wrong with her? After the screaming brakes display on the couch, there was no chance in hell Marcus would brush anything away from her face. He might be the one to push her in front of a speeding bus but touching her again for anything else was out of the question.

Angrily, Alira pulled her jeans up and over her hips. She yanked her tank top over her head and only briefly considered removing it in favor of a bra instead. Nope, she would be more comfortable without the bra. As she slid her oversized sweater on, making sure it sat revealing one shoulder as it was meant to, she steeled herself. She was determined not to show any emotion. Marcus was still in her apartment and likely wouldn't be going anywhere any time soon. Alira knew she would have to suck it up and face him. There was a strong chance that he would break down the door if she tried to hide in the bathroom all day just to avoid him.

Marcus heard her pad down the carpeted hallway. When he turned to apologize, the words caught in his throat. She wore jeans that hugged every curve. Her baggy sweater hung just so allowing her shoulder to peek out and her lovely long hair was loosely braided to hang down her back. He tried not to stare but couldn't seem to look away while Alira pretended that he wasn't even there. She strolled right past him and into the kitchen. He watched as she grabbed a mug from the counter and poured herself a cup of steaming hot coffee. Leaning against the counter, she sipped at the liquid until her phone rang. She jumped at the noise followed by a wince. Setting the mug down, she went to answer the phone.

"Hello?"

Alira listened intently.

"No, I'll be right down. Five minutes," she said before hanging up. Marcus set his fork down on the plate and stood. Alira already had her shoes on with her phone tucked into her back pocket. She reached for her keys, but Marcus grabbed them first. She turned a glare on him that could level a herd of elephants.

"Give me my keys, Marcus," she demanded angrily. He shook his head and tucked them into his pocket.

"Not a chance. What's going on?"

"That's none of your business. Give me my keys," she ordered stepping forward to snatch them from his pocket if necessary. When he didn't hand them over, she reached to take them from his pocket. He grabbed her at the wrist stopping her instantly.

"Fine," she snapped at him. She attempted to step past him, but he blocked her path.

"Talk to me. Who was on the phone?"

Alira glared. She pressed her lips tightly together refusing to answer him. If he wanted her to speak to him, it would need to be a cold day in hell. After his reaction earlier on the couch and the tears she had cried in the shower out of earshot, he was not getting a thing from her. Not a single thing.

"Marcus, you need to leave. I did not invite you here and I do not need you to stay to babysit me. Go home," she said seriously stepping back from him. He was too close. She needed distance from him. She tried desperately to ignore the way his shirt hugged his chest and how badly she wanted to kiss him. Marcus reached for her but seemed to think better of it.

"If that is what you want, I will call Austin and ask if he can schedule someone on short notice. But how will you explain that your husband isn't here to watch over you instead? I can promise Austin has told his employees that you're his sister-in-law already," Marcus told her pointedly. Anyone at Austin's company would know Marcus owned the construction company and they didn't work weekends so it wouldn't make sense that he wouldn't be able to be with her given the circumstances.

Alira felt the anger bubble up from deep inside her. She had forgotten about that. Damnit. That put a wrench into the gears of the machine. It didn't matter. She could just tell anyone who asked that he had left her. No, that wasn't right. She would tell them that she left him. Besides, she meant what she said; she didn't need him to babysit her. She had this handled. His presence in her life could easily go back to just being Karma's older brother. She needed it to go back to the way it was. He was so hot and cold that she couldn't keep up. It wasn't something she could deal with right now. Alira wanted him but it was clear he didn't want her. Logically, that meant she needed to distance herself. She had enough going on as it was. Marcus didn't need to be involved anymore. She had hired Austin's firm. She would be fine.

"You can tell anyone who asks whatever you want to tell them. I don't care," she said louder than she had intended. *I don't care*. Her words hit him hard. He put his hands up in surrender and backed away.

"As you wish," he said softly. Alira nodded and held out her hand for her keys. He pulled them out of his pocket holding them out for her. Alira snatched them away. She slammed the door hard enough to shake the walls on her way out leaving him standing there staring after her. Marcus had no intention of leaving her alone. She would be okay in the building and maybe the time she spent downstairs would help her cool off. In the meantime, he would clean up from breakfast. It was the least he could do after making a mess of her kitchen. He didn't need to give her another reason to be angry with him because she very clearly was plenty angry already.

Alira knocked on the door to the security office. Harold opened it and practically yanked her into the room, closing the door quickly behind her.

"Harold, you're supposed to be at home. Why are you working?"

Harold gestured for her to sit. This couldn't be good. She felt like she was waiting for the principal to lecture her about something she had done wrong in class. Of course, Harold would never do that, but it sure felt like it at that moment!

"Where's your fake husband?"

"Excuse me?" she asked confused before she narrowed her eyes at him.

"Where's Marcus? He's supposed to be with you at all times until your problem is taken care of. He should be here," Harold explained quickly.

The concern she saw on his face made her nervous. She really didn't want to call Marcus. She didn't want to call him for anything but something in Harold's tone worried her. He was truly concerned. Grudgingly, Alira pulled out her phone and sent a quick text message to Marcus. She knew they had the best of intentions, but it still made her want to hide under a rock until this all blew over. The truth was she knew this time it wouldn't just blow over. It was no coincidence that her brother had shown up and shortly after so had her ex-fiancé. Trouble was brewing. It always was with those two.

Marcus walked into the security office as if he owned it. Alira immediately stuffed herself into the corner of the office as far away as she could get from him refusing to meet his eyes. He sighed as he moved to sit in the second chair. He wasn't putting any pressure on her. Instead, he gave her as much space as he could in the small office. She tried not to let her relief show.

"We found this at the main desk. It was just resting on the keyboard," Harold said as he handed an envelope to Marcus. Marcus took it from him. Alira's name was written neatly on the front. Alira leaned over to see. Her curiosity overrode her anger at him. He handed the envelope to her and watched her slowly open it. Her hands shook as she unfolded the paper to read its contents.

Buttercup,

I know he isn't really your husband. You could never be with anyone else. Nobody can love you like I do. Don't worry, baby. We'll be together again soon.

A.L.

Alira couldn't hide her shaking hands as she read the note. She read it again. Her eyes lifted slowly to look from Harold to Marcus and back at the note in her hand. Taking several deep breaths, she turned to Marcus. There was no longer anger in her eyes. What he saw was fear. Real, unbridled fear. She handed him the note and waited. He read the contents. He handed the note to Harold and immediately opened his arms to Alira allowing her to make the decision. She didn't hesitate as she leaned into him.

🔲

"Was there a rose with the note?"

Harold nodded grimly and pulled a red long-stemmed rose from the top drawer of the desk. Alira felt like she was going to be sick. She pulled away from Marcus and dove for the trash can next to the desk. Her stomach rolled violently. Marcus kneeled down next to her, rubbing her back. The only thing that came up was coffee and bile. It made her throat burn and her body screamed in pain as her stomach tried to empty contents that weren't there to expel. When Alira finally sat back on her heels, Harold handed her a Kleenex which she took gratefully.

"It seems we have some things to discuss and we still have dinner at my parent's house tonight," Marcus said quietly as he helped her to her feet. She nodded her agreement. Whether she liked it or not, she needed him. He was right. She was stuck between a rock and a hard place.

He tried to hide his surprise when she leaned into him again. Without thinking about it, he slid his arms around her as Harold angled his head curiously at the scene before him. Marcus kissed the top of her head before she pulled away remembering that she was mad at him. She shoved him as she glared. Her pathetic attempts to knock him off balance could be likened to the wind trying to move the mountain. He chuckled as her glare deepened. The look on her face reminded him of the women in the movies who were about to stomp on the man's foot because he said something that she took offense to. He half expected her to harrumph before she stormed off. He grinned at the image that thought conjured in his head.

"What are you grinning at?" she asked angrily.

"Just how adorable you are when you're mad," Marcus told her with a big grin. Harold burst out laughing. Alira wasn't amused. She turned to glare at Harold but that only made him laugh harder.

"I'm not going in there, Marcus," Alira stated flatly as she stared at the Duvall's house. Marcus killed the engine and turned to face her. His expression was serious. He'd had to toss her over his shoulder and carry her out of her apartment to even get her to the garage where his truck was parked. She had kicked and beat on his back with her fists cursing at him. The elevator crossed over the third-floor threshold before she gave up and hung limply huffing at him. He had even made sure to set her so she was as comfortable as she could be despite the physical discomfort from her car accident battle wounds. She had glared daggers at him for the entire twenty-minute drive to his parent's house just outside of town. The rant that followed when she noticed the resident parking pass hanging from his mirror had been epic. She had demanded to know when Harold had given it to him. Marcus had chuckled but stayed quiet.

Marcus took her hand in his and squeezed. Alira felt her anger slowly ebb away as her eyes met his. She hated to admit it, but it was getting harder and harder to hide her feelings for Marcus. If she were being honest, she really didn't want to hide what she felt. She was afraid that if she said it out loud, he wouldn't feel the same. Growing up, feelings were used against you. Grayson made sure she knew that.

Alira had grown up fearing what would come next. She was terrified of what her brother would do to terrorize her. The history was most definitely there. There was no escaping it. He was a terror disguised as a distinguished gentleman. Mara had been her only ally in the world before she had been sent away for school. Grayson had taken it as an opportunity to make Alira's life even worse. No, she couldn't admit her feelings for Marcus. Not yet. It was too much to think about right now. Though she didn't need to admit them. She could feel them and still keep them to herself. It might hurt less when the charade was over if she didn't say them out loud. And it would keep Marcus safe.

"Alira, I can hear your stomach growling," Marcus told her smiling. Color rose to her cheeks as his finger traced circles on her palm.

"Hey, you crazy kids!"

Alira looked like she was about to jump through the window and make a run for it while Marcus whirled around fist ready to meet someone's face. Austin stood leaning against the truck peering in through the window with a dopey smile. He looked pretty proud of himself for getting the jump on his older brother. Alira knew it didn't happen often despite Austin taking every opportunity he could to try it anyway.

"They're all peeking out through the curtains wondering when you two are going to come in and pretend you're not completely infatuated with one another. I'm starving and mom won't let anyone eat until everyone is here. You're here. Inside. Now," Austin spoke quickly trying his best to make his whining believable. Marcus rolled his eyes. He reached for the handle of his door, but Austin was already pulling it open. Marcus took the opportunity to push on the door, slamming it against his brother. Austin didn't move fast enough to avoid having the wind knocked out of him. He laughed as he tried to catch his breath. Meanwhile, Alira's heart rate was slowly returning to normal after Austin's sudden appearance.

Marcus moved around the truck to help her out. Alira grumbled but allowed him to assist her out of the truck for fear she would fall flat on her face if she attempted it herself. Marcus's truck was massive, and he didn't have running boards because the giant of a man had no use for them. She had ridden in his truck exactly three times and the first two times, she had slipped trying to get out gracefully. Her flailing had been anything but graceful. This was the third time and she was not about to do another clumsy penguin impression.

"This will be fun. Don't worry," Austin said with a wink as he peered around Marcus and wiggled his eyebrows. Alira wasn't so sure. The last couple of days had been anything but fun. She highly doubted that would change for the better tonight. Not after that note. It was going to be an uphill battle for the foreseeable future because that's how it always worked when her ex reappeared. Unfortunately, this had an entirely different feel to it. This was something more menacing.

The Duvall's home was always welcoming. The country-style house had a lovely wrap-around porch with rocking chairs placed perfectly to enjoy a sunrise or a sunset. Between the chairs was an adorable little round table to set your coffee or tea on. Many large windows allowed natural light in throughout the home. Charlotte had decorated the interior to be just as warm and inviting. Family photos hung on the walls and sat on the mantle over the fireplace in the den. It had been a shock her first time out to their sixty-acre property. Seeing that families like ones she saw in movies actually existed. She had been in awe seeing all of the pictures of the Duvall brood from infancy to adulthood. That wasn't her favorite thing though. Alira's favorite thing on the property was the giant hammock bed that hung between two massive oaks in the backyard. It offered a fabulous view of the night sky or you could lay there and watch the horses in the pasture. It was the perfect place.

"Alira! So good to see you up and about!" Charlotte called as she hurried out onto the porch. She always gave Alira the biggest hug. Alira loved it but even after a year of joining them for family dinners a couple days a week, it was still a very new experience for her.

"Mom, take it easy. Remember she's still pretty banged up," Marcus said protectively as his mother moved in for her usual hug. Charlotte laughed and waved him off. Alira smiled as Charlotte wrapped her in gentle motherly warmth while Marcus stood nearby with a worried look etching his handsome features.

"Dinner will be ready in an hour. We will be eating outside on the patio tonight. You go on ahead to your favorite spot. We'll let you know when dinner is ready," Charlotte said releasing her and softly patted her cheek.

Austin handed his mother a book who then passed it over to Alira. Alira smiled as she looked over the cover. She had been reading through Little Women for weeks now but always refused to take it home with her because she didn't need the distraction from work. She read a little here and there whenever she was over at the Duvall's. She adored the movies, but the book had a special place in her heart. Mara had given her a copy before she'd left for school. Grayson had naturally destroyed it when he caught her reading it. He had torn it apart page by page right in front of her taking great joy in her tears as she tried in vain to take what was left back from him.

Alira walked straight through the house to the kitchen. She grabbed a couple of apples from the basket on the counter like usual and headed for the pasture. The horses always came running to the fence when she approached looking for apples or carrots. They made her smile.

Alira had developed a special bond with one horse in particular. Zoe. Zoe had come to the Duvall's property as a rescue. When she had arrived, she had been in bad shape and was terrified of people. Alira had spent hours just sitting along the fence reading to her. As time went on, Zoe always made it to the fence before her herd mates when Alira called to her. She had gained much-needed weight in the six months since her arrival and had really blossomed into a stunning animal. She was an appaloosa that was often referred to as a snowflake appaloosa due to her particular pattern. Her darker body was speckled with white that looked like freshly fallen snow.

Zoe loved to run. Oftentimes, Zoe could be seen galloping around the pasture with her tail held high and mane blowing out behind her. She was in a state of pure bliss when she ran. No matter where she was, she always came running when Alira called out to her. Charlotte was the only other person Zoe allowed near her but her bond with Charlotte was not remotely close to the bond she shared with Alira. They were kindred spirits.

Zoe nickered as she stretched her elegant neck over the fence reaching for one of the apples. Alira laughed as she held it out for her. Zoe munched on the apple happily as Alira shared the other with Maverick, one of the ponies on the property. Zoe finished chewing and rested her head on Alira's shoulder in her version of a hug. Alira scratched her nose softly and whispered to her. The horse's ears perked up as though she understood every word Alira said. Then much to Alira's surprise, Zoe lifted her head and seemed to examine the bruising along her face, touching each tender spot gently with her nose. Alira didn't try to stop her. She allowed the inspection. When Zoe lowered her head and nudged her chest, Alira smiled and scratched her chin.

"I'm okay," she told her as Zoe leaned into the scratches. Zoe lifted her head to rest on Alira's shoulder again pulling her closer into another horse-style hug. Alira wrapped her arms around her muscular neck and rested her head against it.

Marcus stood on the back porch watching the interaction between Alira and Zoe. The bond those two shared never ceased to amaze him. Nobody else but his mother could get near that horse and even his mother couldn't hold a candle to Alira in Zoe's eyes. Zoe had come to his parents severely underweight with patches of her coat missing. She had come with fresh wounds on her rear legs that looked like someone had taken a knife to her. The cuts weren't shallow, but they weren't deep either. They were still bad enough to leave scarring if you looked close enough. The transformation since her arrival was astounding. He never would have believed she was the same horse if he hadn't seen her several days a week.

Alira patted Zoe's neck and gave her a kiss on the nose before leaving her to go to the hammock bed with her book. She pulled the book from her jacket pocket and placed it on the mat so she could climb up without dropping it on the ground. She gave the swing a gentle push and dove on laughing as she flopped. Marcus went inside to grab one of the big down comforters before making his way down the stairs to the swing. Alira always forgot to grab a blanket on her way out and would come in for dinner shivering. Luckily, his parents had patio heaters for the evenings they ate dinner outside in winter. Despite the unseasonably warm weather, it was chilly and with the setting of the sun, the temperature was dropping quickly. The weatherman had said snow was in the forecast for tomorrow evening. There was a crispness in the air that signaled the forecast to be accurate.

"Mind if I join you?" Marcus asked as he tossed the comforter onto the swing. Alira closed her book and looked at him as if she were considering saying no. Instead, she nodded and moved over to allow him room. Marcus grinned. He gripped the edge of the swing, pulled back as far as it would allow, and jumped on. Alira burst out laughing as he landed easily next to her while the swing went high. Marcus covered them both with the comforter and laid back. He held his arm out inviting her to lay with him. She narrowed her eyes before tucking the book into a pocket in the swing and laying down.

Alira settled herself against him only just realizing how chilled she was as the heat from his body started to warm her. While she rested her head on his shoulder, he pulled her hand up to rest against his chest. She didn't fight it. As Marcus wrapped his arm around her while threading his fingers with hers, he couldn't help but think how good it felt.

"I'm sorry I was short with you this morning," Alira said softly as she reached to pull the comforter up around her shoulders stuffing her nose into the fluffy material to warm it.

"You're always short to me," Marcus told her jokingly. She pretended to be offended until he kissed the top of her head and hugged her. Alira lifted her head just enough to look up at him. Tentatively she reached up and traced the line of his jaw with her fingers. He closed his eyes, leaning into her touch. Tiny sparks shot through her fingertips sending shivers down her spine.

"Marcus..." she trailed off unsure what she wanted to say.

"Alira, we need to talk about that note from this morning," he told her giving her an out. She nodded. Yes, they did but she didn't want to. Talking about it made it more real and she'd had just about enough of reality lately.

"Can we just stay here and block out the world for a little while? I don't even want to think about the note right now," she said quietly as she played with the fabric of his t-shirt under his jacket. He tightened his arm around her and rested his cheek on her head. He was okay with that.

The swing rocked gently in the breeze as the sunset gave way to the starry night sky. The patio heaters could be heard humming faintly behind them. Alira shifted just enough that she was still tucked in comfortably against him, but she could see the sky more clearly. Every star twinkled happily above them. There was the occasional shooting star streaking across the deep blue background.

"What did you wish for?" Marcus asked as a star raced across the sky directly overhead. Alira sat up and looked at him seriously.

"I can't tell you because then it won't come true! I know your mother taught you better than that, sir!" she told him teasingly with a poke to his chest for emphasis. He chuckled. She pressed a quick kiss to his lips before she could talk herself out of it and settled back down so he wouldn't see her blush. He held her against him and sighed deeply, content.

"How are you feeling?"

"Emotionally or physically?" Alira responded unsure of what he was asking.

"Physically. How do you feel? You haven't taken any pain killers and I'm sure you're still hurting quite a bit," he said concerned. Alira shrugged. She was very sore, but she could manage as long as she didn't move too fast. Breathing hurt but that was slowly getting better. It would be even better if her brother and her ex would just leave her alone so she could rest without stress. That would be too easy. Nothing in her life was easy.

"Dinner!" Aiden called out to them. The storm door slammed behind him followed by a curse and yelling from Charlotte about not slamming doors in her house. Alira couldn't help smiling. It happened every time they ate on the patio. Someone would accidentally slam the storm door and Charlotte would yell about doors being slammed. It was always entertaining.

Marcus moved first. As soon as he was off of the swing, he held it still so Alira could move off without too much difficulty. Together they folded the comforter. Alira grabbed the book from the pocket on the bed. Marcus held out his hand indicating she should walk ahead of him. At the patio, the temperature was instantly warmer thanks to the heaters. Marcus grabbed the book from her and took it with the comforter into the house before reappearing with a pitcher of tea and one of the side dishes. Charlotte had wrangled him into helping Aiden set the table. Alira sat silently watching him. His leather jacket fit him perfectly, stopping just at his waist. The leather creaked softly as he moved to set the pitcher on the table. She caught her lower lip between her teeth unknowingly as he moved some items around to make room for other side dishes.

"If you don't stop biting that lip..."

Alira raised an eyebrow as she released her lip slowly from her teeth. She couldn't take her eyes off of him. Desire blazed in his eyes as he moved closer to her. He stopped to look around for any potential audience before he placed his hands on the arms of the chair and leaned over. Alira held her breath in anticipation of his next move. When he leaned closer and pressed a soft but demanding kiss to her lips, her hands, seemingly of their own accord, gripped his jacket pulling him closer. Marcus broke the kiss almost as soon as she pulled him in. With another quick glance around the patio, he grabbed her hand and pulled her to her feet.

"Come with me," he rumbled deeply. Alira nodded and allowed him to pull her along as he all but dragged her toward the barn and away from prying eyes. She expected him to guide her inside but instead, he veered around to the side of the barn; the side of the barn where only a single dim light shone. Marcus pressed her against the wall roughly and claimed her mouth with his own. Alira moaned against his mouth as he sucked on her bottom lip, teasing her, asking her to open up to him. When she did, his tongue swept inside to dance with hers. He wove his fingers into her hair at the base of her scalp sending sparks through her as he tugged gently. He leaned down to nibble along the tender skin below her ear. Alira's heart raced as she clung to him losing herself in what she was feeling; what he was making her feel. When he found her mouth again, the kiss was full and intense, unlike anything she had ever experienced before. White-hot fire coursed through her veins as desire pooled low in her belly.

Marcus needed to touch her. He ran his tongue from her collarbone up her neck to her ear, pulling the lobe into his mouth and sucking while simultaneously pressing against the core of her with his palm through her jeans. Alira gasped as her head fell forward against his chest. She gripped his jacket tightly as her moan was muffled by the leather. Marcus encouraged her to look at him. She could feel her heart hammering away in her chest as his fingers fumbled with the buttons on her jeans. She reached down to help him.

"You're so wet," he groaned as his fingers found that sensitive nub between her slick folds. Alira nearly cried out at the sensation. Marcus grinned before pressing his lips to hers again; their tongues dancing together as he teased her. His fingers were like magic. Alira felt the fire he was stroking within her building, feeding it until it blazed out of control and all thoughts in her head scattered. She could feel the explosion coming. It was as if rubber bands were being pulled to their limit, the tension higher and higher until they snapped. She cried out his name as her orgasm washed over her like a tidal wave crashing to shore taking out everything in its path. Alira would have collapsed to the ground if Marcus hadn't been there holding her up. Her legs felt like they were made of jelly. Her heart slammed in her chest and she tried to catch her breath. The aftershocks of her orgasm threatened to overwhelm her as he started to stroke her again.

"Look at me," he ordered as he fed the fire inside her once more. She bit her lip trying to stay quiet as she met his eyes. The desire she saw there made her wild. Alira wrapped her arms around his neck and kissed him hard as she flexed her hips begging for more. He obliged.

"Marcus," she whimpered. "I want you."

"I want you too, love," he whispered in her ear before he nibbled on her earlobe. Alira gasped as the warm moisture of his mouth collided with her cold lobe sending a jolt down her spine. He slipped a finger inside her feeling her slick walls starting to squeeze tighter as her orgasm built again. Marcus kissed a trail down her neck before moving his focus back up, teasing circles with his tongue just below her jaw.

"Dinner!" Aiden yelled from the patio.

Marcus claimed her mouth as her second orgasm shuddered through her muffling his name as she cried out. She broke the kiss to lean heavily against him. He brought his hand to his mouth and sucked her juices from his fingers. A breathless laugh escaped her.

"We should get to the table before they come looking. Wouldn't want them to find you in such a compromising position," he whispered. Alira agreed as she quickly buttoned her jeans. She smoothed her hair back, though her braid would need to be redone. She didn't have time for that. Marcus took her hand in his and together they walked back to the patio where the entire Duvall clan waited.

"Really son? Behind the barn?" Charlotte scolded Marcus.

"I have no idea what you're talking about," he responded as he winked at Alira. Alira felt her cheeks heat up. Karma burst out laughing. Alira glared at her.

"Traitor," she muttered to her as she moved to sit in the chair Marcus had pulled out for her. Karma smiled and shrugged her shoulders.

Charlotte had outdone herself with dinner. She had made the most delicious barbeque-baked chicken Alira had ever eaten. The meat was tender, juicy, and full of flavor! Sweet corn on the cob with homemade scalloped potatoes for the sides. Alira had savored every bite. Despite the amount of food that had been placed on the table, it always amazed her to see how quickly it disappeared. Between the five Duvall brothers alone, they packed it away with ease. Apparently, it took a lot of fuel to maintain the sheer muscle mass they each had. It shouldn't have surprised her, but it always did anyway. Austin's phone rang while Charlotte was inside getting dessert ready.

"Excuse me for a minute," he said eyeing Marcus. Marcus nodded. Alira watched as his entire demeanor changed. He went from happy-go-lucky to serious and calculating. This was the Marcus she was used to, the cold intimidating giant. Whoever Austin was talking to must be important. She guessed it had something to do with her. Austin waved Marcus over. Marcus squeezed her hand gently before he stood. Alira watched as they spoke in hushed tones. She couldn't hear what they were saying but she could see how it was affecting Marcus. The more Austin said, the angrier Marcus became. He didn't even try hiding it. He was furious. The only time his expression changed was when he glanced her way. His features softened but as soon as he looked back to his brother, his anger showed once more.

"Cheesecake," Charlotte called as she and Karma brought plates and the most beautiful cherry cheesecake Alira had ever seen out to the table. The cheesecake had swirls and flowers delicately drawn into it with the cherry filling. It looked too good to eat. She had never seen a cheesecake look so artistically done. Marcus and Austin returned to the table as Karma was passing out plates.

"Alira, I have some bad news about your car," Austin said as he sat back in his chair. Marcus reclaimed his previous seat next to her and took her hand in his. Karma watched curiously wiggling her eyebrows at Alira who just shook her head before focusing her attention on Austin. Austin took a deep breath before getting down to business.

"I had your car inspected after your brother showed up at the hospital and your reaction to seeing him. Your car was sabotaged," he told her seriously. Alira blinked quickly.

"I'm sorry, what?"

Sabotaged? She had so many questions but bit her tongue knowing Austin was going to explain. It was only then that she realized it had become unusually quiet around her. Slowly she looked around the table to see horrified looks aimed at Austin and his revelation.

"Austin, what are you talking about? It was a blown tire. It was an accident," Karma chimed in as she clearly tried to hide the panic that was threatening to overtake her. Someone was trying to kill her friend! Of course, she would be concerned! She knew Greyson was lower than low but this? Poor Alira!

"My guys found a tracking device tucked into your right rear fender. You never would have seen it without getting under the car and actively looking for it. It was anchored in so that no amount of potholes were going to shake it. They also found an explosive device that was designed to blow out your tire using a remote detonation. Whoever triggered the device would have needed to be pretty close to you when they set it off. Your accident was not an accident after all," Austin explained quickly. He waited for Alira to respond somehow. Maybe break down and cry, get angry, something. Instead, she took a deep breath and looked at Karma.

"Shit," Karma muttered and reached for her phone. She and Alira had discussed scenarios like this. It had always been a possibility something like this might happen, so they had made a plan. Karma was texting Mara for her because if they had been tracking her car, it was likely they were tracking her phone somehow too. Her brother certainly could make it happen. Karma typed out a long message and hit send before rejoining the group.

?

"The accident was a warning from my brother," she started as she reached into her pocket for her phone. Marcus watched curiously as she pressed the power button and waited for the phone to shut down before she continued. Austin's eyes widened.

"Wait, you knew this would happen? Do you think he's tracking your phone?" Austin questioned harshly. Alira nodded and held up her hand before he could ask anything else.

"I had no way of knowing for sure, but I always had a feeling it *could* happen. You all know I didn't have the happiest childhood and my family is a nightmare. My older sister was the only one who tried to protect me before she was shipped off to boarding school. Before and after that, my grandfather protected me. He's the only reason I'm even alive. I was unwanted but for reasons unknown to me, my parents decided to keep me when I was conceived and ultimately born. I don't have a relationship with my parents. They used to lock me in the closet whenever they didn't want to deal with me or claimed I had been bad. Sometimes for days at a time," Alira told them. Her voice was sad; shaky as she spoke. She barely noticed when Marcus squeezed her hand. She closed her eyes before she continued telling them about her life growing up.

"When my grandfather learned he had cancer, he amended the terms of the trust he had set up for me so I could receive access when I turned eighteen instead of at twenty-one. He did the same for my sister, Mara, just in case. Grayson on the other hand – well Grayson got nothing. Grayson has always been a monster but he hides it well and the world doesn't see him for the snake that he really is. My grandfather saw him for what he was and made sure he would never get a dime from an inheritance. He thinks there is a loophole somewhere that if I'm gone, everything in my trust somehow goes to him. Reality is, everything gets split between charities and Harold's daughter for school."

"Harold is a dear friend of mine. My ex-fiancé is good friends with Grayson. We technically had an arranged marriage setup because I foolishly believed Alex was safe. For a while, I was safe. Until Alex started acting more and more like Grayson. I was stuck until I turned eighteen but the second I did, I left. I'd had my bags packed for weeks. My parents didn't bother looking for me, but Grayson did. His personal mission in life is to make my life a living hell. Alex is unstable. He's not even supposed to be in the country. I have a restraining order in place but it's just a piece of paper. I am so sorry to have brought this trouble into your lives," Alira said the last part sadly, almost a whisper. She had to leave before they got dragged into her life any further. Her brother would go through them to get to her if he had to. She couldn't stand the thought of any of them getting hurt because of her.

Marcus sat back in his chair as he processed everything he had just heard. He knew there was more. She had given them the short version.

Alira pulled her hand away from his and placed it in her lap, staring down at it as she determinedly avoided meeting anyone's eyes. It had been really difficult to say any of that out loud. It was hard enough thinking it but to say the words – she wanted to throw up. She didn't want to believe her car had been sabotaged but deep down she knew it was true. Austin wouldn't lie to her and he wouldn't hire dishonest people. This was her reality. A living hell of what happens next.

"Hey, Dad, where are the keys to the cabin? I think a vacation is in order for Alira while Austin and his guys do some hunting," Adam spoke suddenly surprising everyone. He and Kenny had been silent throughout listening as Alira spoke.

"I can handle the business for a while. I doubt Marcus is going to allow Alira to go without him," Kenny stated honestly. They all nodded in agreement. Before she knew it, Austin was on the phone calling a meeting while Marcus went to help locate the keys for the cabin. Alira sat in stunned silence as everyone moved around her. Karma was the only one who stayed at the table with her offering her silent support in case Alira wanted to talk. She somehow always knew when Alira just needed a friend to hang out or talk to. Karma offered a reassuring smile as Charlotte requested help clearing the table while the men searched for cabin keys and God only knew what else.

Alira had expected to be shut out. She had been prepared to be told to leave and never come back because their family was in danger simply by knowing her. Instead... Instead, they had somehow managed to bring her tighter into their family and were determined to help keep her safe. Something she never asked them to do and never would have. Not for her. Never for her.

Chapter 7

Alira woke up early to pack for the cabin. Marcus and his brothers had loaded all manner of supplies into his truck the night before. They were set on food and bedding for the cabin which was primarily heated by the wood-burning stove in the kitchen. Alira remembered the cabin from a summer trip with Karma. It was a decently large cabin. Each room boasted its own fireplace. She was going to be incredibly grateful for that fireplace given that the forecast called for a blizzard. Austin had sent a couple of his guys ahead the night before to stock up on wood and make sure the property was secure before their arrival later this afternoon. Alira couldn't deny that she was nervous about the situation. She was comfortable with Marcus, but she knew him. She didn't know Austin's employees. Being snowed in with strange men was not high on her list of comforts.

Marcus had stayed on Alira's couch while she had slept in her bed. He could hear her tossing and turning restlessly. At one point, he had gone in to check on her when he'd heard her cry out in her sleep. He had sat with her for several long minutes while she settled before heading back to the couch for the night. He had wanted so badly to climb under the covers with her but wasn't sure how she would react if she woke up to find him in her bed.

Alira crept through the living room to the kitchen not wanting to wake Marcus who was snoring softly on her couch. She needed coffee. It had been a rough night and she was sore all over from flip-flopping around on the bed. Her ribs were practically screaming at her to stop moving. She vaguely remembered Marcus coming in to check on her and then leaving again. She had almost asked him to stay, but something stopped her. Now she wished she had asked. She may have at least slept better with him in the room.

As the coffee brewed, she pulled out some seasonings she wanted to take as well as some extra coffee supplies. They couldn't run out of coffee. Not when she still had to finish work on the gala. Except now it would need to be done remotely. It was frustrating. She would rather be hands-on with the planning and decorating but she would have to rely on her assistants entirely to handle it. They didn't mind but it didn't stop her from feeling bad about not being able to help more directly.

"Good morning," Marcus's deep voice sounded behind her. Alira spun around to face him.

"Did I wake you?" she asked apologetically. He shook his head.

The scent of fresh coffee had coaxed him from his dreams, beckoning him into the land of wakefulness. Finding her still in the kitchen had simply been a bonus. Without a second thought, Marcus crossed the kitchen and pulled her into his arms. She sighed softly when their lips touched.

"Did I already tell you good morning?" he asked sweetly as he rested his forehead against hers. She nodded with an easy smile that tugged at the corners of her mouth. Alira wrapped her arms around his waist and rested her head against his chest enjoying how it felt in his arms.

"You know, sooner or later we are going to need to talk about whatever is happening here," she said seriously as she tried to pull away.

"I know but not right now," he told her pulling her back against him. "Let's just enjoy this."

Alira finished packing and Marcus loaded her things into his truck. She had run down to the security office to let Harold know that she would be gone. She had wanted to tell him where she was going but he insisted that the less he knew the better. Marcus had agreed with him. The building would operate as usual with the increased security being the only change. As far as anyone would know, Alira was holed up in her apartment still recovering from her accident and working on the final touches for the gala that was rapidly approaching. Nobody would know where she really was. Austin had shown up to discuss security with Harold and his team but not before he inspected Marcus's truck for tracking devices. The last thing they needed was for Alira to be followed to the cabin when there was a blizzard coming. They would be sitting ducks with no way out for days.

Marcus helped her into the passenger seat of his truck. When she was comfortable, he shut the door and went around to the driver's side.

⁂

He hopped in easily. The engine roared to life with the turn of the key and they were ready to go. The cabin was roughly a two-hour drive west. The blizzard was expected to roll in that night. They should make it there with plenty of time to unload and get a fire going to warm the place up. Alira loved a good fire but she wished the cabin had central heating. It had Wi-Fi and electricity but hadn't been set up for heating yet. Karma had described it as a work in progress and since the Duvall's spent very few winter days out at the cabin, it wasn't high on the list of priorities. They had purchased the cabin about ten years ago and had updated it considerably otherwise.

Alira pulled her jacket a little tighter around herself as she watched Cedar Pleasant fade away. Trees zipped in and out of her view as Marcus navigated down the highway. He saw her tense up out of the corner of his eye and realized they were along the stretch where her car had gone off the road. He reached for her hand while keeping his eyes on the road. She didn't seem to notice as she scanned the roadway looking for the tire marks heading for the trees. She inhaled sharply when she saw them.

"Marcus, can you pull over?"

He did as she requested despite thinking it was a bad idea. As the truck rolled to a stop, she unbuckled her seatbelt and hopped out. She zipped her jacket up to her chin and followed the tire tracks through the grass toward the trees.

Seeing the scene in daylight made the entire incident more real. The two trees her car had been wedged between were evident by their missing bark. Any further into the trees and she could have been impaled on a low-hanging branch. There was broken glass scattered around the area. She could easily see the paint from her car on the thick tree trunks. Alira stared in shock as it sank in just how close she had come to being seriously injured or dying. Images flashed through her memory. Marcus had been a strong presence throughout but she thankfully didn't remember much else. She knew she had been scared. That was it.

Marcus stood a few feet away from her watching as she surveyed the area. He remembered the scene like it had just happened. It may have happened four days ago, but it was still so fresh in his mind that he could picture it easily now. He had never felt fear like he had that night when he'd pulled up to see her car trapped between those two massive trees she stood between now. Even the night he had lost Carmen didn't compare. With Carmen, he had been there when she died. He had been helpless but he'd been able to say goodbye to her. The ambulance hadn't arrived in time. When he had seen Alira's car – he had been so afraid he would find her dead. The relief he had felt finding the opposite was palpable.

Alira saw the look on Marcus's face. He was lost. He had seen her accident from an entirely different perspective. Without another thought, she walked over and wrapped her arms around him. She hugged him so tightly that her ribs protested angrily but she didn't care. Her sore ribs and bruises couldn't compare to the pain she saw on his face as he stood there watching her. It was obvious at that moment that he cared for her. Marcus returned her hug.

"Thank you for coming to find me," she whispered as a tear escaped to slide down her cheek. Marcus holding her tighter, buried his nose in her hair and inhaled deeply. When he pulled away, he tilted her face up to look into her eyes.

"Alira, I will *always* come to find you," he told her firmly. The emotion she heard in his voice surprised her. He meant what he said. His dark eyes bore into her as though he was staring into her soul. All she could do was nod as he wiped her tears away. Whatever was happening between them was big. What that was remained to be seen. Regardless, it was there and it was growing.

"Wake up sleepyhead. We're here," Marcus's gentle words broke into her dream. She stirred and opened her eyes blinking against the sunlight. Two men approached the truck as Marcus hopped out. Unbuckling her seatbelt, Alira stretched in the seat and watched as Marcus greeted them. They must be Austin's guys. They were big. Not as large as Marcus but they looked like they could easily hold their own if necessary. Each man had a pistol holstered at his hip. She imagined they probably wore a knife strapped around their ankle in their boots too. Marcus pointed to the back of the truck and together the three of them moved. Austin's men started to unload the supplies while Marcus came to open her door. The whoosh of cold air that filled the cab suddenly made her shiver as her teeth started chattering before she could stop them.

"Nope! Too cold out there!" she squeaked and tried to pull the door closed. Marcus laughed and looked at her with an expression that told her she either got out of the truck on her own or he would get her out himself. She raised an eyebrow challenging him.

"Alira, don't make me drag you out of this truck," he threatened even as he tried to suppress a smile. Alira squealed as he reached into the truck. She laughed when he scooped her up off the seat. Marcus closed the door with his foot and walked up the stairs into the cabin without missing a beat. He set her down on the couch in front of the roaring fire. As he reached for a blanket, she kicked off her boots and tucked her feet up under her. Marcus cast the blanket like he was casting a net before he started tucking it tightly around her. Alira tossed her head trying to shake it off. When Marcus was finished tucking her in, he pulled the blanket down under her chin and pressed a kiss to the tip of her nose.

"I seem to be trapped on the couch. Whatever shall I do?" she feigned indignation. Marcus rolled his eyes in exasperation at her.

"I'm going to go help unload the truck. That blizzard is hitting tonight whether we're ready for it or not," he told her before leaving her cocooned on the couch. She settled in only to realize the remote for the TV was on the stand across the room. With a huff, Alira started trying to wiggle out of the blanket. Marcus had really made sure she was snug in there! Maybe tucking her feet under her hadn't been such a good idea. She struggled to free her feet from the confines of the cocoon. If she could get situated so that she could stand, the blanket would be much easier to get off.

Alira wiggled and bounced until she had somehow wound up on the arm of the couch. Her feet were tangled in the material. Just as she managed to free her arms, she felt herself falling backward. She squeaked in surprise and prepared for the landing that was sure to come on the solid wood flooring. Strong arms caught her before she hit the floor.

"Easy there," a voice said. She opened her eyes to see blue eyes peering at her with concern.

"Camden?" Marcus's deeper voice questioned from the doorway. Alira looked at him confused.

"Wait, Camden? Karma's Camden?" she squealed excitedly. Camden chuckled as he righted her and helped untangle her from the blanket that still had her feet hostage.

"I guess you could say that. Sorry that we're finally meeting like this. Austin keeps me pretty busy," he explained as he dropped the blanket over the back of the couch and went to take the cooler Marcus held. Alira was so excited to finally meet the man Karma was head over heels for. She hadn't expected it to be under these circumstances, but still, she was excited! She had hoped to have them over for dinner at some point when their schedules were all lighter.

"Marcus, your burrito tried to escape off the couch," Camden joked. Marcus laughed. Alira snorted in an unladylike fashion.

"Trucks unloaded. Camden, you going to help me bring more firewood in or what?"

The question was followed by heavy footsteps from behind her. Alira almost jumped out of her skin before she put quick distance between herself and the owner of the voice that was deeper than any she had ever heard before. Marcus saw her wince, but she quickly tried to hide it. The hand pressed against her ribs told another story.

"Alira, you've already met Camden. This other scary gentleman is Duke. He graduated with Karma," Marcus explained as he introduced her other bodyguard. Duke waved but kept his serious expression. Alira couldn't help but wonder if he ever smiled. He was a bear of a man. He was shorter than Marcus. Marcus was lean and muscular. Duke was muscular but he was wide. He looked like someone you would expect to see in a body-building contest. Bulky. That described him very well. Duke was intimidating.

"Smile man! You don't need to be so serious all the time!" Camden told him.

"If I smiled, it would be so dazzling that you would lose your spotlight entirely," Duke replied sarcastically. Camden raised a hand to his chest and stumbled back dramatically like he had been shot. Alira thought she saw the corners of Duke's mouth twitch.

"Well, it's nice to meet you both. Don't mind me and my overly jumpy habits," Alira told them warmly. The dig at her own insecurities was not lost on them. No matter. She was sure they would figure it out soon enough.

Alira moved around the kitchen like a professional. She had chased the men out insisting they would just get in the way. At one point Duke didn't move fast enough for her so she had rather effectively pushed him out of the room. Duke had clearly been surprised because he suddenly found himself in the dining room staring into the kitchen wondering what happened to the jumpy young woman he had met only an hour earlier. The one who had run to the other side of the room when he popped up behind her. They decided the safest place to get away from the tiny angry chef was to go to the game room. There was a pool table to help pass the time.

As she finished breading the chicken to stick in the pan to crisp before transferring it to the oven to finish cooking, she clicked the volume control for the radio turning it up. Alira shook her hips as she started the marinara sauce simmering and hummed along to the music. She danced her way over to the sink with an empty pan to get water for the pasta. While waiting for the water to boil, Alira grabbed plates from the cabinet and utensils from the drawer. She dipped and twirled her way to the dining room to set the table, bobbing her head to the beat of the song pumping from the speakers in the kitchen. When the song changed to one of her favorites, she sang along like it was her job.

Camden set up for his shot, ready to send the cue ball across the table when he stopped to listen. Duke and Marcus had already turned their ears to the door. Camden set his pool stick down on the table and the three of them crowded around the door listening intently. The song ended and the next one began. They could hear her singing just as happily to the next one. Camden cocked his head in silent question. Duke nodded enthusiastically.

"Gosh Duke, if I didn't know any better, I would think you were interested in something!" Camden joked with him jabbing him in the ribs. Duke shoved him before starting down the hall with silent footsteps. Marcus and Camden walked after him. They crowded around the kitchen entrance, unnoticed, as Alira danced around the stove singing into a spatula like a microphone. Marcus stood in awe of her as she hit every note flawlessly. She moved with such grace he would have thought her to be a dancer. Watching her dance around the kitchen now was such a contrast to the clumsy woman who regularly tripped over her own feet.

The song ended. They cheered. Camden yelled for an encore. Alira spun around in surprise and immediately started laughing. She bowed with a dramatic wave of her hand. Marcus stepped forward with his arms out moving in for a hug.

"Why didn't you tell me you could sing?" he asked as he pulled her in.

"I didn't think it mattered," she told him with a shrug. Marcus leaned back with a look she couldn't quite read on his face. The timer went off on the stove and she pulled away from him.

"Alira, you have a beautiful voice!" Marcus praised.

"Thank you. I could have sworn you had heard me sing before. At the same time, it makes sense that you haven't. You made it a point to avoid interacting with me beyond a 'hello' until recently," she stated as she pulled the tray of chicken out of the oven. Camden had moved to drain the pasta for her while Duke had grabbed the pan of marinara sauce and already disappeared with it to the dining room. Camden followed quickly with the bowl of noodles. Marcus stood quietly near the counter as Alira placed the chicken onto a plate for easier serving at the table. The mood shifted and the air grew heavy between them. She refused to look at him.

"I deserved that," Marcus admitted hanging his head. He had avoided her. He had done everything he could to keep his distance from her since his sister had befriended her after that night at Riggs. If he was honest with himself, he had seen her enter the bar that night and considered approaching her then. When her date had cornered her after shot-gunning a beer and two shots almost as soon as he walked through the door, Marcus couldn't just stand by and watch her suffer his advances. He figured when they dropped her off at her building it was the last time that he would see her. Until Karma invited her to dinner at his parent's house. Soon it just became normal to see her at least twice a week or more depending on what events his family was celebrating. Marcus had started trying to pretend she wasn't there because the second he noticed her, he wasn't going to be able to stay away.

Duke appeared cautiously in the doorway. Marcus took the plate of chicken from Alira and handed it to him. Duke took it and left quickly wanting nothing to do with the atmosphere in the kitchen at that time. Alira started to argue that she could take the plate to the table but gave up. She tried following after Duke. Marcus stopped her with a grip on her hand. He pulled her back to stand in front of him and took both of her hands in his.

"You're right. I was avoiding you but I'm not avoiding you now," his voice soft as he spoke; vulnerable. Alira felt the ice around her heart thaw a little bit. Damn him.

"We're talking after dinner," she stated firmly as she withdrew her hands. Marcus didn't argue. He nodded and followed her to the dining room.

Chapter 8

"This is the best chicken parmesan I have ever eaten," Camden said as he enthusiastically helped himself to a third portion. Alira laughed. She was glad she had made plenty. She knew how much Marcus could eat and often did. Looking at Camden and Duke, she figured they would likely eat just as much. Hell, she had seen all of the Duvall brothers eat and it was no wonder their father had started the construction company. It was the only way to afford the grocery bill with six kids; five of whom were bottomless pits. Karma could pack it away too, but nothing compared to her brothers. Alira had been equally impressed and surprised during her first dinner at the Duvall's home watching the brothers eat. They were vacuums. If it was on their plate, they ate it. It was no wonder she had a full kitchen at home. Charlotte was used to shopping to feed a small army. Alira couldn't eat nearly that much.

Duke offered to clean up. His voice still surprised Alira. She had never heard anyone with such an incredibly deep voice. You could almost feel it rumble in your chest when he spoke. She did learn he had other facial expressions beyond serious though. She still hadn't seen him crack a smile no matter how many bad jokes Camden told.

Alira curled up on the couch while Camden headed outside to do a security sweep before repeating the same thing inside. Marcus had disappeared upstairs claiming he was starting the fire in her room so that it would be nice and toasty when she went to bed. She knew he was stalling. They still needed to talk.

Marcus returned downstairs to find Alira dozing on the couch wrapped tightly in a blanket. He knelt down next to her. The fire in the fireplace was slowly dwindling down to embers and there was a distinct chill in the living room as a result. The flickering firelight cast a soft glow over her face. Marcus cupped her cheek in his hand and ran his thumb over her smooth skin softly.

"Hey sweetheart, it's time for bed," he spoke quietly. She mumbled something incoherent and tried to roll away. With a sigh,

Marcus stood. He lifted her into his arms, cradling her against his chest, and started for the stairs. She tucked her face against his neck and inhaled deeply.

"You smell good," she whispered. Marcus didn't say a word in response. Not when her breath on his neck was doing funny things to him. He simply made his way down the hallway and to her room at the end of the corridor. He settled her onto the mattress and pulled the covers up around her while she nestled into the pillows. Satisfied she would be warm enough, Marcus pressed a kiss to her forehead and turned to leave. Her whispered word stopped him in his tracks.

"Stay."

He turned; unsure he had heard her correctly. Her eyes opened slowly and focused on him.

"Stay," she repeated.

Marcus only hesitated for a second before he kicked off his shoes and removed his t-shirt. Alira pulled the covers back for him.

"Let me go grab a pair of sweats. I'm not eager to sleep in my jeans again," he explained. She shook her head.

"Just take them off and sleep in your boxers," she said as a yawn claimed her. Marcus pursed his lips trying to decide if that was a good idea or not. In the end, he removed his jeans, leaving them in a heap on the floor with his shirt.

He laid down and pulled her back against him. She wove her fingers with his and held his hand over her heart between her breasts. She wiggled her hips adjusting to get comfortable. Marcus groaned as blood rushed to his groin. Thankfully, she didn't seem to notice as she quickly drifted off to sleep in his arms with a contented sigh.

Marcus laid awake for what must have been an hour as Alira slept peacefully wrapped in his embrace. The fire had burned out quickly, but he also hadn't built it up too much. It had been just enough to warm the room comfortably for bed. The blankets on the bed would handle the rest through the night. As he lay there listening to her breath, feeling her heartbeat beneath their joined hands, he realized he never wanted anything or anyone so much in his life. Somehow, Alira had broken through his carefully constructed walls. He couldn't pinpoint when exactly it had happened. It just had.

After Carmen had died, he was so sure he would never feel *it* again. Not with anyone. He had been right. He had loved Carmen, but things had never been electric between them. They could go days without seeing one another and he had never had that strong pull to spend every waking minute with her. With Alira? It was different. There was more to it. What he felt for Alira could start a wildfire with a single spark. As Marcus held her, he knew that he would walk through the fires of hell for her if she asked it of him. Embers could easily reignite to a blazing inferno with the right conditions. The realization didn't come as much of a surprise as he thought it would. It had been building. With every glance when nobody was looking, with every hello and goodbye, with every accidental brush of her hand as he walked past in a tight space at his parent's dinners... Those embers had been building.

She rolled in her sleep. Marcus lifted his arm from her waist to make it easier for her to adjust. When she stilled once more, he lowered his arm. She lay facing him; her head tucked up under his chin. Her little puffs of breath tickled the hair on his chest even as her fingers moved reflexively against the bare skin of his stomach. Enjoying the feel of her pressed against him, he pulled her closer and finally let his eyes close.

Alira opened her eyes to the dark bedroom. The fire had long since gone out in the fireplace and the room was cold. Unfortunately, her bladder begged for relief. She was not too excited about having to get out of the nice warm bed but if she didn't, she may explode. Steeling herself against the cold, she rolled away from Marcus and his warmth. Her bones ached without the warmth of a fire. As she scampered across the room and into the bathroom, she wished she still had socks on. The room was too dark to find her slippers on the floor. Socks would have helped a great deal in preventing her feet from turning into instant ice cubes.

As she evacuated her bladder, she tried to prevent her teeth from chattering. Alira finished her task quickly, washed her hands, and practically sprinted back to the bed. There was no hesitation when she crawled under the covers shivering painfully and cuddled up against Marcus. His arm slid around her unconsciously pulling her closer. She happily pressed into him soaking in his heat. The man was his own furnace. She didn't think he ever got cold. Her teeth were chattering, and she was shivering so much that her muscles hurt from the tension. It certainly did nothing to help with the aches caused by the accident though by some miracle she wasn't at the tears stage of pain anymore. Movements were still uncomfortable but manageable. Her ribs were still pretty angry, but the doctor had warned her that they would be for a while.

Marcus was awake the instant Alira moved from the bed. He debated restarting the fire while she was in the bathroom but decided it could wait until the morning. There were two down comforters with flannel sheets on the bed. Between that and their shared body heat, they should be good for the night. If they weren't, there were more blankets in the chest at the foot of the bed and he could restart the fire easily enough.

He listened as she all but ran across the room and crawled back into bed. She snuggled back in with him easily, probably because she thought he was still asleep. Marcus figured if she knew he was awake, she may have questioned it. He could feel her shivering and heard her teeth chattering hard. Her hands were icy cold against his skin as she tried pressing her hands into her shirt to warm them before touching him.

"You okay?" he asked softly. She nodded her head even as she shivered.

"I-I'm f-fine," she stuttered. Marcus held her tighter, maneuvering so he could hold her hands flat against his chest to warm them. She protested that her hands were too cold, but he ignored it insisting he would be alright. She sighed happily when her hands felt almost instantly warmer.

"How much has Karma told you about Carmen?" he asked quietly unsure he wanted to talk about it but knowing he needed to. She needed to hear it.

"Just that you were engaged to her and she died about four years ago. Karma said it changed you because you used to be happy and fun instead of serious all the time," Alira replied just as quietly. Marcus sighed and rolled onto his back pulling her with him.

"Carmen worked as my dad's assistant at the company. That's how she and I met. Dad was slowly handing the main responsibilities over to me. I was spending a lot of time in the main office. Carmen and I grew close. I asked her to marry me after dating a little over a year. One night about four months before our wedding, two men broke into the condo we shared. They thought we were gone for the night so it wouldn't be any trouble," Marcus told her.

Once he started, the words flowed out of him like a river.

Alira listened as he spoke. It was important for him to get it out and tell her what had happened to Carmen. As she listened to him tell everything from that night, she realized that she understood why Marcus was so serious and closed off.

"One of them had a gun. He had it aimed at me but Carmen - she managed to break free from his partner's hold on her. She ran at the gunman screaming. He pulled the trigger in a panic. The bullet missed me, ricocheted off a metal flower on the wall, and hit her. She bled out in my arms before the ambulance ever even arrived. The police caught the guys two blocks away trying to rob another house the same night. I failed her," he told her with a mixture of sadness and anger. She understood why he was angry. She also understood his sadness. That night had to have been traumatic for him. She couldn't even begin to imagine what it would be like to hold someone as they died, let alone someone she loved.

Marcus rolled away from her and got out of bed. Alira stayed put. She watched as his shadowed figure moved to the fireplace and knelt down. He added a couple of logs to the pile and fiddled with some kindling before he struck a match. The fire was slow to start but quickly grew to light up the room. When Marcus stood, he ran his hand through his hair and leaned against the mantle watching the flames dance in the alcove. He didn't hear her get out of the bed or walk across the room, but when her arms slid around his waist to squeeze him tight, Marcus felt his anger soften.

"You didn't fail Carmen. You loved her and she loved you. What happened that night when those men broke in – Marcus, you couldn't have predicted what would happen," Alira told him, her voice soft but carried a serious undertone. Marcus stiffened as guilt washed over him in waves. He removed her arms from around his waist and stepped away from her. Alira tried not to show her emotions but her face betrayed her. It felt like she had been burned. She quickly sat down in the chair beside the fireplace and waited for him to say or do something. When he grabbed his t-shirt and pulled it over his head, she knew the time for talking was over. He left the room without another word, leaving her sitting there wondering what she had done or said wrong.

Marcus stomped down the stairs to the living room. Austin was sitting on the couch reading a book with a lamp on over his shoulder.

"When did you get here?" Marcus asked upon seeing him. Austin closed the book and looked up at his brother.

"Rolled up about an hour ago. Barely made it here before that blizzard started dumping snow everywhere," he explained with a nod to the window. Marcus turned to look outside. The snow was already about a foot deep from what he could see and still coming down heavily. So much for sitting outside in the cold air for a little while to clear his head.

"What's on your mind?" Austin asked him as he set his book down on the end table. Marcus sat with a huff at the opposite end of the couch.

"I told Alira about the night Carmen died."

Austin nodded. He remembered it. He had been the first one at the condo after receiving the call; had arrived just before the police. Marcus had been on the floor holding Carmen when Austin ran in. Blood pooled around them as Carmen's lifeless eyes stared at the ceiling. The paramedics arrived and tried everything to revive her, but she was gone. The bullet had hit an artery. She was dead before anyone could have done anything to stop it from happening. Marcus had to be sedated before they could take her body away. His big brother had been an irrational mess trying to hold onto her. Austin shook his head to rid himself of the memory of it.

"What did Alira have to say?" he asked. Marcus sat with his head resting in his hands. He laughed weakly. Austin waited patiently for him to answer. He lifted his head and stared into the fire.

"She told me it wasn't my fault. Said Carmen had loved me and that I loved her, but you know what? I wasn't in love with Carmen. I loved her, sure, but I wasn't *in* love with her. Not like I am with..." he trailed off.

He stood up unable to sit still and started pacing. Austin watched him with a smile on his face. It annoyed Marcus how his brother could say so much without ever speaking a single word. He imagined his overly observant nature was what made him so good at protecting his clients. Austin could read a person or situation like Marcus could imagine the finished product of a building before they ever started the work on it.

"Not like you are with Alira," Austin finished for him in a hushed tone. Marcus stopped pacing and rested his arm on the mantel as he stared into the flames. He narrowed his eyes. Damnit.

"No, not like I am with Alira," Marcus finally admitted softly.

<u>Chapter 9</u>

Alira put another log on the fire before grabbing her computer to work on finalizing donation deliveries for the silent auction she had planned for the gala this year. The gala was coming up fast and she didn't want to leave anything to the last minute. If she could manage to get final events taken care of then she would be able to take a week off before the mad rush to set up the ballroom at the Cedar Point Hotel. It was the final push and Alira was excited to finally reach the end to see the result of months of planning with very little sleep. As if to drive it home, she yawned as she hit send on her latest email to her assistants.

Marcus knocked softly as he stepped into the bedroom. Alira sat in the chair near the fireplace with her feet tucked up under her and her computer in her lap. She didn't even look up from the screen when he entered. As she tapped away at the keys, Marcus tried to gather his thoughts. He needed to tell her the truth. He also needed to apologize to her for his vanishing act earlier. He moved toward the chair opposite her and started to sit but thought better of it. Instead, he started pacing.

"Marcus, if you wouldn't mind, I really need to get these emails answered so my assistants have the plan moving forward," she spoke without lifting her eyes from the screen. Marcus stopped pacing and looked at her. Assistants? She had assistants? As in plural?

"You have assistants?" he asked surprised. She sighed in exasperation and rolled her eyes.

"Yes, I have assistants. Assistants who have been forced to take on more responsibility than they signed up for with the gala since I was whisked away for safety reasons. No thanks to my brother and my psycho ex. We are now just under three weeks away from the event and trying to finish up last-minute details is difficult via email so if you could stop pacing and huffing at me, I would appreciate it," she said sternly. Marcus was taken aback. There was no quiet avoidance in her tone. She had nicely told him to back off without actually saying the words. She had an edge to her that he rarely saw but he loved when he did. She was tough.

"Let me know when you're done, okay? I'd like to talk. It's important," he told her and quietly moved toward the door.

Alira looked up just as he closed the door behind him. She hadn't meant to be harsh, but she really did need to get those emails answered. Not to mention they were going to be trapped at the cabin for a few days at least, and she did want to enjoy some of it without work involved. Kara and Joey were fantastic assistants and were absolutely capable of handling the rest of the planning with her guidance. They had helped her plan the gala for the last three years since she had been hired to handle it. The gala was her baby. Even before planning for the following gala really started getting heavy, she always had notes ready to go.

"She wouldn't talk to you huh?"

Marcus glared at his brother. Austin put his book down and waited for him to speak. Marcus went into the kitchen for a beer instead. He knew he didn't have a reason to be frustrated but he was. He was frustrated because he had finally admitted out loud that Alira wasn't just his baby sister's best friend. Alira was so much more than that to him and the darn woman wouldn't let him tell her! He heard Austin laugh.

"You're mumbling," Austin called from the living room. Marcus twisted the top off the beer bottle and took a swig. Tossing the bottle cap into the trash, Marcus went back into the living room to flop down in the recliner near the fire.

"There is another elephant in the room beside the obvious," Austin told him with a cough.

"And what would that be?" Marcus asked before taking another swig from the bottle.

"Alira's stalker knows you two aren't actually married," he stated matter of fact as he reached for his own beer on the table.

Alira sat silently at the top of the stairs out of sight listening to their conversation. She knew she shouldn't eavesdrop, but curiosity had gotten the better of her. She had finished the emails she needed to get done and closed her computer. Instead of going back to bed, she decided to go find Marcus and find out what he had wanted to talk about. Imagine her surprise at learning Austin had made it after all. He must have just made it before the storm hit.

"What do you expect me to do? She deserves to make the decision because she wants to get married to someone she loves. Not because she has to get married to help protect herself. Pretending will have to do it. She would never say yes to the real thing," Marcus told him seriously.

Alira stood and cleared her throat startling them. Austin looked up wide-eyed as she descended the stairs while Marcus sat stiffly in the recliner looking mildly embarrassed. Alira couldn't recall a time in the last year that she had seen him flushed. She noticed the beer in his hand and wondered if that had anything to do with it. Maybe he had chugged it and felt guilty? She had seen him drink before so it really shouldn't be that big of a deal.

"Yes," Alira answered quietly. Her hands shook but she hid them in the long sleeves of her shirt. Austin caught the movement and raised an eyebrow in question before quickly glancing at Marcus. Marcus didn't seem to notice. He took a long drink from the bottle he held, emptying it. Austin choked on a laugh.

"Alira, you know you don't have to do this. It was just a suggestion," Austin explained calmly. His voice was soothing as he spoke. Austin was a joker, but he had a sweet side that Alira adored about him. He had a way about him that could put anyone at ease and make them laugh when it mattered. This was one of those times he radiated that calm.

"I do actually. I can't do this on my own and my brother already thinks I'm married. Why not make it official? It's not like I have a choice. I don't get to marry for love. I'm not meant to have the fairytale," Alira stated with certainty as she watched Marcus. He didn't react. She knew he wouldn't. Why would he? His mother had dragged him into this fiasco, and he was just along for the ride. With a sigh, she bid Austin goodnight and turned to go back upstairs. Austin snapped his fingers at Marcus and nodded his head hard in Alira's direction. Marcus rolled his eyes and set the empty bottle on the side table.

Alira closed the bedroom door behind her trying to keep the tears that had formed in her eyes from falling. She had hoped that one day she would marry for love, but fate was cruel. There wasn't a man on the planet who would want to marry an emotionally and physically traumatized woman who had six locks on her door and a psychotic ex stalking her. She had grown up being shown repeatedly that she was unlovable. Her own parents had very little to do with her from the time she was two. If it hadn't been for her grandfather and Mara, Alira didn't know where or even who she would be.

Her grandfather had tried so hard to convince her parents to sign over custody of her, but they had refused. She would never know why they said no. She didn't even know where her parents were or how to get in touch with them. They didn't care to know her. They didn't want her. That had been made perfectly clear when she had been five and they had taken Mara and Grayson to the Bahamas for Christmas. They had left Alira in the care of the maid for two weeks. That was until the maid disappeared and Alira was left all alone in that big house. She remembered being terrified and screaming for her but never got a response. Her grandfather had come by the day before Christmas Eve to deliver presents for her and had found her huddled in the pantry eating uncooked meat. He had immediately taken her home and filed a petition for custody.

Alira tried to shake off the memory but it stayed with her vividly as though it had just happened, and she was watching from the outside. Her parents had immediately picked her up when they returned from their holiday. They had thrown her into the closet when they returned home before ever having their bags brought inside. Grayson had taken great joy in terrorizing her at all hours for the four days she spent locked in the small dark space with nothing but a pad to lay on. As she sat in the chair staring into the dwindling fire, memories slammed into her one after another. She was so focused on them that she didn't hear Marcus come into the room. She didn't even notice when he sat in the chair across from her.

Marcus watched while Alira stared into the flames as her eyebrows knitted together with worry. She was clearly lost in thought. She hadn't even reacted when he came into the bedroom and sat down. Whatever was going on in that head of hers had made her oblivious to anything that may be happening around her.

Alira shook her head and blinked several times to clear her thoughts. He couldn't make out what he saw in her eyes when she looked at him. There was worry mixed with curiosity and something else.

"What do you want from me?" she asked him. Her voice was just above a whisper as her eyes met his.

This was it. She was asking for answers. Marcus took a deep breath trying to slow his stampeding heart. Alira watched as Marcus moved from the chair to his knees before her, taking her hands in his. She almost pulled her hands away but something in his eyes stopped her.

[?]

"You can marry for love and you do deserve the fairytale," he told her honestly. His expression was soft; eyes showing his vulnerability as he knelt in front of her. Alira squinted as if she was trying to see him better. He squeezed her hands. His meaning eluded her. When he let go of one of her hands and reached into his back pocket, her eyes went wide.

Alira's heart started to race as he produced a ring. It was easily the most beautiful ring she had ever seen. The round stone was a stunning sapphire set between two Celtic knots lined with tiny opals and a white gold band. It sparkled brilliantly in the firelight. Her breath caught in her throat as her hand went to her chest.

"Marcus..."

Her voice was breathy and soft when she said his name. He held the ring up to her between two fingers. Alira saw nervousness in him that she had never expected to see. Not from him. Marcus was always so firm; stable and unmoving. To see this side of him – she had no words to describe it.

"I care about you. Let me protect you."

Marcus spoke so softly that she would have missed it if she hadn't been paying attention. She shook her head.

"I already agreed. What more do you want from me?" she asked in frustration.

She still didn't understand why he was making such a big deal out of this. She had already said yes to the marriage. There was nothing left to agree to. They could easily have it annulled once this whole thing with her brother and her ex was over.

Marcus reached up and cupped her cheek in his hand. She leaned into his touch, almost unwillingly.

"You have brought vibrant color back into my life that I hadn't realized was even missing. Since I saw you walk into the bar that night, I haven't been able to take my eyes off of you. I didn't know it then, but I was drawn to you like a honeybee is drawn to the flowers. You are the light shining in the dark, and I have been an absolute fool trying to deny what I feel for you. Alira, let me be your fairytale because – because you're mine," Marcus told her truthfully.

The raw emotion in his voice as he bared his heart to her brought new tears to her eyes. She tried to blink them back, but as he watched her hopefully, they spilled over as the weight of what he was saying hit her full force. Her heart slammed in her chest and her hands shook. He lifted her hand to his lips and pressed a soft kiss to her knuckles. She sniffled and wiped at her cheek with the sleeve of her shirt.

"Ask me," she said in a shaky voice.

Marcus smiled and hung his head in relief. Then his eyes lifted to meet hers once more. His eyes were a soft, almost golden brown as he gazed upon her. Warmth flooded her body as he shifted to kneeling on one knee and held out the ring to her.

"Be my everything. Alira Hervowe, will you marry me?"

Chapter 10

Alira nodded as tears streamed freely down her cheeks.

"Yes?" he asked as he tried to swallow past the lump in his throat.

"Yes!" she replied enthusiastically and threw her arms around his neck.

Marcus couldn't believe his ears! She said yes! He had been so afraid that she would reject him. He fell back pulling her with him, cushioning her landing with his body. Marcus couldn't believe how happy she was. He couldn't believe how happy *he* was! This was happening.

Alira pulled away from him as a blush rose to color her cheeks. Marcus pulled her back against him and captured her mouth with his own, scattering all of the thoughts in her head until there was nothing but Marcus there fanning the flames within her. The intensity of their kiss was almost too much to take. When the kiss broke, they were both breathing heavily. Alira laid her head down on his chest while his arms slid easily around her waist holding her in place against him.

"Shall we see if this thing fits?" he asked her softly talking about the ring. Without a word, Alira pushed away from him into a sitting position. Marcus curled up to sit. Alira shivered as she imagined watching the muscles of his stomach flex with the movement. He picked the ring up off the floor and reached for her hand. Slowly, he slid the band over her finger. It was a perfect fit. The stones glittered and sparkled in the light of the fire as they both admired it.

"Marcus, it's so beautiful but where on earth did you get it?" she asked curiously as she wiggled her finger, fascinated by how the light bounced off the stone. Marcus leaned back on his hand and looked away from her. Alira froze.

"Was this – was this Carmen's?"

"No! No, it wasn't Carmen's. Would you believe me if I told you that I bought it about four months ago?" Marcus asked, cautiously refusing to look directly at her. Alira narrowed her eyes.

Four months ago, she had gone shopping with him looking for a birthday gift for Charlotte because Karma had bailed on helping him find something. Karma had volunteered Alira to go with him since she still needed to find a gift at the time too. He had been a complete grump the entire afternoon. They had gone into a jewelry store over on Ninth Avenue to pick up a necklace being repaired that Karma had asked them to pick up while they were out. She wouldn't have been off work in time to go before the store closed. While Marcus had waited at the counter for the employee to bring the necklace out, Alira had browsed the rings. She was particularly drawn to the sapphires. The way they sparkled in the lights reminded her of the stars in the night sky and the peace that she felt looking up. Marcus had gruffly dragged her out of the store once he had Karma's necklace and she had forgotten about the ring.

"Hang on – Marcus, did you go back to the jewelry store on Ninth?"

He nodded with a sheepish grin.

"Yeah. I did. I saw you looking while we were there for Karma's necklace. You had this soft smile on your face as you admired each piece in the case. The color matched your eyes. I went back after we went our separate ways and bought that ring. I had no idea when I was going to give it to you or what my reason was going to be. Maybe I just hadn't admitted it then..." Marcus didn't finish. He avoided meeting her eyes shyly.

"Admitted what?" Alira pressed him. Marcus sighed but when he lifted his eyes to meet hers, her heart started to race again. The man was going to be the death of her if he kept looking at her like she was the only woman in the world.

"That I was in love with you. That I *am* in love with you."

Alira's eyes widened at his admission. She had misheard him, right? She was tired and she was still fairly sore. Maybe she was imagining this. That made sense. Marcus was still downstairs talking to Austin and she had fallen asleep with her computer in her lap while answering emails upstairs by the fire. This was a dream. A really good dream, but still a dream. Then she felt his warm hand envelope hers.

"I – I don't know what to say. Is this real life?" she stammered out in disbelief.

He nodded.

"It's real and it's okay. There is no pressure on you, I promise," his soft-spoken words were emphasized by his touch on her cheek. The pad of his thumb smoothed over the soft skin as she closed her eyes enjoying the feel of it. Alira opened her eyes slowly. She surprised him as she

?

moved to straddle him. Her arms slid around his neck and her fingers brushed through his hair. He groaned as tiny tingles of sensation moved through him.

"Thank you," she whispered just a breath before pressing her lips softly to his.

Austin was asleep on the couch when Marcus went downstairs to grab a couple bottles of water. Clearly, he had given up on reading but had been either too lazy or too tired to go upstairs to his room. Marcus shook his head and tossed a blanket loosely over him having lost count of how often he found Austin snoring on the couch all the times the family had come out to the cabin. It seemed to be his favorite place to crash. He almost wanted to scare him awake like when they were kids but decided against it. Alira was waiting for him upstairs.

Alira was curled up under the comforters with nothing peeking out. Even her head was covered. The fire had gone out and the room had a distinct chill to it when Marcus returned. They had agreed there was no need to add more wood. Instead, Marcus had insisted they go back to bed. It was the best course when her eyelids started to droop. It was around two in the morning when Marcus carried her to the bed and tucked her in. He hadn't been gone more than a few minutes, but he could hear that she was already sound asleep snoring quietly.

Marcus closed the door softly. He kicked off his shoes in front of the closet and walked through the dark over to the bed. After setting the bottles down on the nightstand, he took his shirt off and picked up their clothes from the floor. He folded the clothing sloppily before placing it on the chair. Marcus pulled back the covers on his side of the bed just enough to slip under but not enough to disturb Alira as she slept. Almost immediately, Alira shifted closer. Marcus pulled her easily into his arms and closed his eyes. This was perfect. She was perfect.

The sunlight had just started to shine through the window when Alira opened her eyes again. Her ribs throbbed painfully making her groan. She rolled trying to find a more comfortable position to ease the pain she was experiencing and rolled right into the solid wall of Marcus's bare chest. Alira held her breath afraid that she had woken him. He didn't seem to notice she had just slammed into him. She let out her breath slowly as her fingers touched his skin. He was warm. As her fingers traced lines across his chest, she momentarily forgot about the pain in her ribcage. Lightly, she traced the line of his jaw. The stubble there tickled her fingertips, making her smile. She kissed his chin. He stirred. Then, she pressed a kiss to his neck. His hold at her waist tightened just a little. Feeling bold, she moved further down and pressed a kiss to his chest as her hand slid slowly down his stomach. He groaned loudly.

"Are you trying to drive me crazy?"

His deep rumbling voice washed over her in a way that sent heat pooling straight to her core. She smiled as she pressed another kiss to his chest before making a slow trail down. When she reached the waistband of his boxers, she traced along the band with her tongue. She felt him tense up and heard the breath catch in his throat.

Alira teased a trail of kisses along the waistband of his boxers driving him absolutely crazy. The instant he'd felt her lips against his neck, he had been awake and hard as a rock. Then she had kissed her way down his chest, his stomach, and lower... He groaned when her breasts pressed against his raging erection. He caught her smile as she looked up at him before squeezing him between her breasts. He inhaled sharply. Holy fuck! When her mouth closed over the tip of him through the material, he couldn't stop himself from tangling his fingers in her hair and tugging. It took every ounce of self-control he had not to thrust his hips. He wanted her. He wanted her more than anything.

"Alira..." he warned through gritted teeth.

She immediately pulled her mouth away from him and moved back up his body. She straddled his hips, grinding against him as she boldly claimed his mouth with her own. Marcus's arms wrapped tightly around her waist as their kiss turned wild and demanding. Alira allowed him to pull her shirt off over her head exposing her bare breasts. He palmed one and then the other. She leaned into his hands with a moan.

Marcus took control and rolled her onto her back. His mouth crushed down on hers, his tongue sweeping in to dance with hers. He ground his hips against her making her moan. Nails raked down his back until her hands reached his boxers. He helped her slide them down before kicking them to the floor. Marcus pressed his mouth to her neck, licking his way across her collarbone and down to the valley between her breasts. Her breath came faster.

When his tongue swirled around one tight bud before he pulled it into his mouth, sucking hard, she arched against him. Her breath hitched in her throat. Alira gripped his shoulders as she bit her lip. She almost came off the bed when cool air replaced his warm mouth over her nipple as he blew against the tight peak. The sensation was more than she could take. She moaned loudly.

"Please, Marcus," she begged and flexed her hips against him. Marcus groaned. He quickly tugged her pajama pants off her hips, sliding them down her long legs as he pressed kisses across her stomach. He tossed them to the floor. Marcus was pleasantly surprised to see that she wasn't wearing any underwear. His cock throbbed painfully as he allowed his gaze to roam over her body.

Alira reached up, running her fingers through his hair, and pulled him down to kiss her. He settled himself between her thighs as he braced his weight on his elbows. His fingers brushed the hair over her ear as he gazed down at her.

"Are you sure?"

She nodded.

"I want this. I want you, Marcus," she told him softly. That was all he needed to hear. Her quiet admission, the desire he saw shining in her eyes, the way she wrapped her arms around his neck and invited him to take her to heights unknown.

Marcus lined himself up with her entrance and slowly eased inside. She felt herself open up to take him in, wrapping around him tightly. She gasped as the sheer size of him stretched her deliciously. He filled her completely. Alira felt her fingers curl and her nails dig into his shoulders. He stilled inside her with gritted teeth, giving her time to adjust to him. His arms shook as he held himself over her, careful not to put too much of his weight on her. She arched against him. It was all he needed as he shifted above her.

Slowly he withdrew. A soft moan from her and he was thrusting back inside her welcoming body.

"You're so tight, baby..." he groaned as he rolled his hips. She felt incredible wrapped around his cock, like she was made for him. Her moans were making it hard for him to keep control. All he wanted to do was thrust into her until she reached that peak and toppled over the other side clinging to him.

Alira arched against him, meeting him thrust for thrust as he took her higher. He withdrew and drove back in. He hit her G-spot like a pro, charging the electricity zinging through her with each thrust. His body moving over her had her craving more. The feel of him as his muscles moved under his skin, the scent of him, his breath against her neck... She was losing herself in him, in what he was making her feel.

Alira moaned his name, spurring him on, begging him not to stop. She could feel her orgasm building. It was still just out of reach. Marcus increased his pace. Then, his mouth came down on hers, nipping at her lip.

"Come for me," he whispered in her ear before pulling the lobe into his mouth and sucking hard. His hand slid between their bodies, his fingers seeking the sensitive nub he knew would send her over the edge.

The slow burn inside her suddenly exploded into an inferno, claiming her, as colors burst forth in a haze of fireworks. Alira cried out his name as her body shook and shuddered, squeezing him tightly with the force of her orgasm.

Marcus thrust into her, giving in to his own release as her orgasm continued to wash over her in waves. Her tight sheath squeezed him as her muscles spasmed forcefully around him. He came hard, pouring his seed deep inside her with a groan.

Marcus kissed her softly. Alira melted into his kiss, but just as soon as it had started, it was over. He pulled out and rolled away from her.

"That was not what I was expecting when I woke up this morning," he told her and grinned slyly. She laughed as she tried to control her breathing. It hadn't been what she was expecting either. She had never experienced anything like that before.

"Hey, you okay?"

"Yes, I'm just surprised. I've never had..." she trailed off as she stared at the ceiling questioning how to explain it to him.

"You've never had...?"

She shook her head. His jaw dropped.

"Wait, you... I wasn't your first, was I?" he asked her. She could hear the concern in his voice. He was afraid he had hurt her. He was afraid he had taken something from her. With a sigh, she rolled onto her side to face him. She reached up to trace his jaw with soft fingertips.

"Marcus, that was wonderful. Better than wonderful. And no, you weren't my first. I just had no idea it could be like that," she told him as embarrassment seeped into her voice. He lifted his hand to cover hers.

"Do you want to talk about it?"

Did she? Did she really want to tell him that her only experiences with sex had been unpleasant and a wham-bam-thank-you-ma'am kind of thing? She didn't want him to look at her differently. People always looked at her differently when they found out. It was Marcus. Marcus wasn't like most people. He wouldn't judge her. Still, the doubt was there scratching in the back of her mind.

She took a deep breath and allowed her hand to drop to the mattress. His hand covered hers again, squeezing gently.

"I haven't been a virgin since I was 15 and my brother locked me in a room with one of his friends. I had no way out. No choice. So, I laid there while he… while he had his fun. I don't know how long I was locked in that room. To be honest, I barely remember it. I went somewhere else in my head and hid there until it was over," she explained to him as she avoided his eyes. She was telling the truth. She didn't remember much of it. She had gotten through it and blocked it out.

"Grayson used to get drunk and watch me and Alex. Alex used to choke me while Grayson watched, jerking off. He never touched me, but he got off watching. It made me sick to my stomach. When Grayson wasn't around, Alex was gentler. It was always quick though. It was always about his pleasure and nothing more. Alex was the definition of wham-bam-thanks-ma'am. I had no idea it could be any other way," she said angrily. Alira rolled to her back trying to get some distance from him.

She was afraid to look at him. She didn't want to see the pity in his eyes, or worse, how repulsed he was by her. She had never told anyone that much before and now she was regretting telling him. The silence in the room wasn't helping. Alira felt like she was damaged goods. Why had she done that? Why had she told him? Fuck! She should have kept her mouth shut. Marcus would never look at her the same way again. All he would see was a mess.

Instinctively, Alira removed the ring he had given her last night and laid it on the bed between them. Quickly, she pulled the blankets up to cover herself and hid her face in her hands hoping he would just go. Just rip the bandage off.

Marcus laid there stunned. What do you say when someone tells you something like that? Were there even words for it? He forced himself to keep his emotions off his face, but she refused to look his way. He was furious for her. What she had been through was something nobody should ever have to experience. And worse, she was embarrassed about it like it had been her fault it had happened in the first place. His heart hurt for her. Even more so when she removed her ring and set it on the mattress between them without ever once looking at him. Did she really think he wouldn't want her now? He picked up the ring and scooted closer to her.

"You're not getting rid of me that easily," he told her softly as he slid the ring back on her finger. He tugged her into his arms and kissed her temple. Slowly, Alira relaxed. He could see the unshed tears shimmering in the blue depths of her eyes.

"You're stuck with me. For however long you're willing to put up with me and my grouchy attitude," he told her with a smile. He kissed the tip of her nose. She laughed as the tears started to fall. She rolled back onto her side and cuddled against him. Marcus wrapped his arms around her and held her tightly to him. Deep inside, he was pissed as hell. Her brother and her ex were going to pay for what they had put her through. He wasn't going to let them get away with it.

Chapter 11

Marcus eased out of bed and made sure to tuck the blankets in around Alira. He stuck a couple logs into the fireplace and got a fire going before he headed downstairs to find Austin. He needed a drink.

"Oh, that's not a good look," Austin said warily as Marcus entered the living room. Marcus headed straight for the kitchen and snatched a beer out of the fridge. He twisted the cap and chucked it across the room to the trash can in the corner. He drank down almost half the bottle before taking a breath.

"You want to tell me what's going on?"

Marcus glared at Austin, who stood in the doorway, before drinking down the rest of the beer. He left the bottle on the counter and started pacing.

"You know how we already knew her brother and her ex are steaming piles of shit? Turns out, they're bigger bastards than we initially thought," he growled. Austin pulled up a chair at the table and listened as Marcus told him what Alira had said. He knew Austin wouldn't say a word about it which he was thankful for because he knew Alira might kill him if she knew he had told anyone. By the time Marcus was finished with the story, Austin was seething.

"Man, I can't believe how grounded she is after all the shit she's been through. What do you want to do?" Austin asked him.

What did he want to do? What he wanted and what was legal were two entirely different things. Grayson was practically untouchable according to Alira. Nobody would believe he was the monster. Nothing would stick without proof. Alex on the other hand could get tagged on charges for breaking the restraining order. It wouldn't be enough to put him away for life, but it would be something. If they could find him.

"Honestly? I want to torture and kill them for what they've done to her. For everything they have put her through. It's the least they deserve," Marcus told him forcefully. He slammed his fist down on the table.

"I'll make some calls," Austin said cryptically and stood. Marcus wasn't going to question him. In Austin's business, he had connections. Some were less than savory connections, but Marcus wasn't going to question it. They just needed to get their hands on Grayson and Alex if they could find them. What happened after that would be anyone's guess.

The room was dark. The window was boarded up and a tiny sliver of light seeped in from under the door. The room spun when she tried to sit up. She felt sick. Where was she? How had she gotten here? Footsteps sounded on the other side of the door. The doorknob rattled and clicked like someone was unlocking it. Then, the door flew open, and a figure filled the doorway. Alira blinked at the sudden brightness in the room.

"Who's there?" She asked shakily even as she already knew the answer.

"I brought you a friend, little sister. I hope you two will have so much fun together," Grayson told her in a sickening tone. Alira shivered. Fear welled up inside her. She had been here before. She watched in horror as Grayson stepped aside and another figured entered the room. His friend, Tyson. Grayson flipped a switch and a single light in the corner came on.

"Just knock when you're done, Tyson. Have fun," Grayson snarled before slamming the door and locking it again.

Alira tried to put some distance between them but realized too late that her ankle was chained to the bed. She started shaking. Tyson crossed the room, already unbuttoning his jeans. He leaned over her, taking a deep breath that made a slight whistling sound as he inhaled.

"Did you really think you would be safe? He always knows where you are. You can't hide," Tyson whispered in her ear as he forced her back on the mattress and climbed on top of her. She started screaming as he shoved her pants down violently.

"What the hell is that?"
A bloodcurdling scream sounded from upstairs.

Marcus moved quickly. His chair slammed to the floor, but he didn't stop to right it. Austin was hot on his heels as they ran out of the kitchen. Duke was already halfway up the stairs when Marcus reached them. He took the stairs two at a time and shoved past Duke. Camden was already in her room when Marcus burst in followed by Duke and Austin.

"Move!" Marcus ordered as he moved toward the bed. Alira was screaming and fighting against something in her dreams. She thrashed and begged them to leave her alone. Camden leaped out of the way as Marcus pushed past him. He sat on the bed and pulled her tight against him. She shrieked and lashed out, still trapped in the dream. Her nails scratched down the side of his face. He didn't care. His focus was her.

"Alira, baby, you have to open your eyes! It's just a dream!" he said and prayed she would hear him through her panic.

"I've got you. I'm not going to let anything happen to you. Please open your eyes! Wake up!"

Alira struggled against Tyson. She felt trapped in his vice-like grip, but still, she fought. She had to get out. She couldn't go through this again.

Then she heard Marcus's voice calling to her. He was begging her to do something. She couldn't quite make it out. All she knew was Tyson was there and she couldn't fight him off much longer. He was too strong. She didn't stand a chance against him. He was going to take what he wanted, and she would be helpless to stop him. When that thought entered her mind, her body, seemingly of its own accord, gave up and she stopped struggling.

"You're okay. I've got you," Marcus told her as he loosened his hold. She had suddenly stopped fighting and gone limp in his arms. He brushed the hair away from her face and silently pleaded with her to wake up. He rocked her, begging her silently to wake up, to free herself from her nightmare holding her trapped in her own mind.

Alira opened her eyes and blinked. She was in her room at the Duvall's cabin and Marcus was holding her, rocking back and forth. Austin, Duke, and Camden were also in the room staring at her.

Oh God.

The dream rushed back in like a freight train and slammed into her. Tears formed in her eyes and spilled down her cheeks. She quickly buried her face in Marcus's chest, his firm arms protectively around her, shielding her.

"He knows. He always knows!" she sobbed.

"Who always knows what?" Marcus asked her quietly as he continued to hold her tightly against him.

"Grayson. Tyson said that he always knows where I am. I can't get away from him!"

"Who is Tyson?" Camden asked from beside Duke. Alira's eyes snapped open. She took a deep shuddering breath before she lifted her head.

"Tyson was one of my brother's friends... and my rapist," she confessed.

Shame washed over her at having said it out loud. She forced herself to meet their eyes, expecting pity, maybe even disgust, but she was surprised by what she saw instead. They didn't feel sorry for her. No, they were angry. They were angry on her behalf. Austin especially. Alira expected it from Marcus. She didn't expect it from Austin. Austin was always happy and smiling whenever she saw him. He liked to joke. This version? This version of him scared the holy hell out of her.

"Marcus..." Alira whispered as she stared wide-eyed at Austin while a new wave of fear tried to pull her down into its depths.

"Austin, you need to tone it down," Marcus warned his brother. The threat in his tone was unmistakable.

Austin closed his eyes and exhaled. He shook his fists out, flexing his fingers. When Austin opened his eyes again, they were clearer, brighter.

"I'm sorry. I didn't mean to scare you," he told her calmly.

Alira shook her head. He didn't have anything to apologize for. None of them did. It wasn't their fault she was like a scared little mouse. She hated that about herself and she liked to think she had grown considerably since getting out of a bad situation. Times like this set her back. Her therapist was going to have a field day with this one.

"I'll tell you all everything. It's only fair that you know the whole story so that you know what you've gotten into, but I need to get dressed and get some coffee first," she explained.

Still, she didn't move out of Marcus's embrace. Warm and safe. She wanted to soak it up a little more before she told them anything else. Austin nodded and offered her a smile before he ushered Duke and Camden out of the room.

"Are you alright?" Marcus asked once they were gone.

"No, but I will be," she replied as confidently as she could. Marcus didn't need to know that her nightmare felt like there was more to it. Like it was some sort of message meant to instill an unshakable terror for her future.

⏾

Alira stared into the black abyss of her coffee as she gripped the mug tightly. She could feel their eyes on her waiting for her to begin. As much as she wanted to put it off, she knew that wasn't possible. They needed to know what they were dealing with. Before she could speak, Marcus started for her. She listened as he told them everything that he knew. When he was done, they all looked back to her for anything else.

"You guys need to understand that I have not even told my therapist about most of this so you're going to have to bear with me. The first thing you need to know is that Tyson is dead. Grayson killed him. He had a bomb planted in Tyson's car about two weeks after he locked me in the room with him. I don't know why. I think he did it because Tyson didn't agree to something else Grayson tried to convince him to do. As a result, Grayson took care of what he perceived to be a problem," she told them quickly. She waited for the questions, but they remained silent as they waited for her to continue.

"Grayson is a good actor. He either fools you into believing that he's a good person or he lures you into his twisted games. He corrupts everything he touches. Alex used to be a decent person until Grayson got to him. Now he's just as sick as Grayson is. The thing you need to understand is Grayson believes he is untouchable and honestly, he is because he never gets caught. There is never anything that can be traced back to him. I've had private investigators try to get something, anything, on him for the last several years, but they always come back with nothing."

Alira paused to take a sip of her coffee. Marcus rubbed her back when she started white-knuckling the mug. She offered him a small smile. Taking a deep breath, she continued.

"Grayson is in trouble. Financially. When my grandfather died, my sister Mara and I inherited everything. When I say everything, I mean everything. Mara only accepted her trust fund and signed everything else over to me. Grayson got nothing. He seems to have this idea that if I'm out of the picture, he'll somehow get everything. My will is very strict on where my assets will go. If I'm married, they all pass to my husband. If I'm not married, they are set to be dispersed between various charities and a friend's college fund for his daughter. Grayson thinks there is a loophole somewhere."

"What about your parents?" Camden asked her curiously.

"They're not in the picture. I don't even know where they are. They weren't exactly model parents," she told him. She took another sip of her coffee. This was stressing her out. It was better to get it out now though. Marcus took her hand and squeezed. She lifted her eyes to his.

"Where do you think this will go from here?" he asked her. He was sure he already knew what the answer would be, but he needed to hear her say it.

"He's going to try to kill me," she stated in a matter-of-fact tone.

Chapter 12

The snow had melted enough that the roads were passable. It was time to go home. It had been almost a week of being stuck in the cabin and they were all going a little stir crazy. She and Marcus had spent most of the time in their room cuddling and watching movies. When they weren't in their room, they were downstairs with the guys losing at monopoly. As it turned out, Duke was a monopoly mastermind and somehow managed to wipe the floor with all of them. Alira whooped their butts at Jenga though. Even when she had been matching shots with Camden before Marcus had cut her off after she fell off the couch laughing. At one point, Austin had suggested they play Twister. They had looked at him like he had lost his mind.

"We can't play Twister. Alira would get crushed to death when one of us fell on her reaching for the damn left hand red!" Camden yelled in his inebriated state. Marcus sat there trying not to laugh. Meanwhile, Alira had burst out laughing at the images it conjured in her mind. She couldn't imagine Marcus playing Twister and when she said as much, Marcus said something about being happy to play Naked Twister with her. Alira turned bright red at his suggestion which had elicited a laugh from Duke. Hearing Duke laugh had surprised them all and led into a round of celebratory shots. They were a mess, and it was the most fun she'd had in a long time, but Alira was ready to get back home. Mostly she was ready to get her hands back into the gala which was a week away. She still had to pick up her gown. Somewhere in the middle of all that, she and Marcus were also getting married at the courthouse. It was shaping up to be a hectic week and it hadn't even started yet.

"It was nice being able to relax but I'm glad to be back," Alira said as she flopped down on the couch in her apartment. Her ribs protested mildly.

She and Marcus had stopped at the courthouse on the way to apply for their marriage license and schedule the date to go before the Justice of the Peace. They would be getting married in two days.

She would be married to Marcus.

It excited her. He excited her. The way he had proposed to her at the cabin had been more than she ever would have expected. Her stomach still did flip-flops when she thought about it. He had been so sincere and open. When he'd confessed that he was in love with her, her heart had nearly burst. She wanted so badly to tell him that she loved him and had for a while. She'd been too scared to tell him because what if, once her brother was no longer a problem, he decided that he didn't really love her after all? It would shatter her if she gave that much of herself to him and he rejected her in the end. She didn't believe Marcus would be that guy but still, the thought took up residence in the back of her mind.

Marcus watched her expression change as she chewed worriedly on her bottom lip. She had been all smiles when they'd been at the courthouse and coming up in the elevator to her apartment. Once inside, all her worries seemed to crash back in, weighing her down. He dropped her suitcase in her room and returned to sit next to her.

"Tell me what's on your mind," he prodded gently.

She shrugged, refusing to meet his eyes. He reached for her hand and tugged her to him. She draped her arm across his stomach as she leaned into him, resting her head against his shoulder.

"Talk to me."

Alira took a deep breath.

"I keep waiting for the other shoe to drop. I know you proposed willingly. When you said..." she stopped and started fidgeting with the hem of his t-shirt.

"When I said that I was in love with you?" he asked her sensing where her train of thought was leading.

"Yeah, that... I guess I just feel like I got carried away, caught up in the moment and I'm afraid once all this is over that you won't really want me. It's a marriage of convenience to help keep me safe. I just don't know if I can go back when everything is said and done," she explained, never moving to look at him. She continued messing with the hem of his shirt trying desperately to hold back the tears that were threatening to fall.

?

He reached to cup her chin and lift it so that he could look her in the eye. She was slow to meet his gaze but when she did, a single tear escaped to slide down her cheek. He brushed it away with the pad of his thumb.

"Alira, I wasn't lying when I said I was in love with you. I think I have loved you since the moment I saw you walk into Rigg's place. I wouldn't lead you on like that. I love you and there is nothing in this world that is going to change that," he told her reassuringly.

Marcus's thumb traced the line of her jaw softly as he gazed down at her. She knew he meant what he said. He had never lied to her and she knew he wasn't lying now. Gingerly, Alira reached up, touching her hand to his cheek, and encouraged him closer. Their lips touched softly, undemanding. When it was over, Alira rested her head against his shoulder once more, draping her arm across his washboard stomach. Marcus wrapped his arms around her and leaned his head on the back of the couch.

Buzz buzz.

"Crap, I forgot we have dinner at my parent's house tonight," he groaned. Alira laughed. She had completely forgotten about it and judging by his reaction, so had he.

"We could always skip it and stay in," she suggested with a wiggle of her eyebrows as she lifted her head to look at him. He laughed and hugged her.

"I like where this is going," he said with a grin and kissed her again.

Marcus eased her back down on the couch as he moved over her. She tilted her head giving him access to her neck which he happily accepted. She moaned when his hot mouth sucked on the tender skin just below her jaw. Alira ran her hands down his back, pulling him closer as she arched against him. Marcus moved, grinding his hips against hers, his desire for her evident by the growing bulge in his pants. She tugged at his shirt, pulling it off over his head and tossing it to the floor before pulling him back down.

"Hey! Open up!"

Marcus groaned into her mouth and broke their connection.

"Go away! We're busy!" he yelled toward the door before reclaiming her mouth in a passion-fueled kiss. They could hear laughter on the other side of the door before the sound of a key in the lock gave them pause. Marcus growled and moved away from her.

"This had better be good or I'll..."

The door swung open to reveal three figures. Austin, Karma, and a woman Marcus didn't recognize. Alira squealed excitedly and practically flew off the couch. She threw herself at the unknown woman, wrapping her in a hug. Marcus stood there watching the interaction with mild curiosity.

"What are you doing here?" Alira questioned as she pulled away, excitement brightening her beautiful features in a way Marcus had never seen before. Marcus glanced between them and it dawned on him who the woman was. He glanced at the mantle to the pictures there. Yep. Sure enough, the woman in one of them resembled the woman in front of him now.

"A little birdie called me and said my baby sister was getting married! I couldn't miss it, so I hopped on a plane and here I am. Karma picked me up from the airport a little over an hour ago," she explained.

"I didn't want to bother you but I'm so happy you're here!" Alira said happily and hugged her again.

Austin cleared his throat as he glanced at Marcus and then at the shirt on the floor. Alira and the woman both turned to look at him. Alira's eyes widened as though she had forgotten Marcus was standing there without a shirt on. She caught her lower lip between her teeth. Marcus knew she probably didn't even realize she had done it, but it was enough to send blood rushing straight back to his nether region like he was some teenage newb with his first girlfriend.

"You must be Marcus. I've heard a lot about you from your sister and brother on the way over. Oddly, not much from my own sister. I'm Mara," Mara introduced herself and held out her hand. Marcus shook it as he glanced quickly at Alira.

"Nice to meet you," he said politely. Alira had bent over to pick up his shirt.

"I can see why my sister is so taken with you," Mara said as she looked him over from head to toe. Marcus felt like he was at an interview with the way she seemed to be assessing him. He took the shirt from Alira when she held it out for him and quickly pulled it on over his head.

"We'll talk soon," Mara told him with a wink. Marcus nodded. Alira grinned and slid her arm around his waist.

"Don't give him a hard time. He's a good man," Alira told her sister as she looked up at him. Marcus knew he could get lost in her beautiful blue eyes and wondered why he hadn't made his feelings clear sooner. Alira was all he had ever wanted. Marcus squeezed her close to him as he leaned down to press a kiss on her forehead. He knew he had to turn his attention back to the party crashers in their apartment before

②

Marcus dragged Alira down the hall to the bedroom to finish what they had started before being so rudely interrupted.

This was the infamous Mara. The sister that had been sent away to school because she had done everything that she could to protect Alira from her parents but more importantly, from their brother. Marcus liked her. She clearly loved her baby sister, or she wouldn't have flown halfway around the world to be there for her when she was going to get married. To see Alira so excited made him happy too. She deserved all of the happiness life had to offer her.

"Mom and dad are expecting us for dinner. Mom has turned it into a big production on account of the upcoming nuptials," Austin said by way of warning. Karma stood next to him nodding with wide eyes.

"It would be embarrassing if it were me, but it's you two so I'm all good," Karma chimed in. Alira laughed while Marcus rolled his eyes. Of course, they would make a big deal out of it. His mom tended to get carried away sometimes. He could only imagine what she had planned for dinner tonight.

"Let's go! Camden and Duke will already be there. We brought the Suburban," Austin told them as he tried to usher everyone out the door. He had already shoved Karma through the door and into the hallway and was reaching for Alira next. Marcus lifted her away and glared at him. Austin laughed.

"We'll meet you there," he growled in annoyance.

Alira placed her hand against his chest, standing up on her tiptoes to kiss him. Any annoyance he may have felt towards his brother's overly pushy behavior faded away the second her lips touched his. That small, simple act had an instant affect on him.

"Oh, dude, you've got it bad..." Karma exclaimed from the hallway. Austin nodded in response.

"You should have seen them at the cabin. It was gross," Austin joked. Alira broke the kiss. She slipped her shoe off and threw it at Austin with a laugh. He dodged it easily.

Thirty minutes later, Marcus had parked the truck in front of his parent's house. They both stared wide-eyed at the banner that hung over the front door.

CONGRATULATIONS MARCUS AND ALIRA!

"There's still time to run," Marcus said half-joking. Alira looked like she was seriously contemplating it. Mara laughed from the backseat.

"Come on, it can't be that bad!" she told them and climbed out of the truck. They watched her walk up to the house. She stopped at the door and waved at them to hurry up.

"Here we go," Alira said, though Marcus could hear the hesitation in her voice. He squeezed her hand in his before hopping out of the truck. He jogged around the other side to open her door for her. Together they approached the Duvall's house.

Marcus and Alira entered the house cautiously, half expecting people to jump out and yell surprise at them. When that didn't happen, they let out the breath they had both been holding. Alira eased the grip she had on his hand too.

"Shall we?"

Alira nodded though she glanced back at the door like she was seriously considering running right back out. Not giving her the option, Marcus released her hand and slipped his arm around her waist instead. She relaxed into him slightly and allowed him to guide her toward the kitchen. Her book was on the counter waiting for her. She smiled.

"Go ahead. I know you want to read some before dinner," he whispered in her ear before he dropped his arm. Alira grabbed the book with a thankful grin, along with a couple carrots from the basket on the counter next to it, and all but jogged out of the kitchen. Marcus chuckled to himself and grabbed an apple to munch on before he followed after her. Alira was already at the barn by the time he reached the porch. He stopped and leaned against the railing, watching her as she gave Zoe the carrots and scratched her neck. Zoe leaned into the scratches and nickered her pleasure. Alira's laugh carried across the yard. He couldn't help the smile that spread across his face.

"She's always had a way with animals," Mara spoke from beside him. He hadn't heard her approach. His eyes on Alira never wavered though he could feel Mara watching him.

"You're good for her, you know," she spoke again as she turned to face him. Marcus hung his head before nodding slightly.

"No, you've got that wrong. She's good for me. If anyone had told me that I would be here a year ago, about to marry the most beautiful and kind woman I've ever known, I would have laughed at them," he told her as he lifted his head to look at Mara. Mara nodded.

"Your sister told me about Carmen. I'm sorry for your loss."

Again, he nodded. He appreciated the sympathies but the more he thought about it, the more he realized they were no longer necessary. Sure, he and Carmen had planned their lives together but looking back, it felt like settling because he had simply been trying to make someone else happy. He hadn't been truly happy with Carmen and it had taken Alira walking into his life for him to acknowledge that. Marcus hated to admit it, but Carmen had just been a filler that he had allowed to take over every aspect of his life and being. Even after she'd died. They had shared loved but deep down, he had always felt like something was missing between them. Watching Alira now, he knew what had been missing. His heart hadn't been fully in it. He had held himself back. He wasn't doing that with Alira, and it was freeing. She was the light to his dark and he would do absolutely anything for her. The minute he admitted how he felt about her, a weight had lifted from his soul and he could imagine their future together.

Marcus hadn't wanted to have children with Carmen. The thought had never even crossed his mind. With Alira, he could picture the whole nine yards. He could see a sweet little girl with her mother's clear blue eyes and caring heart. In his mind's eye, he pictured a determined little boy causing havoc but never wanting to disappoint his mother. He could see it all with Alira. He wanted it all with her.

"Don't be. I can admit now that Carmen and I were just filling space in one another's lives," he told her as he caught Alira's gaze. She smiled a brilliant smile that made his heart skip a beat. Mara watched the exchange between them.

"And how do you feel about my sister? Is she filling a space in your life?" Mara asked him seriously.

"No, she fills my heart. She encompasses my entire being. She is every breath I take. I would do anything for her. Maybe if I had been willing to admit it sooner, none of what she is going through would be happening and your brother wouldn't be a problem because she would have been home with me the night of her accident," Marcus told her honestly. He felt like the blame was on him for being so slow about admitting his true feelings for the feisty but shy woman standing across the yard in ankle-deep snow smiling at her horse.

He and Mara stood in silence for several minutes as they watched Zoe hook Alira's shoulder and pull her closer for a horse hug. Alira wrapped her arms around the horse's neck and leaned her head against her. They stood like that for a long time. Zoe's ears twitched as she listened to whatever it was Alira was saying to her while she scratched her neck. Marcus smiled softly.

"Marcus, I believe you love my sister. Deeply. I couldn't ask for anyone better for her, but you need to understand that my brother will never stop. Our parents have cut him off entirely and he's getting desperate. The only way he will stop is when he's dead or Alira is, and he's already dragged Alex down the rabbit hole with him. Grayson is crazy. He will stop at nothing to get what he thinks belongs to him."

"Alira's inheritance from your grandfather," Marcus said knowingly. Mara nodded.

"Yes. I don't know what Grayson has planned but it's not going to be good and she's going to need you. More than she has ever needed anyone. She's stronger than she knows but she can't do this on her own," Mara told him. The worry for her sister was evident in her words and the expression on her face.

"She won't be alone. She will never be alone in anything ever again if I have my way," he said firmly, mouth set in a grim line. Mara nodded. It was easy to see that Marcus was telling the truth. Marcus loved her sister, and it was clear in everything he did and the words that he spoke. Even now, Marcus watched Alira across the yard and Mara could see that there was nobody else in the world except her. Everyone, everything else, was background noise for him when he stared at Alira.

Chapter 13

Alira was running late. Today of all days. They were expected at the courthouse in an hour, and she couldn't find the dress she had chosen to wear. Mara had been searching the closet for it while Alira ransacked the rest of her apartment, including the guest room. The dress was nowhere to be found. She knew she had picked it up from the dry cleaners and hung it in her closet in plain sight with her shoes placed underneath it so it would be easy to grab and go. Even the shoes were gone. Where the hell were they?

"You ladies ready to go? Whoa, what happened in here?" Camden yelled from the living room. He had been assigned to her for the last twenty-four hours. He'd been with her when she had picked up the dress and brought it home. Marcus's mother had ordered him to stay at his house using the whole excuse that it was bad luck to see the bride before the wedding line. He had grumbled but Charlotte had refused to back down, thus banishing him from Alira's apartment until they returned as husband and wife.

"Camden, my dress is missing and so are my shoes!"

"I don't see it anywhere. Are you sure you brought it in from the car?" Mara asked her, failing to hide the worry in her tone. Alira nodded.

"Yes, because Austin had to return the car to the rental company last night. Camden watched me hang it up!" Alira replied frantically. That was true. Camden has slept on her couch last night. He had carried the dress up for her and everything.

"I'm going to go check the security cameras. Will you be okay for a few minutes?" he asked them as he started to slowly back toward the door. Mara nodded while Alira continued searching her room. They were all startled at the knock on the door. Camden peered through the peephole before opening it. Austin stood on the other side looking angry.

"Alira, we have to go. Now."

Alira glared at him and planted her feet firmly. Austin rolled his eyes at her show of bravado. He wasn't so sure about this sassy new version of Alira that he was coming to know. She was shaping up to be a handful.

"We know where your dress is..." he started but Harold stepped into the apartment, grim-faced, holding what remained of her dress and shoes. Alira gasped.

The beautiful white dress was shredded and muddy. Red lettering covered the bodice.

You're mine.

Alira snatched the dress out of Harold's grasp, surprising him, and angrily shoved it into the trashcan. The destroyed shoes quickly followed it. They all stared at her, shocked at her reaction. This was not what they had expected. Instead of fear, there was rage. Alira was furious.

"How did Alex get into my apartment? When did he get inside?" she yelled turning on Harold and Austin, eyes shining angrily. All these precautions and new restrictions and he had still managed to not only get into the building but had gotten into her apartment. She was scared, but she was also angry, and that anger overrode the fear that wanted to overtake her.

"I have my tech guys looking into it but right now, you have a wedding to get to," Austin told her and gave a gentle shove toward her bedroom. Alira huffed and whirled away from him. Mara followed her down the hallway but was stopped short when the door slammed shut in her face.

Alira went into her closet and searched the hangers for another option. She didn't want to show up to her own wedding in jeans and a hoodie. Not to say that she wasn't considering it as an option. She was marrying Marcus, and nothing was going to stand in her way. Not even her psychotic ex breaking into her apartment could stop her!

Rifling through the hangers angrily, she stopped. How she had forgotten about this dress, she had no idea, but it was perfect. She kicked off her sweatpants and tossed her tank top to the floor. She pulled the dress off the hanger and slipped into it. Carefully zipping up the back, she shimmied allowing the material to settle. Alira grabbed a strappy pair of heeled sandals from a cubby, slid her feet into them, and secured the straps around her ankles.

"Let's go!" Alira ordered as she hurried down the hallway, grabbing her wristlet and phone off the counter as she brushed past her audience. She could hear them scrambling after her. Harold promised to lock up behind them and wished her luck as they piled into the elevator.

Marcus nervously checked his watch for what must have been the hundredth time in the last fifteen minutes. Austin had texted him saying they were running a little bit late but that he would explain after the ceremony. The message had been just cryptic enough to make him worry and mad that he had let his mother essentially bully him into not staying with Alira. It had been strange to be at his house, sleeping in his own bed, after two weeks spending every night with her. He had missed sleeping with her wrapped safely in his arms.

The doors at the end of the hall opened and Alira walked in like she owned the place. Her smile lit up the room when she saw him. He breathed a sigh of relief. She was okay. Mara followed behind her, snatching the wristlet away from her while Camden and Austin pulled up the rear. Alira's pace slowed as she got closer to him, worry marring her beautiful features.

"Are you sure about this?" she asked him as he pulled her into his arms.

"Surer than I have been about anything in my life, baby," he told her honestly. He kissed her on the forehead and pulled her in for a hug. She returned his hug tightly, resting her head against his chest. She took a much-needed deep breath before she pulled away.

The door behind Marcus opened and a secretary appeared.

"Duvall and Hervowe party?" she asked them. Marcus nodded and Alira smiled.

The secretary ushered them into the chamber and explained the process to them. They could have a member of their party stand with them or they could stand off to the side and simply witness. Alira motioned for Mara and Austin to stand with them. Alira thought she saw a tear in Mara's eye, but it was quickly wiped away as Mara smiled.

"Welcome. I hear you two want to get married today!" the judge called out as he emerged from a door in the corner. Marcus chuckled.

"Andrew! It's good to see you!" he said with a grin and held out his hand. Alira watched curiously. Marcus and the judge obviously knew one another.

"I saw it was you on the schedule and knew I had to be the officiant," the judge, Andrew, told him.

"You must be the infamous Alira I have heard so much about from Charlotte. That woman adores you. I'm Andrew. Or Judge Masters. Whichever you prefer," he rambled as he held out his hand in greeting. Alira shook it tentatively still unsure what was happening. Marcus leaned down and whispered something in her ear.

"It's nice to meet you!" she replied happily.

Andrew Masters was Charlotte's baby brother. He was just a few years older than Marcus and was on track to run for Mayor in a couple years. Alira had heard about him but had never met him until that moment. She hadn't seen a current picture of him at Charlotte's house. He looked nothing like his childhood pictures! He stood level with Marcus with similar brown eyes, but his blond hair gave him a unique, though underwhelming look. She never would have known he and Marcus were related if Marcus hadn't told her.

"Let's get this show on the road!" he chimed happily as he clapped his hands together. Alira liked him but could admit that he made her uncomfortable. He was a quick mover, very animated in his actions and in the way he spoke. She leaned a little closer to Marcus seeking his silent reassurance.

"It's okay. He can be a lot to take sometimes," he whispered in her ear understanding what she needed without her saying it. She gave a slow nod as Judge Masters fiddled with some papers on his desk before turning back to them expectantly.

"You may kiss your bride!" Judge Masters told them proudly at the end of the vows. Marcus grinned and cupped her face in his hands as he leaned down to kiss her.

Their first kiss as husband and wife.

Alira's arms slid up and around his neck as their lips met. She threw her head back laughing when he scooped her up in his arms and kissed her soundly once more before placing her back on her feet.

"Congratulations, Mrs. Duvall," Mara said as she stepped forward to hug her sister. Alira laughed as tears slid down her cheeks.

Marcus watched as Alira hugged Mara. Her happiness dwindled slightly knowing that they would be dropping Mara at the airport after lunch to catch her flight back to England and the not-so-secret man waiting for her. He was happy that Mara had been able to be there for Alira. Alira had been so animated since her arrival that he worried how she would be once she left. Alira had assured him that she would still be happy and that she was just excited to see her sister in person and not on a video call after so many years apart. Austin and Camden moved forward to offer their congratulations as well. Marcus shook their hands and smiled though he never took his eyes away from his wife.

"We have one problem," Alira stated flatly once they were back in Marcus's truck after dropping Mara off at the airport for her flight.

"What's that?" he asked curiously.

"Where are we going to live?" she questioned as she turned to look at him directly. This was the same question he had been asking himself. She had her apartment while he had his house. Austin hadn't mentioned anything, but he had a feeling he knew what he would suggest.

"Given the current state of things, I think we should stay at your apartment. I don't have quite that level of security at my house. Once this issue with your brother and stalker blows over..." he didn't finish his statement. His attention had shifted to the person walking over to his truck parked in the garage.

Alira turned to see Harold walking over to them, a grim expression on his face. Then she saw the envelope in his hand. Her smile fell away, and her hands dropped into her lap, twisting nervously. Marcus was already stepping out of the truck and making his way around to her side before Harold reached them. She watched as Harold handed Marcus the envelope. Marcus glanced at her before quickly looking back at the paper. He opened it and read the contents of the letter. Slowly Alira reached for the handle and pushed open the door. Harold tried smiling at her, but she only saw Marcus. She could feel the anger rolling off of him in waves.

"What is it?" she asked. She didn't really want to know but knew she needed to. Marcus met her gaze, his eyes blazing. The fury she saw in his face made her take several steps backward as she slammed into the side of his truck. Marcus made no move toward her. He held out the letter for her. She stepped forward just close enough to grab it from him before stepping away quickly once more. Alira couldn't tell if he was mad about what he had read in the letter or mad at her, but he was definitely scaring her. Seconds before they were talking about where they were going to live and now... Now he was staring at her like she was the devil. Her hands shook as she lifted the letter.

Ask her where she spent last night. Ask her why she couldn't find her dress. That's right. She wasn't at her apartment because she was with me. It doesn't matter what paperwork you have; she'll always be mine.

A.L.

Alira stared in horror at the paper in her hand as she reread its contents. Surely, Marcus knew this was a lie. Camden and Mara had both been with her! Yet, when she looked up, Marcus was walking away.

"Marcus!" she called out. Still, he kept walking. She started to run after him, but her heel slipped on the concrete and broke. She fell to her knees, scraping her hands as she put them out to catch herself. Harold rushed forward. He helped her to her feet and reached for the letter still clutched in her hand. Her palms were raw and bleeding where she had landed. Harold read the note and cursed.

"Marcus!" Alira screamed after him. Marcus disappeared around the corner of the garage and out onto the street, ignoring her.

"Let's get you inside. He'll come back," Harold said trying to reassure her. She nodded but she didn't believe him. This was exactly what Grayson wanted and he was winning. Marcus hadn't said anything about her wardrobe change at the courthouse even though he had helped her pick out the dress in the first place. The fact that she had been wearing an entirely different dress only solidified what was in the note, even if it wasn't true. Her heart shattered. If he would have stayed, she could have shown him the dress in the garbage. Instead, he chose to walk away.

Harold helped Alira into her apartment. He handed her a new set of keys since he had the locks changed while she was out. She thanked him and said goodbye. He offered her a sad smile that was meant to reassure her before he pulled the door closed behind him. As soon as the locks clicked into place, Alira collapsed to the floor and sobbed. All of the pain in her life came pouring out of her violently. All she could see was Marcus walking away. He hadn't bothered talking to her. He just left. He had believed the lies in that damned note and he wasn't coming back.

"Karma, it's Harold. Alira needs you. Marcus – he left," Harold said once she answered the phone. He had heard the locks click into place as the door closed behind him. Then he'd heard her. The sound of a heart being broken. Harold had known her long enough to know that she wouldn't want anyone to see her fall apart, but that she needed a friend, and he knew Karma was pushy enough to get through. Karma cursed loudly, relayed what had happened to someone in the background, and told Harold she was on her way. Harold thanked her and leaned against the wall outside of Alira's apartment waiting.

Harold didn't know how long he had been sitting in the hallway but boy was he glad when the elevator dinged and out stepped Karma with Austin, Kenny, and Camden in tow. He gained his feet and met them halfway down the hall. He handed Karma the letter. She read it quickly and passed it to Austin.

"Son of a bitch," Austin muttered as he handed the paper to Camden.

Karma held out her hands for the keys she knew Harold had. He handed them over easily and followed slowly as she walked down the hallway past him to Alira's door. She slid the keys into the lock and pushed the door open. When it hit something, she cursed again.

"Alira, let me in."

Alira crawled across the floor away from the door and pressed her back against the wall in the dining room. Harold peered through the door and had the strong and sudden urge to punch Marcus the next time he saw him.

"Come here," Karma spoke softly as she slid down the wall to sit next to Alira. She wrapped her arms around her and held onto her as Alira cried. She smoothed her hair back and rocked gently as if she were soothing a small child.

Marcus sat in the dark booth with a line of shots laid out on the table in front of him. He hadn't even touched them yet. The waitress kept coming over and checking on him, leaning uncomfortably close to him as she flashed her cleavage. He cringed. He had ordered the shots intending to drink them but there they sat, untouched, taunting him. He didn't know what had come over him. He had noticed that Alira wasn't wearing the dress she had picked out originally. Marcus just hadn't thought anything of it. Maybe she had gotten a stain on it. She was gorgeous no matter what. She could have shown up in a potato sack and would have been the picture of perfection as far as he was concerned. Then Harold had handed him that blasted note! He knew it wasn't true, but something had come over him and he just – he couldn't stay there. Not with her looking at him the way she was. The fear he had seen in her eyes. The fear of *him*. When she had called out to him, he'd ignored her. He couldn't take her looking at him that way.

Buzz buzz.

"Where are you?"

Marcus took a deep breath as he read the text message from Austin. He typed back a response and waited. Any minute now, Austin would come barreling into the bar ready to rip him a new asshole. The door opened and he was surprised to see Kenny walk in ahead of Austin. The look on Kenny's face was dangerous. Austin and Kenny spotted him immediately, moving in his direction. Kenny slid into the seat across from him while Austin slid in next to him, shoving him against the wall.

"What the hell are you doing?" Kenny snarled at him. Marcus shrugged. He didn't have an answer for him. What could he possibly say that would make sense? He read the note, got mad, and scared the hell out of Alira before he stormed off leaving her in the parking garage of her building? Yeah, that would go over really well.

"I assume you read the note?"

"Yeah man, we saw the note. What we don't understand is why the hell you're here with enough shots to knock out an elephant when you should be with your wife. You know, reassuring her that you know she wouldn't step out on you," Austin told him flatly with a sharp elbow jab to his ribs. Marcus winced.

"Karma wants to kill you. She's trying to do damage control, but you should have seen Alira," Kenny growled as he leaned forward, fist ready. Judging by Kenny's behavior, he was with Karma. Austin held up his hand between Kenny and Marcus. Kenny settled back in the seat and glared daggers at his brother.

"I fucked up," Marcus said out loud. He reached for a shot. Kenny slapped the shot out of his hand before his fist connected with Marcus's nose. Blood poured down his face instantly as his hand flew to his face. Kenny sat shaking out his hand, a triumphant look on his face as Marcus stared at his blood-covered hand in surprise. The waitress screamed and ran over with a wad of napkins. She leaned across the table, pinning Austin against the seat as she shoved the napkins at Marcus.

"That looks awful, sweetheart! Here, let me help!" she squawked as she tried to position herself to appear helpful while still revealing as much of her cleavage as possible. She glared at Kenny.

"You should be ashamed of yourself!" she told him unhappily. Kenny smiled a sickeningly sweet smile at her.

"No ma'am. I will never be ashamed of decking my *married* brother in the face for walking out on his brand-new wife," he told her as he slid from the booth. The waitress stared after him in shock before slowly turning back to Marcus and slamming him in the face with the napkins. She scooted back across the table and stomped away muttering something about how all men were pigs. Austin laughed and shook his

?

head. There was never a dull moment with the Duvall brothers, it seemed.

"I have to go talk to Alira."

Marcus tried to push Austin out of the booth, but he wouldn't budge.

"That's not a good idea right now, bro. You left a big mess and if you go back to Alira's right now, you'll regret it. If you can get past Harold and he doesn't kill you, Karma definitely will. Duke is on his way over there now. Karma and Camden are there, and I'll be heading back over there after I get you home. She'll be plenty safe tonight. You need to go home and cool off. Give her some time to calm down. You can try to talk to her in the morning. That is if Karma and Kenny will even let you in the building," Austin told him half-joking. Marcus groaned. His phone rang, buzzing against the table.

Mom.

Austin laughed. "Scratch that. You're a dead man now. Mom knows."

"Mom…" Marcus answered and winced.

Charlotte was yelling the second he answered her call. Marcus was sure Austin could hear her word for word as she went off on him. He had never in his twenty-nine years on that earth heard his mother speak that way. She was furious with him and he wouldn't have been surprised to see her come strolling through the door of the bar with a leather belt in her hands ready to have a go at his backside like he was a disobedient child. She wouldn't even let him get a word in.

"How is Alira?" Marcus asked his brother once he had hung up with their mother. Austin just shrugged and shook his head. Fuck. Fuck. Fuck.

Alira crawled under the covers and hugged her pillow tightly. She was fairly certain she didn't have any tears left until she caught his scent on his pillow. The tears came anew, welling up and pouring out. She didn't bother trying to hide her sobbing. There was a living room full of people who had seen her broken and raw already. She couldn't bring herself to care anymore. She begged for sleep to take her so she wouldn't feel anything, even if it were just for a little while.

"I'll kill him!" Karma muttered from the couch as they all listened to Alira crying in the other room. Alira had insisted she needed to sleep and that she would be okay, but they all knew the truth. Marcus was on their shit list. Kenny had happily walked back into the apartment after punching his brother in the face. A fact he made sure to share with a little dance in his step. Duke had arrived just minutes before Kenny's return and had only gotten a quick rundown of what they knew had happened. Camden had to talk Duke out of going and finding Marcus. Camden had somehow managed to convince Karma that Kenny and Austin could handle it and that his and Duke's job was to keep Alira safe.

"I just don't understand how he could do this. What was he thinking?" Kenny asked nobody in particular.

"He wasn't. This is what my brother does. He plants doubt and it grows freely," Alira's small answer sounded from the hall. They all looked in her direction.

"I didn't mean to interrupt. I just came to get some water," she explained as she scrubbed her face with the sleeve of her shirt. Duke jumped to his feet and rushed into the kitchen.

"I'll get it!"

Alira thanked him as she took the glass from him before padding back down the hallway to her bedroom. The door closed softly behind her, clicking into place. They all exhaled the collective breath they had been holding.

Marcus raised his hand to knock but let it drop. He did this half a dozen times before Harold appeared at the end of the hall.

"You going to knock or just keep almost high-fiving the door?" Harold asked him. Marcus sighed. He honestly had no idea. He had caught a cab from his house at seven in the morning because his truck was still parked down in the garage of the building. Austin had dropped him off at his house and told him not to call or come over to the apartment until the next morning. He had told him that it would give everyone some time to calm down and wake up feeling a bit more refreshed.

"I don't even know if she's in there," Marcus whispered once the older man reached him.

"She's in there. She's got a small army in there watching over her. I've been watching the cameras all night. That door has not been opened once since your brother came back," Harold informed him.

"Good luck," Harold said with a growl and knocked on the door for him before continuing down the hall on what Marcus assumed was his final building check. Locks clicked and the door swung open. He came face to face with Duke. Marcus had never been afraid of anyone, but the expression on Duke's face made him stop and think that maybe he should be at least a little concerned. Duke immediately pushed him back into the hallway, following him out in the process. He left the door open a crack behind him.

"You have some nerve," Duke's deep voice ground out.

"Who is that?"

Karma appeared in the doorway. She leveled him with a stare that would topple skyscrapers. Marcus felt his shoulders sag as his baby sister stomped over to stand directly in front of him, shoving Duke out of the way as she went. She jabbed him in the chest with her finger hard enough to knock him back a step.

"How dare you, Marcus! The nerve to show up here after what you did yesterday! Not even a full three hours after saying 'I do' and you walked out. What the hell were you thinking? I'll tell you what you were thinking! You were thinking only about yourself! How could you?!"

By the time Karma was finished, she was yelling at him. He knew he deserved the raging fury he saw in his sister's eyes as she glared at him.

Movement inside the apartment caught his attention.

Alira stood in the living room, staring wide-eyed at him. He could see her struggling, glancing down the hallway toward her bedroom. Her eyes were red and puffy like she'd been crying all night. She stood stiffly, seemingly rooted in place with her fists balled up at her sides. Suddenly, she turned and ran down the hall back to her safe haven. Marcus started after her, pushing past his sister but Duke stepped to block his path.

"I don't want to hurt you, Duke," Marcus growled at him as he tore his eyes away from where he'd last seen Alira.

Duke cocked his head and stared, challenging him. Marcus glared. He really didn't want to do this, but it didn't appear they were going to let him see his wife without a fight. Marcus shifted his foot and launched himself forward. Duke braced to stop him. At the last second, Marcus dropped his shoulder and slammed into Duke, knocking him backward into the apartment. They landed in a pile on the floor. Marcus quickly scrambled to his feet and jumped out of Duke's reach as Karma came back into the apartment screaming at him. Austin grabbed her as she went to leap onto his back. Marcus only caught a glimpse of the amused expression on Camden's face as he blocked Kenny from joining in the fray.

Marcus strode down the hallway, barely stopping at the closed door. He reached for the knob and started forward only to stop in his tracks as the door opened.

"I'll have my lawyer draw up divorce papers this afternoon, Marcus. You don't need to be here," she sniffled and turned toward the bathroom. He caught her wrist in his hand and spun her around to face him. She slammed into his chest and immediately tried to get away from him.

"That's not what I want," he told her softly, his gentle grip holding her in place. She refused to meet his eyes. He closed the door with his foot to keep out the prying eyes of their angry audience. It was just him and Alira. He moved his hands to cup her face.

"Please look at me," he begged her as she closed her eyes tightly. One breath. Two. Three. Four. Five. Just as he was about to give up, thinking it was truly over before it had really begun, Alira opened her eyes. Her brilliant blue eyes shifted up to his face and he started breathing again. Her hands lifted to cover his as tears fell down her cheeks.

"I am so sorry I hurt you," he whispered as he dropped his forehead to hers. She whimpered and backed away from him. It broke his heart watching her retreat. The fear and mistrust he saw in her eyes, on her face, all because of him. He would give anything to have her look at him like she had only the day before. Hesitantly, he stepped toward her, not thinking. Alira quickly moved across the room away from him.

"Please don't be afraid of me. I would walk through fire for you if you asked it of me," Marcus choked out as he fell to his knees. He didn't know what else to say or do. She stood in the corner by her dresser, watching him with a guarded expression.

Karma glared at Marcus as he walked down the hall following Alira. Camden kept a tight grip around her shoulders. He wasn't about to let her move off the couch. Duke sat at the dining table grumbling about how Marcus better watch himself if he ever did anything like that to Alira again. Kenny was nowhere to be seen while Austin was busy pouring himself a cup of coffee.

Marcus tried to ignore them as he followed her to the kitchen. She quietly reached for a mug and pour herself a cup of coffee. Austin handed her the creamer without a word and raised his eyebrows at Marcus. Marcus shook his head.

"Marcus, I swear to..." Karma started before Camden clamped his hand over her mouth shutting her up. She glared. He shrugged.

"I know. I know. I was a complete idiot and let them get to me. I screwed up and I'm sorry. I'm so incredibly sorry for it," Marcus said though it was clear the last bit was aimed at Alira. She met his eyes briefly with her own before glancing away again. He couldn't blame her. He had been the moron that fell into the trap with that note. Marcus knew he should have just talked to her and trusted her. Somehow Carmen flashed through his mind and he cringed. He knew why he had reacted that way. It was no excuse. Alira was not Carmen.

"We should head out and let you two, uh, talk. Camden and Duke will be back tonight for guard duty and we'll see you at the Gala on Friday night!" Austin said loudly as he rinsed out his coffee cup before leaving it in the sink. His message was obvious. Clear out. Camden leaped to his feet, nodded to Alira with a grin, and dragged Karma across the living room to the door. Karma did a throat slicing motion at Marcus but didn't say anything. Duke nodded to Alira and glared at Marcus. Austin gave a half-assed wave just before he closed the door behind him.

Alira and Marcus stood in silence for several painful minutes. She sipped at her coffee refusing to look in his direction. Marcus knew she was dragging it out. Any other day she would have already been pouring her second cup of coffee. She took slow sips as she stared determinedly at a spot on the floor. Marcus nodded and went into the living room. He grabbed the remote and found her playlist in music on the TV. He scrolled through until he found what he was looking for.

Something Just Like This by The Chainsmokers began playing through the speakers filling the apartment with the music.

Alira lifted her eyes as Marcus reappeared in the kitchen with a grin on his handsome face. He gently took the mug from her setting it down on the counter. Then, he gripped her hand and tugged her after him to the living room. He took her in his arms, spinning her and dancing with her around the living room. When he started singing along, she laughed. She couldn't help herself. When the song ended, she looked up at him.

"You're my superhero, you know," she told him honestly. He pulled her against him, hugging her tight.

"I'm no superhero, baby. I'm just a guy from a small town in the middle of nowhere," he said quietly. She laughed.

"Superman was a small-town Kansas boy," she reminded him. It was his turn to laugh. She had him there. He could be her superhero. He would be anything she needed him to be.

Marcus followed her when she moved to sit on the couch. She pulled her knees up to her chest, hugging them as she rested her chin on her arms. She stared at him. It was clear she wasn't entirely sure where to start or what to say. He didn't really know either.

"I tried to go after you," she told him as she inspected the scrapes on her palms.

"I know."

"I didn't think I would see you again," she whispered. The words caught in her throat.

Marcus scooted off the couch and knelt down in front of her. He reached for her hands, but she jerked back. He didn't let her pull away from him. He reached for her hands again. This time, she didn't move. She simply allowed it to happen. Marcus turned her hand over and kissed the scrapes on her palm. He did the same with the scrapes on her other hand. When he lifted his eyes to hers, he saw the tears there. It killed him inside to know he was the reason for her tears. It had never been his intention to make her question him. At the moment, he hadn't known what else to do. A tear slid down her cheek. He reached to brush it away and she leaned into his hand.

"Carmen cheated on me. I guess that note just reminded me of that time and I got lost for a minute," he explained quietly as he hung his head. It was her turn to make him look at her. Her touch, encouraging him to look up, to see her.

"Then Carmen was a fool because you are the best, most amazing man a girl could ever ask for, Marcus," she told him softly. She leaned closer and pressed a tentative kiss to his mouth. He held his breath for a second before kissing her back. Without missing a beat, she slid off the couch and into his lap, wrapping her arms around his neck, deepening the kiss. Marcus groaned when she pulled back abruptly.

"Marcus... I love you," she whispered. The words were so quiet he almost missed them. A smile broke out across his face as he shook his head in disbelief.

"Say it again," he asked her.

"I love you," she said a little louder this time. He let out a thankful laugh before pulling her tightly against him and claimed her mouth with his own.

Chapter 14

"You can't be serious!" Alira yelled at her phone. People were due to begin arriving at the Gala in five hours and the caterer was late! They hadn't given a reason. Just a quick voicemail left on her phone. Kara and Joey appeared next to her.

"We just heard!" Joey exclaimed. Kara nodded beside him. They had been working their butts off to get this event going off without a hitch! Alira wanted to scream. Instead, she took a deep breath and formed a plan. The caterers were simply late. They hadn't canceled altogether. That would have cost them a lot of money plus their deposit.

"Alright, Kara, go talk to the hotel manager and ask if we can borrow some of his staff for a couple hours to finish setting up the ballroom. The caterer will still be here, but they won't have enough time to finish setting up the ballroom and begin serving on time. Joey, please call my husband and ask him to bring my gown now since I won't have time to run home to grab it before the hairdresser arrives which should be in fifteen minutes," she ordered as she glanced at her watch. Kara and Joey disappeared to do as she asked while Alira finished adjusting some place settings that were already out.

"I'm heading up to the suite! I'll see you both up there!" Alira called out to her assistants as she left the ballroom. Duke followed closely behind her. He held the elevator doors until she was safely inside before hitting the button for the top floor. The mayor always reserved the penthouse suite for Alira and her assistants so that they could get ready for the gala "in style" as he put it. It was his way of saying thank you for all their hard work.

"You know, Duke, Kara won't stop talking about you," Alira told him with a wink. Duke visibly tensed.

"Oh?" he asked trying desperately to sound relaxed. Alira laughed.

"I'll give you her number, but you should ask her to dance tonight!" Alira told him. Duke grinned. Alira thought she caught a twinkle in his eye. Duke wasn't as unbothered as he wanted the world to think. It was obvious he was trying to contain his excitement. He and Kara had been making eyes at each other for two days and Kara couldn't stop talking about how cute she thought Duke was whenever he was out of earshot. Naturally, Kara was afraid to approach him first and Duke was afraid to approach her. Alira had taken it upon herself to encourage them to step up.

"Where is she?" Marcus asked Austin as he adjusted the tie at his throat again.

"Dude, knock it off. I'm not going to help you retie that damn thing again," Austin growled and knocked his hands away from the tie. Marcus huffed and shifted back and forth on his feet. He could feel their eyes on him. He hated it. He had already turned away several young women asking him to dance or asking for his number. They were completely ignoring the wedding ring on his finger. One of them had even had the gall to say that his wife didn't have to know and that they could just head into the coatroom really quick. Marcus had been less than polite in telling her off. Now he had resorted to using Austin as a shield. His patience was wearing thin, and the night had barely begun. There was still no sign of Alira either. He had brought her gown as requested but hadn't seen her when he dropped it off. He had handed it over to her assistant, Joey, and bolted. He still had to pick up his tuxedo and get changed before making his way back to the hotel for the main event.

The music picked up the tempo and he watched as several couples moved to the dance floor. Austin spoke into the mic at his wrist and nodded to Marcus before he shifted away, heading to the other side of the ballroom. Marcus followed after him, trying his best to avoid making eye contact with any of the women trying to catch his attention. He shivered. He understood why women got angry with men who acted like they were nothing but a piece of meat. Women did it to men too. It was obnoxious.

The music stopped and feedback sounded throughout the ballroom.

"Good evening!" a happy young voice sounded over the speakers. The audience turned to face the stage. Marcus saw her and his heart nearly ran away with him. Alira stood on the stage in a flowing glittery red gown. There was a slit along the right side of the gown that stopped mid-thigh. The heels she wore matched the dress and made her slender legs appear even longer. The bodice was snug and perfectly fitted to her shape, allowing her breasts to almost spillover. She wore a simple necklace that pointed delicately down to her chest only drawing more attention there. The sweet teardrop earrings complimented her necklace as did the bracelet that hung delicately around her wrist. Her dark tresses were piled on top of her head with little wisps of hair framing her heart-shaped face. She was flawless.

"Whoa…" Austin said beside him. Marcus nodded his agreement unable to take his eyes off of her. She was breathtaking.

"Hello everyone! My name is Alira Duvall and I'm the mastermind behind this beautiful event! I'm really only up here to introduce you to our Master of Ceremonies for the evening, Mr. Carson McNally!" Alira spoke into the mic introducing the MC. She smiled and clapped with the audience as Carson stepped onto the stage and performed an exaggerated bow.

"Thank you for that lovely introduction Mrs. Duvall!" he said as he leaned in for a hug. Alira smiled and hugged him. Carson covered the mic and said something that made Alira laugh. She scanned the audience before she spotted him. Marcus felt their eyes on him, but he couldn't take his eyes off of Alira.

"Our stunning party planner is newly married! Please join me in welcoming them to the dance floor for their first official dance as husband and wife. They didn't have the chance to do the big deal wedding because our beautiful hostess was busy planning this lovely charity event for us!" Carson spoke into the mic. The crowd cheered and applause sounded loudly in the ballroom. Alira descended the stairs with Duke's assistance. The crowd parted as Alira made her way over to Marcus. She smiled and held out her hand.

"Shall we?" she asked him with a curtsy. Marcus laughed and accepted her hand.

The music started as they made their way to the dance floor. Marcus heard the whispers around them ranging from how beautiful she looked to how she didn't deserve a man like him. Marcus ignored them all as he swept her onto the dance floor. He only had eyes for her. Alira was the most beautiful woman in the room, and she was all his.

Marcus and Alira were sitting at their table with Austin and Karma as they waited for their meals. Karma still hadn't forgiven him for his mistreatment of Alira. He figured it would be a while before she did. He had messed up pretty badly, so it was only logical he had some making up to do for hurting her best friend the way he had.

"Have I told you yet how absolutely stunning you are?" Marcus asked as he leaned over to kiss Alira. She leaned in and granted his request for a kiss easily. She was smiling when she leaned back.

"No lie, you look amazing," Austin told her with an appreciative nod. Karma agreed.

"I'd do you," Karma said jokingly. Alira laughed.

"Alright, you two. She's already taken!" Marcus told them with amusement as he rested his arm around Alira's shoulders pulling her closer. Austin and Karma laughed as a waiter brought over two plates. The aroma was mouthwatering. Karma thanked him as he placed her plate down on the table in front of her. Austin nodded his thanks as he dug into the garlic chicken on his plate. Alira just shook her head.

"Animal," she muttered at him as a waiter placed her meal down in front of her. It smelled so good! She couldn't wait to dig in. That was until she spotted the woman making a beeline for their table. She groaned. Marcus gave her a curious look as he chewed the piece of chicken he had just popped into his mouth. He followed Alira's gaze and groaned. Coatroom request woman. Karma was already glaring.

"Alira," the woman greeted coldly though she never took her eyes off Marcus.

"What do you want Denise? Or are you going by a different name this week?" Alira asked in a cool even tone. Marcus swallowed the chicken and leaned back in his chair with a raised brow watching their exchange. Alira sat stiffly as she stared expressionless at the woman.

"Funny, I remember you were going by Bridget when you were with my brother. Oh, and when you were with Alex, it was Shannon. It's so hard to keep all of your alter egos straight," Alira said with a false sweetness Marcus had never heard from her before. It made him sit up straighter.

"Marcus, may I introduce you to Denise, as is her *legal* name," Alira stated flatly. She never took her eyes away from Denise as she spoke.

"We've met. She tried to coax me to go into the coatroom with her," Marcus growled as he slid his arm around Alira's shoulders once more. He was suddenly feeling possessive and hearing that this tramp had slept with both Grayson and Alex, he was going to make it very clear she was not welcome. Karma and Austin sat watching them closely. Karma held her knife as if she was ready to use it if the need arose. Austin appeared calm but Marcus knew he was anything but calm as he said something into the mic at his wrist. Duke and Camden suddenly appeared close by, steady and ready. Denise noticed them immediately.

"Calling your watchdogs, I see," she snarled. Alira flinched. It was the only sign she was nervous. Marcus traced along her arm softly, reassuringly. He wasn't going anywhere.

"I think it's time for you to leave," Camden told her forcefully as he stepped forward. Duke flanked her on the other side. Alira nodded her agreement and Camden gripped Denise's arm to pull her away. Denise started laughing.

"You really think you're safe? They know where you are. You can't escape him," she said cackling like some evil witch in a movie. Camden didn't waste another second before he yanked her away from the table. Marcus watched as Denise was escorted from the ballroom by Camden and Duke. Austin was on his feet following behind them quickly.

"Alira?" Karma asked cautiously. Marcus turned to look at her and saw that all the color had drained from her face.

"I'd like to go home now if that's alright," she spoke quietly staring at the closed doors Denise had just gone through. Marcus nodded. Karma stood, tucking the knife into a hidden pocket of her skirt. Marcus would have laughed at the absurdity of it, but he knew better. His baby sister was always packing something. He imagined she probably had a knife strapped to her leg. Austin had taught her that little trick after one of her boyfriends had roughed her up in high school.

"I just need to grab my things from the penthouse, and we can go," Alira told them quietly.

"I'll go with you. Marcus, we'll meet you at the elevators coming back down?" Karma asked as she moved around the table. Marcus could only nod. He wanted to go with them, but he needed to talk to Austin when he came back in. He had this nagging feeling that something wasn't right. He didn't know what it was yet. Alira and Karma would be fine going up on their own. It was a private elevator that could only be accessed by a keycard for that specific penthouse.

Karma rode up to the penthouse with Alira. Alira had walked confidently into the elevator putting on a show of confidence. The instant the doors closed behind them, she collapsed against the wall. She took several deep breaths in an attempt to prevent the panic from bubbling up even further. Denise was somehow helping Grayson and Alex. Of course, they knew where she was. The whole city knew about this event. It wasn't impossible to think outsiders wouldn't know about it. People came from all over for this! It drew big names with fat checkbooks handing over donations for a good cause.

The elevator door dinged open, announcing their arrival to the penthouse suite. They stepped into the entry together. Alira knew immediately that something wasn't right. The hair on the back of her neck stood up and she reached to pull Karma back into the elevator with her, but it was too late. Alex came out of the coat closet next to the elevator, knocking Karma hard on the side of the head. She fell to the floor almost instantly. Karma struggled to get up, reaching for the knife that Alira knew was tucked into the folds of her dress. Alex kicked her square in the stomach.

"Stop it!" Alira screamed and lunged at him. He caught her in a vice-like grip laughing at her pathetic attempts at getting out of his grasp. Grayson appeared around the corner holding a knife to Kara's throat.

"Alira, you're going to come with us or your lovely assistant here and that hell creature on the floor will be leaving here with some new holes," he told her smoothly, coldly. He spoke like this was a completely normal situation and everything would be okay. It wouldn't be okay, but he sure spoke as if he believed it! Alira immediately stopped struggling and went limp in Alex's arms.

"Good girl," he praised and tossed Kara away from him roughly. Kara hit the floor hard, knocking a vase off the table as she fell. Kara scrambled away from Grayson staring in horror at him.

"Alex put her down. She'll behave herself," Grayson ordered. Alex obeyed like the puppet that he was. Alira stood tall in an attempt to display confidence she didn't feel. How had they gotten up here? Nobody had access except Alira, Kara, and Joey. Joey! Where was he? Was he alright?

"Grayson, you have really lost your mind, haven't you?" Alira asked him though she already knew the answer. She needed to bide her time. Karma tried to stand but Alex kicked her down again. Karma groaned as she clutched at her stomach in obvious pain. Alex laughed. Kara was pressed against the wall watching Grayson with quick glances to Alira and Karma on the floor.

"Kara, where is Joey?" Alira asked her. Kara pointed to the bathroom.

"They knocked him out and tied him up. He's bleeding. I don't know what to do!" Kara explained with fear in her voice. Alira fought down her own rising panic. She could do this. She had to stay calm. If she stayed calm, they would all get out of here.

"Say goodbye to your friends. You won't be seeing them again," Grayson told her as he strode forward and gripped her arm painfully. Alira winced but refused to cry out. She wouldn't give him the satisfaction of it. Grayson dragged Alira along behind him as Alex brought up the rear. Alira tripped, trying to slow them down. That only served to have Alex toss her over his shoulder like a sack of flour and trudge down the stairs. She had already tried screaming. That had resulted in a gag in her mouth and her hands being tied together. They reached the garage and Grayson hit a button on a remote. The liftgate of a nearby SUV opened as the vehicle started up. Alex dumped her in the back and slammed the gate closed. This was it. Nobody would know where she was. She was on her own.

"Marcus!" Karma screamed as she fell out of the elevator. Kara stumbled out after her. Austin and Camden ran to them immediately. Marcus reached for Karma and only then noticed the knife protruding from her side. Karma held her hand around the knife trying to keep it in place while Kara did her best to help support her weight, which she gratefully passed to Marcus. Camden rushed to take her from Marcus as Marcus frantically checked the elevator for Alira while Austin called 9-1-1. Duke appeared huffing and puffing.

"Security… cameras shut… off…" he panted out. Austin ordered him to sit down and catch his breath before he said any more. Sirens sounded outside. Paramedics rushed in with a gurney and their gear bags. They helped get Karma settled on the gurney.

"Marcus, they took Alira…" she told him as they started to wheel her away.

"I'm going with her!" Camden said knowing nobody would argue with him. He ran after the paramedics and Karma.

"What did she mean?" Marcus yelled, turning on Kara. Kara jumped back so hard she slammed into the wall. Austin stepped between Marcus and Kara. He gave Marcus a hard stare before turning to face Kara.

"Kara, who took her?" Austin asked her more calmly, though he was anything but calm.

Kara proceeded to tell them everything. She and Joey had gone up to the penthouse to clean up and make sure their things were ready to go when the event ended. They could just grab their bags and go home.

Two men had been in the penthouse when they arrived. She had thought they were staff at first but then things took a turn and Joey had been knocked out. They had tied him up and left him in the bathroom while they waited for Alira to come upstairs. Alex stabbed Karma when she tried getting up off the floor the second time. They had demanded Alira go with them and nobody else would get hurt. Alira had agreed. Kara was sobbing hysterically by the time she was finished telling them everything.

"I'm so sorry! I had no idea who they were!" she cried and buried her face in her hands. Duke hugged her tightly. Austin quickly called the police and his firm. Marcus slammed his fist through the wall.

Marcus hit his knees, breathing hard. When he lifted his head again, his eyes were blazing.

"I'm going to end them," he growled.

Chapter 15

Alira opened her eyes. Her heart nearly stopped when she realized where she was. It was the same dark room Grayson had locked her in years ago when he had turned his friend loose on her. The same friend he had killed not too long after. The one difference was the window was no longer boarded up. Iron bars had replaced the wood nailed into the frame. She already knew the door would be locked. Alira was trapped and the only way out would be getting past Grayson when he opened the door.

She looked down. She was still in her dress from the charity gala. Alex had knocked her out when she wouldn't stop kicking the seats in the back of the SUV. Her head throbbed painfully. Reaching up, Alira could feel the knot where Alex had clubbed her.

Glancing around the room, Alira saw a folded pile of clothes. Grey sweats, a larger than her size matching grey t-shirt, and a pair of socks. She knew Grayson wouldn't have thought or cared to leave them for her. It must have been Alex. He was still in there somewhere. Maybe Grayson hadn't corrupted him entirely. She hoped that was the case. If it were, she had a chance.

Marcus paced the office like a caged animal. He should have gone with them. He shouldn't have let them go up to the penthouse by themselves. They should have been safe! How Grayson and Alex had gained access to the penthouse was still a mystery. The hotel manager couldn't explain it. Austin had his tech guys going over the system but so far, they hadn't pulled anything. The cameras had been shut off remotely on what was supposed to be a closed system. The only camera that had been active at the time of Alira's abduction was the one in the garage that focused on the elevator and stair access. Grayson, that smug bastard, had looked straight into the camera and smiled as Alex carried Alira to a waiting SUV. Then the feed cut out. They didn't have a plate number. Just the make and model of the vehicle.

"They found the SUV!" Camden hollered as he slid to a stop in the office at Austin's firm. All eyes turned to him. He was leaning over, hands on his knees, huffing like he had run a marathon.

"Where?" Marcus demanded.

Camden held up his hand, signaling that he needed a minute to catch his breath. Duke entered the room holding an envelope. He looked angrier than Marcus had ever seen him.

"They dumped the SUV but left this," Duke informed them, indicating the envelope in his hand.

"They had this planned because this is some serious tech. This wasn't a quick and easy job to do with just a few days' notice," a tech said over the phone as he finished going through the hotel's system.

"Get back here with the data," Austin ordered and ended the call. He held out his hand for the envelope. Marcus reached for it, but Austin grabbed it first. It took more restraint than he realized not to knock Austin on his ass and take the envelope from him. Austin seemed to understand the struggle and nodded to Camden and Duke. They flanked Marcus, prepared to grab him if necessary.

Marcus watched as Austin opened the envelope and pulled out the folded letter. He unfolded the paper and read the contents. After what seemed to be an abnormally long time to read the letter, he lifted his head and Marcus saw a darkness sweep over him.

"Duke, get everyone in here. Now. I want every available guy in the meeting room ten minutes ago," he barked the order, his tone cold but firm. Duke nodded and left the office quickly. Austin turned to Camden then.

"Alira's apartment is bugged," he informed him. That was all it took. Camden went from easy-going to all business in mere seconds. Then Camden disappeared after Duke. Marcus stood in silence waiting. For what, he wasn't sure. Austin sat down in the chair and tossed the letter on the desk. Several long painful minutes passed before Marcus finally caved and sat down in the chair across from him. His shoulders slumped, defeated. Marcus and Alira had made up. He had literally been on his knees apologizing to Alira for being an idiot just two days ago! She had forgiven him! Now, they didn't know where she was or if she was alright.

Footsteps sounded in the hallway. A lot of them. Marcus turned to see who it might be. Austin was on his feet quickly and moving forward. Marcus stood to follow. He was surprised by what he saw. It was as though a small army had descended upon the building. They marched toward the meeting room. Austin didn't say a word as he watched his guys stroll past his office. None of them spoke. They all had the same expression on their faces; steel and determination.

Marcus quietly followed Austin to the meeting room that was practically packed to capacity. The more time that passed, the worse Marcus felt. They still had no leads on Alira's whereabouts.

He remembered the fear in her eyes when she had seen her brother standing in her room at the hospital. Her quick actions when Alex had reappeared. The resignation at knowing she had to get married followed by the excitement of knowing that she was going to marry a man she loved. The same man who loved her in return. Unconditionally. He remembered the pain he heard in her voice when she called out to him as he walked away in the garage. Dancing with her in her apartment. Her musical laugh. What if he never heard her laugh again? No, he couldn't think that way. They would get her back! They had to.

Alira sat huddled in the corner on the bed watching the door. The room was cold and the clothes she had been given to wear didn't provide much in the way of warmth. She could see her breath each time she exhaled. Her stomach growled loudly. It was the only sound in the quiet. She had no way of knowing how long she'd been locked in the room. It was hard to keep track.

Denise had shown up at their table and ruined her appetite, so she hadn't gotten more than a bite of her meal. If she had to guess, it had only been a few hours since Grayson had abducted her. Reaching for the discarded dress, Alira wrapped it tightly around herself hoping it would help provide some warmth. The sound of a key turning in the lock made her jump.

"Alira…"

Alex's voice called out to her as he opened the door. Light flooded the room, temporarily blinding her. She crouched, ready to pounce like an angry cornered animal. She knew she didn't really have a chance at getting the jump on him, but she had to try. She needed to get out of there. She needed to get back to Marcus.

Alira blinked against the light, praying her eyes would adjust quicker but the door closed quickly, and she was plunged back into darkness. Alira threw herself at the door, banging on it, begging for him to come back and let her out. She felt the tears stinging her eyes. She would not cry now! Crying didn't unlock doors.

"Alex! Alex, let me out!" she screamed. She thought she heard footsteps. Pressing her ear to the door, she listened. Maybe it had been her imagination. But then, she heard it again.

"Alex, please, it's cold..." she begged. Nothing. No footsteps, nobody breathing on the other side of the door. Just silence. Alira turned and pressed her back against the door before sliding to the floor. She pulled her arms into her shirt hoping it would help warm her. This was too much. Cold, hungry, and terrified. She had been here before. It was not any better now that she was an adult. If anything, this was worse. As a child, being locked in the closet with just a bucket for a toilet and a pad to lay on was a walk in the park. Now? It was like living in a nightmare because this wasn't just Grayson doing this to her. She had nobody to pull her from the darkness. How could she? Nobody knew where she was. She didn't even know where here was!

"Move away from the door," Alex ordered from the other side. Alira hadn't realized she had dozed off until his nasal voice sounded through the door behind her. She cringed. Her bones ached; muscles stiff as she moved to obey his command. The key turning in the lock sounded throughout the room once again before the door swung open. She stood with her back pressed solidly against the far wall, unprepared in the moment to try and make her escape. Alex's small frame filled the doorway. His arms were loaded down with a blanket, a small tray of food, and... wait, was that some sort of craft? What the hell was he playing at?

"Don't try anything. I don't want to have to hurt you again," he said as he eyed her. The way his eyes roamed over her body made her feel sick. She tried to stay still, tried to stay calm, but the panic welled up inside her threatening to boil over. She choked it down and cleared her throat.

"Thank you, Alex. You always take such good care of me," she whispered trying to sound grateful even as the bile rose up in her throat. Alex placed the tray down on the little table by the door and tossed the blanket to the bed. He set the small box of craft supplies on the floor.

Alex stepped toward her and it took every ounce of control she had not to scream. She froze when his hand reached out. She turned her face away, shutting her eyes tightly when his fingers touched her cheek and traced a line down her jaw to her neck. She cringed at his touch. It felt like her skin was on fire. She was going to be sick.

"You'll love me again. You'll see," he told her quietly. Alira didn't move. The second the door closed behind him, she ran for the bucket in the corner and emptied the meager contents of her stomach into it.

⏾

"Alright crew, this is what we know as of now. Grayson Hervowe owns several properties. We already have teams heading out to search for them. We know Alira's apartment was bugged. We believe a man named Alex Loftin is helping Grayson. You have already been briefed on when Alira was abducted and how. Unfortunately, we don't have a whole lot of new information but we're sending it out to you as we get it. This is on us to find her. The local PD doesn't have the resources or manpower to offer much in the way of assistance. We're flying under the radar here. Keep your eyes peeled and ears to the ground," Austin said as he dismissed the meeting.

It felt like a waste of time to call them in there for no real new information, but it was the easiest way to do it. If anyone had new intel, that would have been the perfect time to share it with the entire squad. Austin glanced over at his brother sitting in the corner of the room. He didn't know any other way to help him. Marcus had barely eaten, and he was running on so little sleep it was a wonder he wasn't a walking zombie by that point. They had been following any and every lead that came their way in the week since Alira had been taken. His guys were exhausted, but they weren't giving up. They would find Alira. One way or another.

"Camden just checked in. Their property was empty. Said it didn't look like anyone had been there in years," Duke reported as he walked purposely into the meeting room. Marcus stood up, slamming the chair hard against the wall as he did.

"It's been a fucking week and we're no closer to finding Alira! We have no idea if she's dead or alive and every damn lead so far has been cold!" he yelled furiously. Duke visibly flinched. Austin sighed. He truly wished that he had some better news. He wanted Alira back as much as anyone. It was hard enough not being able to go out into the field to help search Grayson's known locations. Someone had to stay back to coordinate the teams.

Austin's secretary came into the room then and handed him a stack of papers before she handed an envelope to Marcus. Marcus eyed it suspiciously before accepting it. He carefully opened it and pulled the folded paper out. Taking a deep breath, he read its contents.

You'll never find her. She's in a dark place now. I know your brother has his entire staff searching my properties. She isn't there.

"The bastard is taunting us," Marcus growled as he reread the letter. Austin took the letter from him and read it out loud.

"What about calling her sister? Maybe she would know something?" Duke suggested in his deep rumbling voice. That was actually a great idea. As Austin was reaching for the phone, his secretary came on over the speaker saying there was a phone call for him.

"Who is it?" Austin demanded.

"Sir, it's Mara Hervowe."

Austin and Marcus exchanged a look before Austin told her to put the call through.

"Mara?" Austin said answering the phone and hitting the speaker button.

"Austin? Is Marcus there with you?" she asked. Her voice shook as she spoke. Something wasn't right. She was scared. They could hear it. Marcus had a feeling it had nothing to do with Alira.

"Grayson just called me. He tried convincing me to come back to the states. He said if I didn't come on my own, he was coming to get me. He told me that he already had Alira. What did he mean?" she asked panicked. Nobody had told Mara that Alira had been taken. The thought hadn't even crossed their minds.

"Shit," Austin said angrily before launching into an explanation about what had happened and what they were doing to find Alira. Marcus felt useless. Completely and totally useless. He listened as Austin and Mara went back and forth. Austin told her where his men had searched already, and Mara added more locations to the list. Grayson had far more property than they had found in records so far. The longer the list got, the lower their chances became of finding Alira soon.

"Have you checked Alira's properties? Our grandfather had a rather large estate. There's a guest house hidden away in the woods. I don't think even Alira knew about it. It's a run-down little house that our grandfather left to rot years before Alira was born," Mara told them quickly. Austin cursed. They hadn't thought to check into Alira's properties. They had assumed Grayson would use one of his. Marcus thanked Mara for the information and Austin ended the call.

Alex had been coming into the room to bring her meals and to replace her bucket with a fresh one. Alira hadn't seen Grayson once. She didn't ask about it either. Seeing Alex every day, talking to him, trying to get close to him hoping for an opening was hard enough. She knew Grayson would never fall for anything she tried but Alex would. Alira had spent the hours she was alone in that room slowly and methodically dismantling the mattress. She had no idea how old the mattress was. It was musty and stained with holes where a wild spring had poked through. She had struggled in the beginning when she first started to form her plan. Her hands and fingers ached from the effort in the cold to bend the metal away from the frame. Once she figured out the quickest way to detach the springs themselves using a spoon Alex had left for her soup, she made quick work of detaching several springs before Alex reappeared with her evening meal.

As soon as she heard the key in the lock, Alira dropped the mattress back down and threw her dress over the large hole she had created. She moved quickly to flatten herself against the far wall as he entered carrying a tray of food and a fresh change of clothing for her. She eyed the door, but he didn't seem to notice. Alira was positive that Alex didn't even realize that he always followed the same path when he entered the room. Open the door, put the tray down on the table, set clothes on the tiny dresser, step forward to touch her face or her shoulder, and then turn to leave. He never changed it up. He was predictable as always.

"Alex?"

He stopped and turned to face her expectantly.

"When can I come out?" she asked him, keeping her voice small and unsure.

"As soon as you admit that I'm the only one who can love you and take care of you. Grayson won't accept a lie," he told her and left without another word. The key turned in the lock. Alira counted to ten before she moved away from the wall.

If she had been tracking it correctly, she was given two meals a day. Her bucket was changed out once a day in the morning. She had been given twenty-eight meals which meant she had been locked in that room for fourteen days. Two weeks. Was anyone even looking for her? Were they getting closer to finding her or did they think that she was dead by now? She shook her head to rid herself of the thoughts crashing around in her mind. She had no way of knowing. What she did know was that she needed to get out of there no matter what.

Two weeks. Two damn weeks and still nothing! They were running on fumes. Austin and his men had been spread thin searching properties and since the list had increased exponentially, they were stuck. They could only cover so much ground at once. They had received word that Grayson had boarded a flight overseas two days ago. They hadn't heard a thing from Mara since. Marcus hoped it was because she had gone into hiding and not because Grayson had somehow gotten ahold of her too.

"We think we found the property but there's a problem."

Austin glared waiting. Marcus's heart started pounding in his chest. He had heard this before but the hope that was always there broke free and burst out. They needed a win. He needed a win. He had reached the point a few days ago where Austin had to forcibly restrain him and have him sedated. Marcus could admit it hadn't been his finest moment. Days of not sleeping and tracking leads with Austin's guys had made him desperate.

"It's a hundred-acre heavily wooded property. We can't get any drones out there until morning," Camden told him standing stiffly, wary.

"I want men out there now, on foot if necessary," Austin ordered. "Marcus, you stable?"

Marcus nodded. He had a thin hold on his temper and getting out there searching helped. Every lead so far had turned up nothing. If there was a slight chance that Grayson was keeping her on her own land, he was going to be there when they found her. He had to be there. He had been going out of his mind with the what if's. It was making him crazy.

"Load up then," Austin ordered. The room cleared in seconds. Marcus slipped his flack on and secured the straps.

Chapter 16

Austin barked orders through his walkie as Camden drove the truck following the directions of the GPS. Marcus sat in his seat watching out the window. He listened intently to the voices crackling over the radio. Austin's guys were already on scene and working to set up a makeshift command post. It was really just a van with some monitors and radio equipment inside, but it got the job done. They would be searching the hundred-acre property on foot with only two search dogs available. That van was the central control point. They hadn't needed to search the property in secret or gain permission to search because technically, Marcus owned it now that he was married to Alira.

"Please let us find her. Please," Marcus whispered to the universe as the truck turned off the highway and onto a paved road. He had never been a big believer in higher powers and all that, but it couldn't hurt to try. They had been hoping and praying for two weeks. The more time that passed, the higher the chances were that they would never find her and if they did, she wasn't likely to be alive. Grayson was sick and there wasn't a single person that would expect him to keep her alive if he thought he no longer needed her. The experts always said that the first twenty-four hours were critical to finding a kidnapping victim alive. Chances of finding the victim dwindled drastically after that. It had been three hundred and thirty-six hours since Alira had been taken. It was a number that haunted him. It flashed like a neon sign in his mind.

Three hundred and thirty-six hours of failure.

Three hundred and thirty-six hours of not knowing.

Three hundred and thirty-six hours of wondering if Alira was alive or dead.

Three hundred and thirty-six hours of living in hell.

Camden turned the wheel quickly, guiding the truck off the paved road and onto an unmarked dirt road that they would have missed if they hadn't been paying attention. Marcus gripped the suicide handle at the sudden jolt of the truck.

Alex was late. Alira paced the room nervously. She had been awake all day and most of the night bending the wire from the springs into a makeshift weapon that she could use. She knew Grayson was gone because Alex had told her but had no idea when he would be back. This might be her only chance. She just needed to get past Alex and she could get out. Grayson wouldn't be there to stop her. She could escape. She had to escape. There was no chance that she was going back to Alex and Alira sure as hell wasn't willing to die in that cold, damp room with the ghosts of her tortured past. She had spent far too much time in that room. Her hands were sore and scratched from bending the metal together into what could only be described as a shiv. It was all she had.

"Alira, I'm coming in. I have your dinner. I'm sorry it's late," Alex called through the door. She heard the key slide into the lock. Listened to the gears as the locking mechanism shifted before the bolt moved and the door swung open. Alira stood in her usual spot, pressed firmly against the wall. Alex walked in but he didn't set the tray down on the table. He glanced at her only for a second before he moved toward the mattress. Her dress from the gala was spread out over the hole she had made as she worked on unwinding the springs inside it.

Shit!

"Alex... I – I'm ready to go back to you," she spoke softly hoping to distract him. "I made a huge mistake leaving you. I realize that now. Can you forgive me?"

She flexed her fingers around the handle of the shiv she had tucked behind her back. Her hands shook. She tried to keep her breathing even, eyes downcast. It was enough to distract him from the dress. He set the tray and clothes down on the mattress without another thought and turned toward her. A chill ran down her spine. Alex smiled. He stepped closer until he was standing directly in front of her. Bile rose in her throat when he reached out to touch her cheek.

Don't throw up! Don't throw up!

"Do you mean it?" he asked softly. He trailed his fingers down her neck to her chest, grazing her breast. Alira could only nod.

"I've waited so long to hear you say the words!" he told her as he yanked her up against him and slammed his mouth down on hers painfully.

⏱

It was now or never!

Alira raised her hand quickly. She slammed the shiv down, piercing his neck. Once, twice, three times. Blood spurted from the holes in his neck spraying her, covering her in the red sticky fluid. Alex staggered back with his hand over his neck staring at her in shock. The blood spurted out between his fingers. She screamed and dove at him again, this time aiming for his chest. Alira flew at him, falling to the floor as she stabbed him.

"W... why?" he choked out. Blood oozed from the corner of his mouth. She could see it coating his tongue. He coughed and sprayed her.

Alira watched as Alex took his last shallow breath. His hand fell away from her arm as his lifeless eyes stared up at her. She scrambled off of him quickly and slipped on the blood slick floor. She fell. Alex's blood soaked into her clothes and she felt her stomach roll in disgust. She couldn't hold it down any longer. The vomit rose up, squeezing her insides violently as her stomach revolted. Alira barely reached the bucket in time. That was when she realized he hadn't closed the door behind him when he came in. He'd been distracted by her dress on the bed in the same place it always was. Without thinking twice, Alira was on her feet and running.

Alira didn't recognize the house she was in. She had never seen it before. It didn't matter. She could get out. She was no longer locked in that room and with Grayson gone, she could make it. She could do it! Alira slid around a corner and realized she was in what should have been the kitchen. Spotting the far door, Alira ran for it. Unlocking it, she threw it open and almost cried. A cold gust of wind blew in making her shiver. Snow-covered trees never looked so good in the moonlight! There was a pair of galoshes next to the door that she slipped on. It would provide some level of protection on her feet as she trudged through the snow. Then it hit her. She had just killed someone. She had gotten out.

She ran. She ran as fast as her legs would allow.

Marcus trudged through the snow with Austin and his team. They were one of six groups searching the woods. They were searching in the dark with headlamps and flashlights. Their team had one of the two search dogs. It was a slow process with how deep the snow was in some areas. So far, Marcus was convinced the dog was useless.

Static crackled over Austin's radio, breaking the silence.

"We hit a dead end here. Circling back around," Duke's voice crackled through.

"Ten-four."

"Hang on, the dog picked up on something," Duke's voice crackled back over the radio.

Their team waited for Duke to come back on but there was silence. Austin signaled for them to keep moving. Marcus wanted to hit him. Why wasn't he demanding more information? A phone buzzed. Austin stopped moving. The backlight on his phone brightened the darkness around them.

"What is it?" Marcus demanded. Austin ignored him. The radio crackled again.

"Boss, we found the house. Entering now," a voice Marcus didn't recognize crackled through the static. "There's blood. A lot of it."

Marcus felt like the world was crashing down on him.

Please no.

Alira ran until her lungs burned and her muscles screamed at her to stop. The snow was up to the middle of her calves but still, she pushed herself to keep going. Putting distance between herself and that horrible little house was the only goal she had in her mind. She couldn't think about anything else. She knew she was leaving a trail of bloody footprints behind her, but she couldn't stop. If she stopped, she was sure someone would be coming after her. She needed more time. There had been so much blood. It felt like most of it was on her. Her stomach rolled. Alex's dead eyes stared back at her in the darkness. He was everywhere she turned.

Snow crunched behind her. A flash of light flickered through the trees. Unsure of what else to do, Alira dove behind the biggest tree she could find, which in the dark was difficult to gauge. She was sure whoever was following her could hear her heart pounding in her chest. She could see lights bobbing toward her in the dark. Footprints crunched through the snow, growing louder, closer. Alira held her breath. Something touched her in the darkness. She screamed and tried to run in the opposite direction. She slammed into a large figure dressed in black. It felt like she hit a brick wall. She fell back, landing on her butt in the snow, and screamed while she scrambled backward trying to get away.

"I won't go back! You'll have to kill me!" she screamed at the figure.

Alira somehow managed to get her feet under her just in time to run smack into another wall of a man. This time she didn't fall. Instead, the figure gripped her tightly in a bear hug. Instant regret smacked into her. She should have taken the shiv when she ran. It was stupid to leave it behind. She hadn't been thinking about that. Her opening had presented itself and she had jumped for it. Alira fought. She fought with everything she had left in her. Grayson's goons wouldn't take her alive if she had anything to say about it. One of the thug's arms was a little too close and he had no idea. She angled her head and chomped down hard on his arm. He howled in pain and loosened his grip on her. It wasn't much but it was enough. She slipped from his grasp and hit the ground running.

"Alira!"

Alira kept running. She was running from hell itself and nothing was going to stop her from getting away this time.

"We found her! She's running scared. She bit Carson and bolted!" Duke's voice crackled over the radio.

"Repeat! Clarify, you found Alira?" Austin yelled into the mic of his radio. No response. Austin repeated the order into the mic. Still nothing.

"Camden, turn Bazzle loose. Track him on his collar," Austin ordered. Camden immediately unhooked the tracking line from the dog's collar and gave him the order to search. Marcus watched as the dog disappeared into the trees ahead. Camden pulled up a little monitor and waited for the signal to bounce back.

"Bazzle is loose. I repeat, Bazzle is loose!" Austin spoke into the mic as they began following Camden through the woods as he tracked the little dog on the screen in his hand. Marcus wanted to run ahead of them. He wanted to find her. She was alive.

"Alira! Stop!" a deep voice yelled after her. It was enough to break through the curtain of fear separating her from the rest of the world. She slowed her pace, gasping for breath. Bright lights shone into her eyes, blinding her. She held her hand up trying to shield her eyes.

"Jesus..." the voice told her between breaths.

"Duke!"

Alira felt her knees give out beneath her as relief washed over her. Tears welled up in her eyes and poured free, sliding down her cheeks leaving little trails through the blood that had dried on her face. She collapsed in the snow. Strong hands were on her, examining her, searching for the source of the blood covering her.

"It's not mine," she choked out. A cold wet nose hit her cheek, followed by a gentle lick. She sobbed.

"Bazzle, out!" Duke ordered. The dog backed away and sat, waiting patiently.

"We've got her. Bazzle is with us," Duke spoke into his radio. Cheers erupted through the speaker. Lights bobbed through the trees around them at breakneck speeds.

Marcus raced towards the lights that he could see ahead of them. Adrenaline coursed through him, urging him faster. Even in the deep snow, he passed Austin and Camden with ease. He broke through the trees into a little clearing where several of Austin's men stood. His eyes immediately landed on the two figures in the middle of the circle. Duke was kneeling in the snow and wrapped there in his arms was Alira. Small, shivering, and sobbing. Marcus ran forward, sliding to a stop in front of her, landing hard as he did so. He didn't care. They had found her.

Duke held her tightly as she sobbed uncontrollably. She was safe. They hadn't given up on her. A gentle touch to her shoulder nearly made her jump out of her skin. Then she heard it. His voice saying her name. It was smooth like butter. Slowly, so slowly, she lifted her head and looked into his chocolate brown eyes. Duke released her and she threw herself into Marcus's arms.

"What the hell happened to her?" Austin asked when he looked down at Alira wrapped tightly in Marcus's embrace, still covered in blood. Duke stood and dusted the snow off his pants.

"You need to see it to believe it," Duke told him.

"Alira, sweetheart, can you tell us what happened?" Austin asked kneeling down to her level. She shook her head.

"I can show you," she told him after several deep breaths. Marcus held her tightly, rubbing her back, trying to soothe her even as his own heart was racing. Marcus wanted to get her home and cleaned up. She didn't need to go back to wherever she had come from, but she had insisted. She tried to explain what had happened and hadn't been able to form the words. She kept getting tongue-tied and mixing up her words. She was in shock. Austin had shrugged off his coat and draped it over her shoulders as Marcus held her, never wanting to let her go.

"Fucking hell..." Austin said as he entered the house. The trail of blood was easy to follow back to the source. Alira had stayed out in the clearing with Duke and several of the men while Austin, Camden, and Marcus entered the building. Austin and Camden had their guns drawn, ready if needed. Austin found the room first. Marcus and Camden were right behind him. Marcus couldn't believe his eyes. Now he understood the 'so much blood' comment over the radio. It was everywhere in the small room. Then he saw the bed. The dress she had worn at the gala was laid over it, spread out like it was concealing something.

"What's that?" Camden asked pointing to something. Austin and Marcus followed his line of sight. Whatever weapon she had used was sticking out of Alex's chest. Austin glanced over at the bed. He walked over and lifted the dress revealing the gaping hole in the mattress.

"I'll be damned..." he breathed. "She's resourceful."

Chapter 17

The truck pulled into the garage at Austin's firm. Alira was wide awake, staring blankly out the window as they pulled to a stop. She had refused to sleep for the hour drive. Marcus had held her snugly against him in the backseat as Camden drove along the empty highway. Alira had barely blinked. When Camden pulled into a parking space, Austin jumped out quickly and opened the rear door. He carefully scooped Alira up and out of the truck. He waited for Marcus to get out before he transferred Alira back into his arms. She never argued or said a word. She simply shifted when she needed to shift.

"You can use the shower in my office. I'll bring in some clean clothes," Austin told him as he showed him into the building and up to his office. Marcus thanked his brother and closed the door. He set Alira down, keeping his hands on her arms for support. She stood unmoving.

"I'm going to start the shower," he explained softly.

Alira looked around the bathroom. She felt numb. Then she caught sight of herself in the mirror. She didn't recognize the person staring back at her. Who was she? Her once grey clothing was now a dark crimson color with a smattering of grey. There were streaks down her face where her tears had washed away some of the blood spray but not all of it. Her dark tresses were matted in spots and stringy in others. She looked like she belonged in the wild with the animals.

"Come on. Let's get you cleaned up," Marcus said coming up behind her. Her eyes met his in the mirror. A tear slid down her cheek, but she brushed it away. She was so tired of crying. It was exhausting.

Marcus helped her into the shower before stepping in after her. She stood under the water in her clothes, letting it soak her. Alira turned her face up into the stream and scrubbed. Marcus grabbed her hands to stop her. He reached for a washcloth, wet it, and gently wiped the blood off her face. She watched as the water ran red at their feet and circled the drain before disappearing into the abyss.

"Knock-knock," Austin called as he opened the door a crack.

"You're good," Marcus responded never taking his eyes off of her. The door opened and Austin walked in, ducking his head so he wouldn't see anything he shouldn't. Alira burst out laughing startling them both. She laughed so hard her stomach hurt. She bent over clutching her stomach but couldn't stop. It kept coming like it had taken on a life of its own. Austin and Marcus stared at her with wide, concerned eyes.

"I'm fine," she laughed. "This is all completely normal!"

She took several deep breaths to get control before she stood up straight again. It didn't work. The laughter kept bubbling up within her, bursting forth taking on a life of its own as tears streamed freely down her face. Austin glanced between her and the door like he was trying to decide if he should just leave now or wait to see what happened next. Apparently, he chose to stay because he didn't move once he set the towels and clothes down on the counter.

None of this was normal. It never had been. Ever since she was a little girl, her entire life was just one thing after another. Her marriage to Marcus had been brought about by a lie his mother had told to protect her. Only it had taken him and his family further down the rabbit hole of her life. They had spent two weeks searching for her for Christ's sake! They would have been better off just letting her stay lost. It would have ended for them and Marcus could have moved on with someone else. He could have been happy. Instead, he was saddled with her mess. She was messy. She made the lives of those around her messy just by existing.

"You should leave. Both of you. You should all get as far away from me as you can before Grayson comes back," she told them honestly. Marcus was already shaking his head while Austin narrowed his eyes at her.

"Don't you dare! We've been through this. I'm not going anywhere," Marcus growled in response. Austin nodded his agreement.

"You're stuck with us. The entire Duvall clan has your back so get cleaned up and get moving. We have plans to make and guess what!" Austin said with a wink. Marcus gave him a questioning look.

"What?" she asked unable to hide her curiosity at his statement.

"One down. One to go," Austin said and walked smoothly out of the bathroom pulling the door closed behind him.

Marcus turned back to her with a smile. Austin was right. They had work to do, and the first order of business was getting her cleaned up and home. The rising sun was already shining its light through the window of the bathroom, warming it. Marcus made quick work of stripping her clothes off. He followed quickly. She allowed him to wash her. The only thing left to wash was her hair. It proved to be a difficult task. Two weeks with only a fork to comb it out meant they had to comb the mats out and used a lot of shampoo. Once Alira was able to get a comb through her hair without a fight, Marcus slathered conditioner through her hair, massaging her scalp as he went.

"Are you ready to go home?" he asked after she rinsed the conditioner from her hair. She yawned in response. He grinned.

"Let's get out of here and dried off then. You deserve a nice hot meal and a comfy bed," he told her as he turned the water off. Alira reached up to touch his face. She ran her fingers across his jaw before sliding her hand around to the back of his head and pulling him down for a kiss. Her lips brushed his softly. Just as quickly, she ended the kiss and stepped away from him as she reached for a towel.

"Welcome home! There have been some changes. First thing, the apartment has been swept for bugs. It's clear. The locks have also been changed. Again. And third, you now have a keypad entry. If you don't have your key and the code, you're not getting into this apartment. I, Marcus, and yourself are the only ones with the code. Harold refused it saying the fewer people that had it, the better," Austin told her happily as he threw open the door to her apartment.

Alira stepped inside and inhaled deeply. She didn't want to be there, but it was the safest place for her. As soon as Grayson was no longer a problem, she was moving. Too much had happened here in recent weeks and not all of it was good. Somehow, Grayson or Alex had not only gotten into her building, but they had gotten into her apartment. It was no longer her safe haven from the nightmares. The only saving grace was Marcus. If he weren't there with her, she wasn't sure she would have been able to set foot inside. Austin closed the door. The sound caused her to jump. She noticed there was a new chain lock at the door too. Marcus touched her arm. Alira flinched at the contact.

"I'm okay," she told him and offered a small smile. His eyebrows knit together as he looked down at her.

"I'm just really tired. Didn't get much sleep the last couple weeks," she said half-joking. She hadn't gotten more than a couple hours of sleep here and there. Only when she knew Alex wouldn't be coming in. The idea that he would come in when she was asleep had terrified her. The idea of Grayson showing up was worse. She had never fully understood the warning to sleep with one eye open until she had been kidnapped. Now, she understood it better than ever. Every little sound had woken her.

"Austin, you're welcome to crash in the guest room. I'm sure you haven't slept much either."

Austin nodded thankfully and after making sure the locks were all secure, he walked sluggishly down the hallway to her guest room. The door clicked closed behind him and they heard him flop down on the bed. Alira was positive he hadn't even bothered removing his boots. She wouldn't blame him. Marcus looked dead on his feet too.

"Come on. It's time for you to get some sleep," Alira told him as she took him by the hand and pulled him down the hallway to the bedroom. She kicked off the tennis shoes Austin had materialized in her size and pulled the comforter back. Marcus watched her. He looked like he was having trouble deciding if he wanted to ask the question that was so clearly written in his eyes or bite his tongue and keep it to himself. It was clear what he wanted to ask. He couldn't be blamed for it, but she wasn't going to answer an unasked question. She was too tired for that.

Marcus watched her as she kicked off her shoes and pulled the logo sweatshirt off over her head revealing the black tank top underneath. She tossed the sweatshirt at him before crawling under the covers. A quiet sigh escaped her lips as the soft mattress molded around her. She patted the space next to her, inviting him over. It was all he needed as he stripped out of the sweatpants and t-shirt he had on. He crawled in next to her. When she scooted closer to him and rested her hand on his chest as she had most every night since her accident, he let out the breath he didn't realize he'd been holding. Her head settled against his shoulder. Marcus wrapped his arms around her, swearing to never let her go again, and closed his eyes.

Alira screamed. There was blood everywhere and she couldn't get away from it. If she moved across the room, it followed her. She tried climbing up on the bed to get away from it and the room began to slowly fill with it like a pool filling with water. She was choking on it. It was everywhere. Alex's strangled voice asking her why sounded in her ears as his corpse floated closer to her. She pushed him away. His body just kept coming back to her until his dead arms wrapped around her and squeezed. A copper taste flooded her mouth and she realized she was choking on her own blood. When she opened her eyes, it was Grayson's face staring at her, smiling maliciously.

"I told you that you wouldn't make it out alive," he sneered at her as the room continued to fill with blood. She searched frantically for the

door, but it was gone. There was just a wall where the door should have been. Alex's corpse was nowhere to be seen. This wasn't right! This wasn't the way it ended for her! It couldn't be! She was supposed to have Marcus's baby! They were supposed to be a family!

Marcus was frantic. He couldn't wake her up. She was choking like someone had their hands wrapped around her throat. Alira was gasping for air. Austin must have heard her because he stumbled into the room searching for danger. He stared in shock as Marcus shook Alira trying desperately to wake her. She was trapped in a nightmare. Not knowing what else to do, Marcus yelled at her as loud as he could. He yelled her name, yelled for her to wake up. That did it. His booming voice had broken through to her. Alira's eyes popped open. She sat quickly upright coughing and sputtering. Marcus immediately pulled her into his arms and cradled her against his chest.

"What the fuck just happened?" Austin asked from the doorway with wide eyes. He had never seen anyone have a nightmare like that. He could face down an armed gunman and play bodyguard to celebrities but none of that compared to what he had just witnessed.

"It was a night terror," Marcus explained as he rocked Alira. She clung to him breathing hard.

"Does that happen often?" Austin asked, his voice a little higher than he probably intended it to be. Marcus shook his head. Austin moved his mouth like he was going to say something, but nothing came out. He stared, unsure of what else to do. Someone having a nightmare they couldn't wake up from? He never would have believed that was a real thing. If anyone had told him that happened in real life and wasn't just a horror movie plot twist, he would have laughed thinking they were joking.

"No, but they happen often enough."

"For me, they usually happen due to sleep deprivation... and trauma," Alira responded softly as she caught her breath. She pulled away from Marcus and crawled to the edge of the bed.

"I need my phone and some water," she whispered without meeting their eyes. Austin jumped at the opportunity to leave the room while Marcus shifted to rub her back. Austin returned a few minutes later with a glass of water and Alira's fully charged phone. Marcus took both from him. He could see that Austin was acutely uncomfortable which was a rare sight. Sadly, it wasn't one he could enjoy. His concern for his wife easily overrode his desire to poke fun at his brother.

Alira scrolled through her contacts list until she stopped at Karma's name. She tapped out a message and hit send. Marcus watched her curiously with a nice helping of caution. Her phone pinged back with a message.

Be there in 20.

"Why is Karma coming over?" Marcus asked her. Alira took a deep breath. He needed to know about her dream. So, she told him. She left out the pregnancy part of it though. It didn't seem relevant at the moment. He listened intently and held her as she told him all of the gory details of the nightmare. By the time she had finished, there was a knock at the door. They could hear Austin grumbling about not being paid enough to be a personal butler answering the door. It made Alira laugh. He was crabby. She couldn't recall a time where he wasn't happy and joking. Clearly sleep deprivation brought out an entirely different monster.

Karma appeared in the doorway of her room a minute later holding a small brown paper bag in her hand. She looked like she was going to start crying when she saw Alira. Karma rushed over and hugged her. Alira understood. Everyone had thought they would never see her again. Hell, she had been almost convinced she would never get out of that nightmare house. Some people far into the future would have found her bones and nobody would have known how she came to be there. Her story would have ended without a happy ending. When they pulled apart, Alira smiled gratefully and took the bag from her before she kissed Marcus on the cheek and scooted off the bed. Marcus watched as Alira walked into the bathroom and closed the door.

"There's a pregnancy test in that bag, isn't there?" he asked his sister without ever taking his eyes off the door. Somehow, he knew.

"Yes," she answered easily and headed for the living room. No denying it. Just a simple answer and then she was gone, leaving him to contemplate his next move. Alira clearly wanted to be alone but he also got the impression that she didn't want to bother him either. Not unless she had to. He knew what he had to do.

Alira read the directions several times before she was certain she understood them. *Here goes nothing.* She opened the package and took a deep breath. She willed her bladder to cooperate as she peed into a little specimen cup Karma had thankfully added into the bag. Alira set the cup on the counter, cleaned herself up, and dipped the stick into the cup. Counting to ten before removing the stick from the cup, she laid the test flat and set the timer on her phone.

A knock sounded at the door. She grimaced.

"Just a minute," she called quietly. Another knock.

"Alira, you're not doing this alone," Marcus's strong but firm voice said through the door. He waited for her to answer him. Alira stood up and moved to open the door. She swung the door open to find Marcus there in front of her, filling the space of the doorway, gazing at her with a look she could only describe as reserved for her. She stepped forward and wrapped her arms around his waist.

"Thank God," he whispered before kissing the top of her head as he wrapped his arms around her. Marcus had almost been sure that she would try to turn him away, but she hadn't. His heart flip-flopped in his chest. He had an argument ready to go if she tried to send him away.

His heartbeat was solid, steady in his chest. Alira closed her eyes and allowed it to fill her up, calming the storm that raged inside her. The last few weeks had been harder than anything she had ever known so far but Marcus was there. Her knight in chipped armor. They both had scars, but they also had been slowly healing one another and this was no different. This was powerful. *They* were powerful.

The timer went off on her phone. Her eyes snapped open as she stared at the flashing screen on the bathroom counter, suddenly terrified to see the result. She knew what it would say. The test was just a confirmation of what her dream had already told her. What she had already known a week ago but hadn't wanted to admit yet. Marcus looked at her, concern evident on his face.

"I already know what it says," she told him softly, eyes downcast. She was scared to look at him. Scared to see what he thought. Marcus walked over the counter and picked up the directions. He read them quickly and then looked at the plastic stick on the counter. Alira refused to meet his eyes. If she saw resentment there, as she suspected she would, she didn't know if she could handle it. She wrapped her arms around her stomach and slowly backed away from him. This was too much. It was too soon but felt too late all at the same time. Grayson was still out there, and they had no idea when he would reappear or what he would try next. She and Marcus hadn't had any time to be a normal couple let alone a normal married couple.

"How did you know?" he whispered coming up behind her and sliding his arms around her waist. Alira felt his hands move over hers, his thumb rubbing gentle circles, like always, as he held her. All the worry she had fell away as she leaned back against him. He wasn't mad. He almost sounded... hopeful.

"I suspected it the day we got married. My period was late and I'm never late," she replied turning in his arms to face him. His arms hung loosely around her waist as she gazed up at him. He had a look of wonder on his handsome face that took her breath away.

"I started feeling sick about a week after they... After I was taken. I thought it was a fluke the first time. Alex had brought a tray of food in for me and when he touched my cheek, I felt nauseated. It kept happening. It was worse whenever Alex came into the room, but he never did more than brush my cheek with his hand. Then that dream, I was panicking because in the dream I was drowning. All I could think about was how we never got to meet our baby and be a family. I was scared you might think it was Alex's and you wouldn't want me anymore," Alira explained quickly. Marcus rested his forehead against hers and smiled softly.

"I would never have thought that. I love you and I am going to love our baby. I do have one question though," he told her leaning back and staring at her with a quizzical brow. Her eyebrows knit together. She knew what he was about to ask her.

"Why didn't you tell me?"

Yep, there it was. She glanced at the door to make sure there wasn't anyone standing in the hallway that may overhear them. Alira took a deep breath before responding and meeting his eyes.

"Well, I was going to talk to you about it the night of our wedding but... and then everything happened," she replied quietly and tried to pull away from him. Instead of letting her go, Marcus pulled her back and kissed her deeply. It was all the reassurance she needed as she melted in his arms and moaned into his mouth. Marcus closed the door with his foot, never once breaking away from her as he moved.

Chapter 18

Marcus stretched and opened his eyes. He checked the time on his phone. It was after five and he had a text message from his brother, Kenny.

Heard you guys found Alira. Don't worry. I've got the office covered. Don't you dare try to come back in here until she's sick of seeing your ugly mug and kicks you out.

Shaking his head, Marcus set the phone back on the nightstand and rolled out of bed. The sound of laughter drew him to the living room where the delicious aroma of coffee and bacon washed over him, making his stomach growl. Rounding the corner, he spotted Austin and Alira sitting on the couch. Austin was doubled over laughing while Alira sat with her legs tucked under her, hands wrapped around a steaming mug of coffee, and an amused smile on her face. Her smile brightened further when she saw him. Marcus crossed the living room and leaned down to kiss her.

"Hey, remember that time you tried to ride that little Shetland pony mom had? What was his name? Firecracker?" Austin asked him and burst out laughing once more. Marcus glared at his brother. Alira tried to stifle her laugh but Marcus turned his glare on her. She pretended to innocently sip at her coffee though he could still see the amusement in her eyes. He kissed her again. He couldn't help it. Marcus would spend all day kissing her if he could. Those soft lips of hers begged for it.

"There's food in the kitchen. Karma cooked and ran," Alira explained as she set her coffee down on the table beside the couch. Marcus nodded and headed to the kitchen.

None of them had eaten a whole lot over the last two weeks while they searched under every rock and in every hole for her. His stomach growled again, demanding sustenance immediately, while he loaded a plate with bacon, scrambled eggs, sausage, and pancakes. He slathered syrup over the pancakes and sausage before he poured himself a cup of coffee.

Alira sat watching him move around the kitchen. Marcus had come down the hallway in nothing except his boxers and she had almost melted into a puddle right there on the couch. Vivid memories of their earlier activities sprang into her mind as she watched the muscles of his shoulders flex when he moved. She could still see the marks along his back from her nails. Her scalp tingled where he had run his fingers through her hair and tugged her head back before nibbling along her neck. The way he moved...

"Alira, your lip," Marcus said, his voice low and husky, as he entered the living room with his plate. He had stopped mid-step and was staring at her mouth with an intensity that made her gasp as white-hot heat pooled low in her belly. Austin stared wide-eyed between them, holding his fork halfway between his mouth and his plate.

"It's okay! I was done eating! I'm just going to go, uh, shower. Yup. Going to go take a really long shower and leave you two alone," Austin said as he dropped the fork onto the plate and leaped to his feet. Alira barely noticed as he set his plate on the side table before he bolted down the hallway, slamming the bathroom door behind him. Marcus set his plate down on the dining table, never once taking his eyes away from her. In a flash, he crossed the living room and pulled her off the couch into his arms. When his mouth crushed down on hers in a passionately demanding kiss, she moaned. Marcus slid his hands down along her sides, over her perfectly round ass, and pulled her roughly against him. His erection, heavy and throbbing, pressed against her stomach as her arms wrapped around his neck demanding more. She wiggled her hips making him groan. He gave her ass a squeeze before lifting her up. Alira wrapped her legs around Marcus's waist as he walked over to the couch. He sat with her straddling him. Pressing featherlight kisses along her collarbone to her shoulder and back again, Marcus moved his hand between her legs, feeling the wetness there. She was practically dripping for him. With a quickness he hadn't expected, Alira jumped away from him to shimmy out of her pajama bottoms. Marcus quickly freed his erection from the confines of his boxers before hauling her back onto his lap.

Alira straddled him once more. The mushroom tip of his cock pressed insistently at her, begging for entrance. When she eased down onto his thick member, inch by slow inch, allowing him to fill her up, her fingers curled into his hair holding him in place as she kissed him. Marcus groaned as her tight pussy gripped him, taking him all the way inside until he was firmly seated within her warmth. She rotated her hips, teasing him as she nibbled along his stubbled jaw.

When Alira began to move, it took all of Marcus's control not to take over and drive his cock into her hard and fast. She was making him crazy with the way she was moving, rotating her hips, gliding up and down, and changing the pace, all to tease him until he couldn't stand anymore. The woman knew exactly what she was doing to him and relishing in the power she held over him. Marcus pulled a budded nipple into his mouth, sucking through her t-shirt. She gasped at the sensation of it. Sparks shot out, moving swiftly through her body straight to her core where they fed the heat growing inside. Alira was chasing it now, needed it, demanded it.

Marcus held her hips firmly, fingers digging into the tender flesh, as she rode him. He knew she was close. So was he. Her little moans in his ear as she climbed higher and higher, closer to that peak, were making it difficult for him to focus on making sure she found her pleasure before he got his. She rode him hard, grinding down on him with nails digging into his shoulders painfully as she reached the peak. When she threw her head back moaning his name as she rode the waves of her orgasm, Marcus found his release with a shout of her name. She squeezed tightly around him, milking his cock for every last drop, as her entire body quaked. Alira collapsed against him, breathing hard, as he felt himself begin to soften inside her. She started laughing. It sent a jolt through him as blood started to rush back to his cock with each squeeze of the muscles.

"Alira, sweetheart, I need you to stop laughing or you're going to kill us both," Marcus groaned when she laughed again. His fingers curled into her thighs when she leaned forward and pressed a teasing kiss to his throat before lifting herself off of him. When she leaned over to pick up her pajama bottoms from the floor, she made sure he got a full view of her ass. Marcus growled and reached for her. She squealed as she hopped out of his reach.

"Tease," Marcus joked with a lopsided grin. She threw his boxers at him, hitting him in the face.

"Only because you make it so easy," she replied with a saucy smile. Marcus pulled his boxers on and stood. Alira watched him carefully, a grin on her face. He lunged for her. Alira laughed and danced away from him, but he wasn't letting her go so easily. Marcus chased Alira down the hall, scooping her up just before she reached the bed. Her laugh was musical and carefree as she wrapped her arms around his neck, holding him tightly while she pressed a soft kiss to his lips. Alira's fingers teased through the hair at the back of his head and down to the nape of his neck sending tiny shivers down his spine. Her touch made him feel alive, unlike anything he had ever known. He couldn't get enough of it.

"Hey guys, can I come out now? Is it safe?" Austin called out as he opened the bathroom door a crack. Alira giggled. Marcus kissed her again before setting her back on her feet though he kept his arm around her waist.

"Yeah, it's safe. You can come out. We promise to behave," Marcus called back. They heard the bathroom door creak open before Austin poked his head out and peered around the corner. He spotted them standing in her bedroom. A dopey grin broke out across his face as he wiggled his eyebrows at them.

"Did you guys have fun? Because it sounded like you had fun. I'm pretty sure after that, the entire building needs a cigarette now because damn. I mean who would have guessed under that shy sweet exterior there would be... Shit!" Austin didn't get the chance to finish what he was saying as Marcus dove for him. Austin turned and ran down the hall with Marcus hot on his heels. Alira ran after them laughing. She reached the living room just in time to see Marcus tackle his brother. As they wrestled around on the floor as brothers do, Alira couldn't help but laugh at the scene before her. The whole thing was light and carefree. It was nice. It felt so good to laugh despite the weight that was on her shoulders knowing that her brother was still out there.

Marcus managed to get Austin in a headlock. He rubbed his fist over Austin's hair as Austin struggled to get out of his grip, trying to escape the noogies. Austin jokingly claimed that Marcus was messing up his perfect sleek look and now there were no ladies that would want him. The wrestling match ended when there was a knock at the door. Marcus and Austin exchanged a look before Austin stood and helped Marcus to his feet. Marcus moved to stand in front of Alira, shielding her, while Austin went to answer the door. Alira watched as Austin peered through the peephole and then turned back to them with a grin.

"It's mom."

Alira let out the breath she didn't realize she had been holding. That knock at her door, the way Marcus and Austin had moved from silly and playful to ready for the worst-case scenario – it had been a harsh reminder that there was still trouble out there coming for her. She had temporarily forgotten that. Stupid. Incredibly stupid. Until her brother was dealt with, she needed to remember that allowing herself to relax was simply not an option. Grayson's plans had been foiled and he would, without a doubt, be coming for her. Alira just wished she knew when that would be.

Austin opened the door and Charlotte breezed through with a confidence Alira only dreamed of. Marcus wrapped his arm around Alira's waist protectively and glared at his mother.

"Mom, slow down. Alira doesn't need you rushing her like some crazy person!" Marcus snapped at her. Charlotte stopped short and puffed up like an angry mother hen. Marcus held his ground though Alira could feel his fingers twitch against her hip.

"Marcus Duvall, you will mind your manners! You are my child and I love you but Alira is my daughter-in-law, and I love her like my own. Your overprotective behavior is completely unnecessary right now and if you don't back up two steps so that I may hug this gorgeous young woman, I will hurt you," Charlotte told him threateningly.

Charlotte glared up at her eldest as he towered over her, waiting for him to make his decision. Alira and Austin stood silently watching the standoff between mother and son. It made Alira uncomfortable. She almost felt like a toy they were fighting over and damnit, she really needed a hug from Charlotte. She needed that motherly affection and reassurance that Charlotte gave so freely without strings. After spending her whole life craving something she had never been given and unexpectedly finding it with the Duvall's, it wasn't something she was willing to give up easily.

Marcus looked down at Alira to see what she wanted him to do. Charlotte softened as she watched her son allow Alira to decide what she wanted. He was leaving it in her hands. He must have seen it in her eyes, the silent acceptance because he dropped his arm from her waist and took a step back. Almost immediately Charlotte stepped forward and wrapped her arms around Alira. Alira happily accepted the hug she so desperately needed. It felt like Charlotte was taking some of the weight off Alira's shoulders and holding it herself. Alira suspected it was some sort of Mom Magic.

"I am so sorry, sweet girl," Charlotte told her softly as she hugged her tightly. Alira felt the tears forming, threatening to fall. She also felt a strong urge to get away as quickly as she could. It was all suddenly too much, and it was absolutely terrifying. A year ago, Alira was alone. A year ago, she didn't have many friends. At least none she could spend time with regularly. A year ago, she had settled into the rules that life had given her and she was content to follow them, mostly. Now, she had friends, an amazing husband and with all of that, she had a family. A wonderful, fantastic, loving family and it overwhelmed her. They were in danger as long as she was in their lives, but they weren't going to leave her to fend for herself. She was a walking curse for them, and they were such an incredible blessing for her. She felt terrible for what she was putting them through just by existing in their world.

"I'm sorry," Alira said quickly and pulled away from her mother-in-law. They watched as she turned to run down the hall to the bedroom. The door slammed behind her. Charlotte watched her go with a sad look on her face.

"Go on. She needs you. She's overwhelmed and struggling," Charlotte explained knowingly. Marcus thanked her for coming and jogged down the hall after his wife. Marcus knocked softly before opening the door. Alira was laying on the bed with the light off, curled up in the fetal position, clinging to her pillow. He closed the door behind him, plunging the room into darkness. Marcus moved slowly to the edge of the bed and eased himself down beside her.

"What do you need from me?" he asked her quietly as he reached out to touch her. Marcus didn't know if his touch would help or if she would even care. Even if she didn't want his touch, he needed to touch her. He needed some way to reassure her that he was always going to be there, that he would never leave her. Alira stayed silent. The only acknowledgment of his presence was the hitch in her breath when he reached out to her. They stayed that way for who knew how long. All he knew was that she would come to him when she was ready. He didn't want to push her.

Alira stared at the house from the passenger seat of Marcus's truck. He sat waiting patiently for her to gather her courage. They were due for dinner but Alira was embarrassed over her behavior the night Charlotte had come to check on her. Deep down, she knew it was alright and not a single person in that house would fault her for anything, but it was still hard. She had spent an hour worrying about what to wear despite Marcus reminding her repeatedly that they were just going to his parent's house and not a steakhouse where there would be other people. In the end, she had settled on what she had started with – black leggings, an oversized t-shirt, and an even bigger hoodie. Over that, Marcus had insisted she wear her coat too. It was below freezing outside, and he refused to allow her to leave the apartment without it. In the end, Alira was extremely grateful for it when the icy breeze blowing through the parking garage hit her.

"We can turn around and go home. We don't have to do this tonight," Marcus said quietly as he squeezed her hand. Alira turned to face him, offering a weak smile. He touched his palm to her cheek.

"We still agree?"

Marcus smiled and nodded. They had agreed that morning that they weren't going to tell the family that Alira was pregnant until after the first sonogram. Alira had wanted to have more time to adjust to the knowledge they were going to be parents but the real truth of it? She wanted to be able to make it a big surprise for the Duvall's. Marcus had readily agreed. She and Marcus had spent the morning thinking up reveal ideas too. He liked to think they had come up with some great ones, but time would tell.

They had an appointment in the morning to confirm the pregnancy. From there, they would schedule further appointments while keeping things hush hush. Karma had been sworn to secrecy though it was obvious it would drive her crazy knowing and not being able to talk about it. Austin knew out of necessity because he would be the one accompanying them to the appointment in the morning and it would be obvious why they were there in the first place. Nobody else knew. Not even Camden and Duke despite still being assigned to Alira's detail.

Karma appeared on the porch tapping her foot impatiently. She waved at them to hurry up as she wrapped her coat tightly around herself. Alira grimaced. A wave of nausea washed over her, forcing Alira out of the truck with just seconds to spare. Marcus rounded the truck hastily. He gathered her hair, holding it back for her as she emptied the meager contents of her stomach. Austin appeared with a bottle of water. Alira offered a weak smile as she took it from him before her stomach rebelled again.

"I think I'm okay now," she said as she straightened and twisted the cap off the water bottle. She got a good mouthful of the liquid and swished it before spitting it out. Alira rinsed her mouth out several more times before she was ready to go inside. With a deep breath and a tight grip on the plastic bottle, Alira and Marcus started toward the steps with Austin jogging ahead to open the door. Alira almost regretted telling Austin anything because now it seemed as though he was acting like she was going to break. It was increasingly frustrating because Marcus was acting the same way.

Marcus squeezed her hand before letting her go. He knew exactly where she was going. As Alira grabbed some apples out of the basket on the kitchen counter, Marcus considered giving her his leather coat to wear over her own coat while she went out to see her horse. She had been shivering and he knew she would be out there in the cold with Zoe for as long as she could stand it. She shouldn't, but she absolutely would. Instead, he followed her through the house to the back porch. Marcus stopped at the railing, as had become his habit over the last several months, to watch her. Alira trudged across the yard to the fence line, calling out to Zoe as she moved. Zoe nickered her usual greeting and trotted over, tossing her head happily.

"Just think, if you had admitted your feelings sooner, I wouldn't have given you so much shit about watching over her," William spoke behind him. Marcus spun around to see his father sitting quietly in one of the rocking chairs.

"Damnit, Dad! Warn a guy, will ya?" Marcus grumbled. It wasn't often someone could get a jump on him, but his father was a pro. It always amazed Marcus and his brothers how their father was able to go unnoticed until he wasn't. The man would always be bigger than life in Marcus's eyes, so it was a tad unnerving that William seemed to blend into his surroundings like he was a part of them from the beginning.

"That wouldn't be any fun," William chuckled and rose from his chair to join Marcus at the railing. They stood next to one another, leaning against it, watching Alira across the yard. She leaned over the fence with her arms wrapped around Zoe's neck. Zoe appeared to be hugging Alira more than usual. When Alira leaned away from the horse, Zoe lowered her head. Marcus watched as Zoe inspected Alira's stomach intently before gently nudging her. Alira scratched the horse's neck and smiled. They couldn't make out what she said to the horse, but it was safe to assume she told Zoe that she was right.

"Well, I'll be. How long?" William asked watching the exchange between his daughter-in-law and the horse.

"How long what?" Marcus asked him, trying to keep his tone calm and light but inside he was freaking out. His dad was using those superpowers he seemed to have. He knew! Marcus suddenly felt like he was a teenager again and about to get in some very real trouble for not fessing up immediately. He tried to shake off the nerves. He was a grown married man and they had simply done what married couples do!

"Son, I have been around horses my whole life. You really think, with the bond those two shares, that horse wouldn't have known right away?" William said and turned to face him. Marcus coughed in an attempt to hide his surprise. Of course, his father saw right through him. That damn horse had given away the secret and Marcus felt his shoulders slump in defeat.

"We see the doctor tomorrow to confirm and get a better idea how far along she is. Don't say anything to anyone. Alira and I wanted to do something special to announce it," Marcus explained. William patted Marcus on the shoulder soundly and smiled warmly. Their secret was safe with him. Marcus breathed a sigh of relief.

"Marcus, I'm happy for you. Not shooting blanks!" William said with a hearty laugh. Marcus burst out laughing at that. Leave it to his father to crack that joke proudly. William patted him on the shoulder once more before heading into the house.

The screen door slammed shut behind him. Marcus shook his head when he heard his mother yelling at his father for allowing the door to slam instead of closing it properly as he entered. William yelled back something about it being his house and he would slam the door if he wanted to. Marcus pushed away from the rail with a grin and started down the stairs toward his wife.

Alira gave Zoe a kiss on the nose and offered her one of the apples. Zoe took the fruit gently. She chewed the crisp fruit, sending spit and apple bits every which way. Another wave of nausea washed over Alira and she had to turn away as Zoe enjoyed her apple. She took several deep breaths and waited for it to pass. There was nothing left in her stomach to come up. When she felt better, Alira turned and tossed the remaining apples over the fence for the other horses.

"Hey, you," Marcus whispered gruffly as he slid his arms around her waist and nuzzled her neck. Alira leaned back against him, covering his arms with her own, as she watched the horses. He was warm. Alira turned to face him. She slipped her arms into his thick leather jacket and around his waist. Marcus kissed the top of her head as she rested her cheek against the solid wall of his chest.

"Dad knows."

Alira's head snapped up and she glared fiercely at him.

"Your horse gave it away," he explained laughing. She relaxed again, leaning her head against his chest once more as he tightened his arms around her.

"Naturally. Leave it to the horse to spill the beans," she grumbled. Her voice was muffled by his coat when she spoke. Marcus couldn't help but chuckle.

When he looked up, the sky was colored brightly with orange and pink as the setting sun splashed its colors across the sky. The air was quiet save for the subtle breeze rustling through the leaves on the trees. It was peaceful. Despite the cold that could make your bones ache and the uncertainties of the future, there was nowhere he would rather be. With

Alira in his arms, anything and everything was possible. Everything would be alright. They were going to get past this hurdle with her brother and get to really enjoy being a family.

Alira had no idea how long they were standing outside in the cold. All she knew was she could breathe. It was the first time since the gala that she truly felt capable of taking a deep breath and feeling it course through her, relaxing her. Marcus helped a great deal too. His steady presence had a grounding effect as she felt herself start to spiral out of control when worry over the future weighed heavily on her shoulders. Despite every attempt to push him away for his own good, he had continually refused to listen to her. He was her rock. The lightning in her storm ready to strike anything if she so willed it. Marcus was amazing and she absolutely loved him with every fiber of her being.

"We should get inside," Marcus whispered against her hair. Alira nodded as a shiver ran through her despite the heat radiating off of Marcus.

Marcus and Alira entered the house to a wave of tantalizing scents drifting through the air signaling that dinner was almost ready. Alira kicked off her shoes by the door so as not to track in any snow and slipped out of her coat. Marcus hung it up on the hook for her, followed by his own, before he draped his arm around her shoulders and guided her to the living room. Kenny, Adam, and Aiden sat around the coffee table playing a game of Spoons. Karma sat in the recliner pouting. It was clear she hadn't lasted long in the game. Alira made a silly face at her to make her smile before settling down on the couch beside Aiden to watch the game. It wasn't long before Alira's eyes started to close, and she dozed off while a new round started.

Chapter 19

Alira found Marcus making breakfast in the kitchen. She remembered dozing off on the couch at the Duvall's shortly before dinner. Marcus had tried to wake her to eat, but she had shooed him away claiming she wasn't hungry. The truth was, she had been starving. She'd also been exhausted, and sleep had won out. After her rebellious stomach had expelled everything, she hadn't been too inclined to eat anyway. Not when the nausea was waiting there in the wings to rear its ugly head. Besides, Alira felt very well rested as she wove her arms around his waist, resting her cheek against his bare back.

"Morning, sleepyhead," Marcus said in a husky tone. Her breasts pressing against his back was just enough of a distraction that he almost burned the pancake he had in the pan. Alira pressed a kiss to his shoulder.

"Morning," she spoke softly.

Alira inhaled deeply. He smelled good. Really good. Marcus said something else but Alira hadn't heard him. She had been too distracted by the feel of the muscles moving smoothly under his skin as he flipped the pancake he had been cooking. The feel of his abs under her palms, twitching as her fingers traced light circles above the waistband of his jeans.

"If you don't stop that, I will have to drag you back upstairs to the guest room," Marcus rumbled as he placed the pancake on the growing stack next to the stove. Alira was tempted to keep teasing him but realized that everyone would be waking up soon. She wasn't anxious to be caught with her hand in the cookie jar, so to speak.

With a huff, Alira dropped her arms and turned to walk away but not before Marcus was pulling her back. With one arm around her waist holding her snugly against him, his free hand moved to cup the back of her head, fingers tangling in her hair and tugging gently. He captured her gasp with his kiss. Alira melted against him as his tongue slipped into her mouth to dance with her own. Her arms slid up his chest and over his shoulders to wind around his neck. She wanted him closer, needed it.

"Whoa! Get a room!" Aiden said from the doorway. Alira jumped in surprise at the sudden intrusion. Marcus growled. It sent shivers up her spine in a delicious way. This pregnancy, even this early, was definitely messing with her. Despite her embarrassment at having been caught practically climbing all over him in his parent's kitchen, she had an almost desperate desire to jump his bones and she didn't care who knew it. Her husband was a marvelous specimen of human perfection. She slid her arm around his waist when it was clear he wasn't going to let her go anywhere. Not that Alira minded.

"We have an appointment to get to," Marcus whispered in her ear before pressing a kiss to her temple. Alira's eyes widened. She had almost forgotten about it. With a grin, Alira slipped her hand down and pinched his butt before she all but skipped out of the kitchen.

Marcus and Aiden watched her go. Aiden didn't try to hide his surprise. Who the hell was that person wrapped in the Alira packaging that just skipped past him?

"Did she just...?"

"Yup," Marcus replied with an amused grin.

"Is she always this saucy in the morning?" Aiden asked him still staring after her.

Marcus shook his head. He strode past his brother to follow his wife back up to the guest room. It was clear she was in a mood and he wanted to be a part of it. He wanted to be a part of it in a big way. Marcus could hear Aiden laughing as he raced up the stairs after Alira.

Marcus burst into the room to find Alira waiting for him. The second he closed the door behind him, making sure to lock it in case someone decided to come in, Alira was on him. She threw herself at him, wrapping her arms around his neck while her legs wrapped around his waist. His response to her was instant as he claimed her mouth in a demanding kiss. Still kissing her, refusing to break their contact, Marcus moved to the bed.

Marcus and Alira stared at the screen. The doctor checked some measurements and had shown them where the baby was. Alira was about five to six weeks along by the doctor's estimates based on the information Alira had given him regarding her last period and what he was seeing on the sonogram.

"Everything looks good so far. Do you have any questions?" the doctor asked them. They both shook their heads. He'd already done the job of answering any questions they had so far during the appointment as he checked, measured, and made his notes in her file. He handed them printouts of the sonogram with a smile and told them the tech would be in to schedule them for the next appointment. Marcus didn't appear to have heard him. Alira saw him staring down at the pictures with a look of what she could only describe as wonder on his handsome chiseled features.

They were having a baby.

Marcus was silent for the rest of the appointment and the drive home. Alira sat watching out the window as he drove. Trees, houses, and office buildings speeding by as he maneuvered the truck through town toward her apartment building.

"Will you be okay? I have to get to the office and get some work done. Aiden is already upstairs until Duke can get here. The schedule is a little weird right now," Marcus explained, worried she would be uncomfortable. He didn't want to leave her, but he had been absent from the office for a while and needed to make an appearance at the very least. He knew Kenny had everything covered but he felt bad for putting it all on him. Marcus knew from experience that it was a lot to handle. Until recently, he had spent more time at the office than he had at home. Home? Alira was his home. Admittedly, she had been his home since that first night at the bar. Lord, he had gotten sappy.

"Do you still work here?" Kenny asked when Marcus walked into the office. Marcus laughed. He should have known Kenny would crack that joke as soon as he entered. The only reason he was there now was that Kenny had told him there was paperwork he needed to handle. Otherwise, he wouldn't have left Alira's side. Being the man who signed the paychecks meant he was also the only one to sign off on major projects and orders. Marcus hated the paperwork side of the job. Maybe it was time to officially set things up so Kenny could handle it too. Kenny was the paperwork nerd. He practically lived for it, got this weird glint in his eye over it and everything. Marcus had always been more hands-on in the field. Offices were stifling. Marcus hated how it felt like the walls

⁇

were closing in on him the longer he sat at the desk going over orders and records before signing off on them.

Kenny stood up from the desk with a grand flourish for Marcus to take his seat. Marcus rolled his eyes and gave him a brotherly shove as he moved around the desk to the chair.

"It's good to see you back in here," Kenny told him as he turned to leave. Marcus didn't respond. Instead, he grabbed the nearest file and began going over its contents.

"Hey, Harold. What's up? Aren't you off today?" Alira asked when Duke opened the door revealing her friend standing on the other side. Harold smiled warmly as he stepped past the threshold. Duke closed the door quietly behind him and went back into the kitchen where he had been boiling water for tea.

"I'm covering for Alex. His girlfriend went into labor this morning," Harold explained. Alira grinned. She adored Alex and his girlfriend Sophie but since they no longer lived in the building after having purchased a house out in town, she didn't see them nearly as often as she would have liked. Alex worked two jobs despite the raise Alira had given him once she found out they were expecting. After learning Sophie was considered high risk, Alira understood why he was working as much as he was. Sophie couldn't do the tasks necessary to perform her job and maintain a pregnancy to term so Alex was picking up extra work where and when he could.

"Well, I'll have to send them a gift or something!"

What she was going to send, she had no idea. Flowers were pretty but not practical. Perhaps something for the nursery? Maybe a meal delivery for a couple of weeks? Nobody wanted to worry about dinner when they were exhausted and had a new baby. They should focus on bonding with their new little bundle! It was perfect. Alira made a mental note to set that up for them.

"I just wanted to bring this up," Harold explained and produced an envelope. Alira took the envelope tentatively from him. Duke appeared around the corner with two mugs of steaming hot tea as Alira opened the envelope. Her eyes widened.

"She did it?!"

Harold's face broke out into the biggest smile. He was one proud papa! All the hard work that Cammie had put in and the proof of her

KRYSTAL ZOPPA

success was there in Alira's hands. Cammie had been approved for early graduation. She was graduating high school two years early! She had worked so incredibly hard to pull it off with summer and night classes on top of her regular classes at school. It had been a process to get approval for her to do the extra classes, but it was paying off!

"I'll be there. With a big graduation present!" Alira spoke excitedly and hugged Harold. This was a big deal. Huge!

Harold left a few minutes later since he was technically on the clock. Alira practically bounced with glee as she waved the graduation invitation around excitedly. Cammie had been convinced she wouldn't get through those horrid math classes, but the proof was in the pudding, so to speak, and she had survived! Duke set Alira's mug down on the end table and made himself comfortable on the couch with his own while Alira put the graduation information into the calendar on her phone.

"Ready to continue our movie marathon?" Duke asked her as he handed over the remotes. Alira laughed.

"Do fish swim in the ocean?" Alira asked him as she grabbed the remote and hit play. Duke was a closet musical fan. They had started with watching Greece and were halfway through The Greatest Showman. Duke had tried to convince her to watch The Sound of Music but that was one movie Alira had adamantly rejected. Alira had burst out laughing when she realized Duke knew all of the songs to everything they watched too. He could belt it out!

The lights flickered and the TV shut off. Alira and Duke looked at one another, mildly concerned. Shaking it off, Alira pressed the power button on the remote to turn the television back on. Just as the TV powered back on, the lights flickered once again, and a loud crash sounded in the hallway outside of Alira's door. Duke carefully set his cup down on the end table, eyes on the door and motioned for Alira to move down the hallway out of sight. Alira scrambled off the couch and hurried down the hall. She took her cell phone with her, making sure it was on silent.

"Open the door little sister or your precious friend is going to get seriously injured!"

Alira peered around the corner as Duke moved toward the door. He angrily waved her back as he peered through the peephole. Alira crept closer despite her better judgment. She should listen to him. He was there to keep her safe after all but if it was true and Grayson really did have Karma, she had to know.

"Grayson?" Alira called out through the door. Duke glared at her and tried to wave her back again, but she ignored him.

189

"My sweet sister! You are there. I knew you would be," Grayson responded. He sounded off. Grayson didn't sound like his usual controlled self. A chill ran down Alira's spine.

"How do I know you have Karma?"

Duke peered through the peephole. He hung his head and motioned for her to look. With quiet steps, Alira moved closer and looked through the tiny glass piece. Grayson held up a cell phone with a picture of Karma. Alira gasped.

"Let her go, Grayson!" Alira yelled through the door at him. Grayson laughed.

"You have one hour to decide before I make the decision for you. I'll see you very soon," he spoke menacingly through the door. Alira reached for the doorknob. Duke gently but firmly pushed her away, effectively blocking her from opening the door.

"You can't play into his hands. You're staying right here, and we let the agency handle it. They'll get her!" Duke growled hoping to reason with her into compliance. Alira shook her head. Not this time!

"No, he'll kill her before they get anywhere close. We don't even know where she is!"

She could practically see the steam coming out of Duke's ears. He was furious. He knew she had a point. Grayson clearly wasn't bluffing. In the picture, Karma had been tied to a chair and gagged. It was clear she had been beaten. Alira looked at the clock. They had an hour to figure this out, but she could only see one way to get Karma away from Grayson and to safety. She didn't like it and she knew Duke wouldn't go for it but there wasn't any other course of action.

The power flickered again. It was quickly followed by the blaring of the fire alarm throughout the building. They could hear doors opening and closing as people emerged from their apartments in a hurry making their way to the nearest fire exit. Alira and Duke didn't have any other choice but to join them.

"He isn't going to follow through on the hour," Alira told Duke knowingly. Duke grimaced. It wasn't a surprise. Grayson had never kept his word so why start now? Whatever his game was today, Alira knew what she needed to do. This had to end. She couldn't continue living in fear of her brother and she sure as hell couldn't allow him to terrorize her family and friends.

Alira slipped her tennis shoes on quickly and tucked her cell phone into her bra in such a way that it wouldn't be obvious it was there at all. Duke held out his hand. Alira took it.

"Stay close to me," he ordered and withdrew the gun he kept in his shoulder holster. Alira took a deep breath and nodded. She had no intention of listening to him. He must have known because he held onto her hand tightly, almost painfully so. Alira winced at his grip.

Chapter 20

"Breaking news! Authorities are requesting the public stay away from Cedar Point Luxury Apartments and the surrounding area after receiving reports of a bomb threat in the building. We will have more information for you as we receive it."

Marcus's hand froze mid-signature as he lifted his gaze to the TV on the wall of the office. There was ariel footage from the Channel Six chopper circling Cedar Point Apartments. Alira's building.

Kenny slammed through the door of the office, a look of panic on his face. He followed Marcus's eyes to the TV and his jaw dropped as he read the scrolling message.

"Alira slipped her detail. Grayson has Karma," Kenny all but yelled at him.

"How do you know that?" Marcus asked, his voice a shaky whisper, unable to take his eyes off the television. Kenny showed him the forwarded text message he had from their brother Austin. From Duke. Austin had specifically sent it to Kenny and not him. Why? Marcus knew why the second he questioned it. He would do anything it took to protect those he loved, and his methods weren't usually subtle. Marcus had always had a raging bull mentality, charging in first without really thinking it through. He saw red.

Marcus leaped to his feet, his chair slamming back against the wall hard enough to leave a hole in the drywall. Marcus tossed the office keys to Nigel, one of the crew foreman's, on his way out with Kenny hot on his heels. Nigel stared after them wondering what the heck had just happened as his eyes landed on the television. Kenny and Marcus hopped into Marcus's truck and sped out of the lot. Marcus didn't even bother using the driveway. He went straight over the curb and onto the road.

"Grayson, where's Karma? I'll go with you, but you have to let her go first," Alira spoke calmly, trying desperately to keep her voice even so her brother couldn't hear the fear she was trying to conceal. He would feed on it like insects on a decaying corpse if he knew how truly scared she was. This had always been a fear. Getting close to someone, anyone, and Grayson using it against her.

Grayson stepped around the corner. Alira couldn't help but jump at his sudden appearance. He held something in his hand. It looked like some sort of remote. His hair was disheveled. He wasn't wearing his usual suit. Instead, he was wearing dark-washed jeans and a black button-up shirt. The top three buttons were undone. The shirt itself was wrinkled and untucked. Grayson had a wild look in his eyes that sent cold shivers through her. He had finally snapped. His head twitched every other minute or so as though he had developed a tic.

"Sweet, beautiful baby sister! It's so nice of you to join us!" Grayson spoke just as smoothly as he always did despite his unusual appearance and obvious twitching. Is this what crazy looked like when it finally won out?

"Grayson, where is Karma? You have to let her go. She has to be safe before I'll go anywhere with you or give you anything," Alira said in a firm voice.

Her cell phone was warm against her chest. She had called Austin on the way down the stairwell after ditching Duke in the crowd of people moving down the stairs to safety. Alira had quickly explained what she knew was happening and begged him to stay on the line with her. She had told him though he would be muted, he could hear every single word spoken between them. She knew Austin would be outside. Duke would have called him immediately when she slipped his grip and disappeared into the crowd. She hoped he wouldn't call Marcus. Marcus needed to stay safe. He didn't need to be there.

"Come. She's tucked away safely in the security office," Grayson told her with a grin that made her skin crawl. He quickly turned knowing Alira would follow him. He had her right where he wanted her to be, and he knew it. Alira suspected this had been his plan all along. Kidnapping her had just been a play in the book leading to the final round.

Grayson gestured for her to enter the office, standing just outside the door. Alira scooted past him, trying to keep as much distance as she could while still going into the office. Karma sat slumped over tied to one of the chairs. Alira rushed to her side.

"Karma?" Alira whispered. *Please open your eyes!* Karma opened her eyes as if she had heard Alira's silent plea and slowly lifted her head. Karma grinned upon seeing Alira. Her face was streaked with dried blood from the cuts Alira could clearly see were still weeping. A split in her lip was bleeding slightly. Her right cheek was heavily bruised with the eye almost swollen shut. Alira tried to cap her anger. The last thing she wanted Grayson to see was how much this affected her. Seeing her best friend in such a state tore at her heart. This was her fault. If she had just kept her distance, none of this would be happening. The Duvall's wouldn't be involved. *You're a Duvall now.*

"Grayson, let her go. She's done nothing to you."

"Very well. You may escort her to the door, but don't you dare set one toe outside or the whole block blows. Do you understand?" Grayson snarled. Alira nodded quickly and began working at the ropes binding Karma's wrists. As soon as Karma was free, Alira helped her stand. Karma's arm hung around Alira's shoulders heavily as Karma leaned against her trying to stay on her feet. Alira knew that Karma didn't want to lean too much on her for support. She didn't want to appear weak.

"Not one toe," Grayson warned as he stepped back into the shadows of the lobby to watch them.

Alira and Karma shuffled to the entrance at an agonizingly slow pace. Karma whimpered with each jarring step. Alira's heart squeezed in her chest at her friend's pain, wishing desperately that she could take that pain into herself. Karma whispered something but Alira shook her head. She had to play by Grayson's rules. It was the only way to make sure her friend got out safely. There was no alternative.

"Tell Marcus I'm sorry," Alira whispered in Karma's ear as the door opened and Austin appeared with a police officer to help Karma out. He reached for Alira, but she stepped back quickly out of his reach. She shook her head. Austin's eyes darkened. Alira was sure he would try to grab her and pull her through the door, but he must have seen something in her expression that changed his mind.

"Get Karma out of here. I have to stay so nobody else gets hurt," Alira explained quietly. She could feel Grayson's eyes burning a hole through her. He was expecting her to make a run for it. Alira wouldn't give him the satisfaction. She was tired of being afraid. She was so incredibly tired of living in fear of what he would do next. One way or another, this was ending today. No more terror. No more games.

Alira stood in the doorway long enough to see that Karma was safe. The building tenants were huddled across the street in the park. Alira spotted Harold and Cammie among them. She scanned the crowd, hoping that somehow Marcus would be there, but she knew that he wasn't. He didn't know what was happening. How could he? Had he known, Alira was sure he would come raging into the building... and Grayson would blow it to kingdom come.

This was it. Sucking in a lung full of air, Alira turned to face her brother. The lobby door closed softly behind her.

Grayson stood leaning against the wall just behind the pillar near the lobby desk. Alira assumed he was positioned to avoid being visible from outside.

"Your little friend is safe," he grumbled as he made air quotes at the word *safe*.

Grayson twitched. Something was very wrong with him. Alira had always known that to be true but now it was manifesting physically. She had no way of knowing how long she had before he lost it entirely. She just hoped it would be long enough for the bomb squad to find the bomb and disable it. Despite this stupid show of bravery, Alira was terrified beyond words. She wanted to live through this disaster. It took all she had not to move her hand protectively over her stomach. Grayson couldn't know. It would only make things worse. Alira stood with her hands fisted at her sides as she stared at her brother.

"Gray... I know we've never been close, but I can see that you're hurting. I want to help you," Alira said quietly as she snuck a glance toward the security office. She just needed to get inside and close the door. That's all she needed to do. Grayson barked out a laugh.

"Help me? Help. Me?" he growled. "You can help me by dying. Then everything that should have been mine will be and I'll get the sharks off my back!"

Alira felt herself start to shake. He still thought her inheritance would go to him if she died. What in the world ever made him think that?

Three more steps. Just three more and she would be at the doorway. Grayson wasn't even paying attention to her. He was pacing and muttering angrily to himself. His hand gripped what Alira assumed was the remote trigger for the bomb somewhere in the building.

"It doesn't work that way. Everything goes elsewhere upon my death. It's been set for years," Alira told him, her voice laced with the slightest amount of venom. Grayson's head jerked up when she spoke as if he had forgotten she was there for a moment.

"No. I'll just kill your savior husband too. He'll never get a dime!"

Alira laughed then. It was a startle response. Marcus wouldn't get anything. He had signed forms at his insistence on it. He had been adamant that everything continued the way Alira had it set out. It was the only way to keep everyone safe, protected. Every single asset Alira had would go to her chosen charities as long as Grayson was still alive. No exceptions. He would stop at nothing to get what he thought was his to claim and Alira couldn't allow him that kind of power. He was dangerous enough.

One more step.

Grayson noticed her slow steps closer and closer to the office. A dark grin spread across his face.

"Do you think you can lock yourself in there? Do you think you'll be *safe* in that office?" he hissed out with a menacing step closer to her. Alira took the chance. She leaped into the room, managing to slam the door behind him. She locked the bolt and pulled the barrier bar down, locking it into place. Grayson wasn't getting through that door any time soon. Sagging against the door, Alira pulled her cell phone out of her bra and unmuted it as she looked around the room for what she needed.

"Austin, are you still there?"

Silence.

"Yeah, sweetheart, I'm still here," Austin's quiet voice sounded through the speaker. Alira breathed a sigh of relief. She wasn't alone.

"Austin, I'm sorry. Tell Marcus that I'm sorry and that I love him. I wish I could talk to him," she said whispering the last part. Alira sighed and listened. She didn't know what she was listening for.

"We're going to get you out of there," Austin's voice sounded through the speaker once more. Alira didn't stop the tears that escaped her eyes to slide down her cheeks. She heard the determination in her brother-in-law's tone. Could practically feel it but inside, it was pointless. Nobody could help her now. She was effectively trapped in a box with a maniac outside who wanted her dead because he thought he was entitled to everything she had.

Marcus bounced the truck up over the curb and slammed it into park, leaving the keys in the ignition, not caring if anyone stole his truck. Nothing else mattered but getting to her, getting to Alira. He would rip her brother limb from limb with his bare hands. Marcus ran across the park as fast as his legs would carry him. Kenny was racing after him. The police had the roads blocked. Marcus hadn't had the choice but to run the distance across the park. It was the size of a football field. Finally reaching the other side, Marcus spotted the crowd. The police were trying to move them back further away but not having any luck.

"Sir, you need to get back!" an officer ordered as Marcus got closer. Marcus dropped his shoulder and barreled through him. He would deal with any consequences later. The officer dropped to the ground like a sack of potatoes.

"Where is she?" Marcus bellowed. Silence descended upon the crowd as everyone turned to face him. Harold hugged a young woman before releasing her and moving toward Marcus.

"Alira's still inside. We don't know anything else," Harold explained sadly. Marcus shoved him aside intending to run up to the building, but Kenny had finally caught up with him. Kenny grabbed his arm, trying to hold him back. Marcus turned and leveled his brother with a murderous stare. Kenny released his arm in surprise.

"Marcus!"

Marcus was already halfway across the street when Duke tackled him to the ground. Quickly Austin and Kenny were there helping hold him down.

"Let me go!" Marcus yelled enraged.

"No! You'll only get yourself killed if we do!" Austin growled at him as he put a knee to Marcus's chest. Marcus struggled against him but with Kenny and Duke also pinning him, he wasn't getting far. Harold appeared beside them with the young woman Marcus had seen him with seconds before.

"Marcus?"

Austin reached for his phone and tapped the speaker button.

"Go ahead Alira. He's here," Austin spoke calmly into the speaker before holding the phone in front of Marcus's face.

"You've had her on the phone this whole time?!" Marcus raged at him and struggled against his brothers and Duke once more.

"Marcus, I'm sorry. I love you! I wish we had more time!" Alira's words sounded through the phone. They could hear her sobbing, could hear Grayson's muffled yelling in the background. There was a loud banging sound. It sounded like metal on metal.

"Oh, little sister! Little sister! Open the door! I'll press this button if you don't!" Grayson could be heard yelling in the background.

Marcus fought harder against them. He had to get to Alira. She needed him. The fear in her voice, the sorrow in it heavy. Harold appeared at his head and pressed his hands down on Marcus's shoulders, helping hold him down. A weight suddenly covered his legs and Marcus could barely make out the figure of the young woman Harold had been standing with. She was holding down his legs.

"You're going to press that button anyway Grayson! We both know it so stop threatening and follow through for once in your pathetic life!" Alira yelled back angrily through her tears.

Everyone had heard it. She was still on speaker. Austin hadn't muted her. Austin turned and stared at the building, shifting his weight against Marcus's chest just enough. Marcus felt his muscles coil tightly throughout his body and with a sudden burst of strength, he managed to throw his brothers off. Adrenaline was a powerful thing. Harold and Duke made a good effort of maintaining their grip on him, but Marcus's burst of energy had managed to toss Austin off him as well as the young woman. Kenny quickly moved Harold out of the way and locked Marcus in a headlock while he was trying to free his arm from Duke's solid hold. It was enough to give Austin the chance to get a grip on him again.

"Let me go!" Marcus roared angrily at them.

"No can-do brother. Alira seems to know what she's doing," Austin yelled back at him forcing him to hear him.

How could she possibly know what she was doing? Grayson was insane. There was a fucking bomb in the building! She was going to get herself killed and Marcus was powerless to stop it. The fight left him. He was going to lose her. They were going to lose their future. The future he so desperately wanted more than anything he had ever known in his life. He wanted Alira. He wanted their baby. Marcus wanted to grow old with her. Her son-of-a-bitch brother was taking that away from them!

Austin must have felt the fight leave his brother because he motioned for those restraining him to let him up. Marcus stood carefully, glaring at each of them but didn't move. He stood still as stone staring helplessly at the apartment building. If he tried to get to her, they would stop him. He understood. As much as it killed him, he understood. It devastated him knowing that he had no choice but to stay out there with the crowd instead of going to Alira.

"Austin, take care of him!" Alira's calm voice sounded through the speaker on his phone. They could hear metal on metal again, only this time, Grayson's voice wasn't muffled in the background. Alira must have let him into whatever room she was hiding in.

Please, God, no...

Austin grabbed the young woman that had been sitting on Marcus's legs. He swung her around, tucking her between himself and Marcus in a flash just as the building exploded. The sound was deafening while the force of the explosion knocked them back. They landed hard on the ground several feet back from where they had been. Marcus groaned as the weight of two people landed on him roughly, forcing the breath out of his lungs.

Debris rained down as people began screaming and running. Austin grunted and Marcus saw a pained expression cross his features. The trembling woman sandwiched between them moved as Harold grabbed her arm and pulled her away to huddle behind a nearby police car leaving the brothers to help one another. Austin pushed slowly into a standing position, grimacing as he moved. He pulled Marcus to his feet. Marcus couldn't take his eyes off the burning building before him. Marcus hit his knees and stared, despair washing over him in waves. He gasped for breath. Nobody could survive that. Nobody.

Duke waved Austin over. Duke was standing with Harold and they were speaking quickly, glancing at Marcus. They ducked when a secondary explosion sent more debris flying through the air. What the hell? They looked around the ambulance to witness more of the building falling.

Marcus felt the heat from the fire. He couldn't bring himself to move away. He had barely flinched when the second explosion happened, leveling more of the building. The flames danced in his eyes as he watched it burn, knowing Alira was inside and powerless to reach her.

Pain seared through him as he fell back catching himself with his hand.

"Marcus!" Austin shouted and ran the short distance to his brother. Blood poured out around the metal pipe sticking out of his abdomen. Marcus looked down as his hand went to his stomach where the pipe protruded from. He grasped it, about to pull it out but Austin stopped him. The one-inch pipe protruded from his abdomen.

"That's just a bitch and a half," Marcus choked out as he released the pipe with a weak laugh. Paramedics surrounded them, moving quickly. Austin stepped back as they pushed past him to assess the injury. Kenny stood beside him, eyes wide, watching them work. He looked like he was going to be sick.

"The pipe went straight through," one paramedic said. Another nodded as they started an I.V. line. Austin watched as they packed around the pipe to secure it in place, maneuvering Marcus to lay on his left side. Someone had put duct tape over the ends of the pipe to cap it. Presumably to prevent any debris from getting into it and causing more problems at the hospital when they removed the pipe.

"Call mom. Ride with him to the hospital. Don't tell mom anything about Alira right now. Not until we know for sure," Austin spoke loudly over the roaring fire and sirens.

Mom would have enough to worry about with Marcus. She didn't need her heart broken any further. Chances were that she was already at the hospital with Karma, but he had no way of knowing. He prayed that they weren't watching any news channels while there either. Kenny nodded silently and gave Austin a weary look before he turned to follow Marcus into the ambulance just as the paramedics finished loading him in. Austin had work to do. He couldn't afford to be emotional. Pushing his brother and sister from his mind, he turned to Duke and Harold who stood waiting by a squad car.

"The fire chief isn't happy but he's going to let us in behind them on the condition we suit up as soon as they clear the building," Harold explained quickly as he waved at them to follow him. Austin and Duke walked silently after him over to one of the firetrucks.

A gruff-looking man stood there glaring, barking orders into the mic on his shoulder as they approached. He glanced at them before turning his attention back to the building and listening to what his crew was saying. Voices crackled over the mic. Austin only caught part of what came through, but it was enough for him to snatch the offered gear, pulling it on quickly. Duke and Harold followed his example. Unfortunately, it would still be several hours before they could get into what was left of the building. The fire chief was taking an enormous risk even agreeing to let them in after all was said and done.

Chapter 21

The siren blared loudly as the ambulance sped through the streets. Marcus was numb. He knew he should feel something, but he didn't, couldn't. If he closed his eyes, he saw the building exploding. He pictured Alira's face, her beautiful smile.

Austin, take care of him!

The words rang through his mind. The last thing she had said was for his brother to take care of him. Her last words had been for him. Not for herself. For him. His sweet, selfless Alira.

Marcus closed his eyes, unable to keep them open any longer. He was tired. So incredibly tired. He couldn't hear the siren anymore, could no longer feel the motion of the vehicle as they rode to the hospital. They had to be close by now.

Kenny wheeled Karma into the family room of the hospital where the rest of the family waited impatiently for news on Marcus's condition. Upon arrival at the hospital, Marcus had been taken immediately into surgery. Two hours later, they still had no information. Aiden paced the waiting area restlessly. Every time a nurse or doctor walked past, everyone jumped to their feet anxious for news only to sit back down disappointed with their worry increasing. What would they be told when they finally received an update?

"Karma! Sweet girl! How do you feel? Do you need anything?" Charlotte fired off the questions as soon as she saw her daughter. Karma tried to wave her off, but Charlotte wouldn't have it. Two of her children had been seriously injured and nobody would tell her anything about her daughter-in-law. She looked as frazzled as they all felt. While Charlotte examined Karma's face as only a mother could do, a doctor appeared with a nurse beside him.

"Duvall?"

William stood. He had been sitting calmly, quietly in the corner until that point.

"I'm William Duvall," he stated flatly though there was a wobble to his voice as he spoke. The doctor raised an eyebrow when the Duvall family flanked William.

"Marcus is stable. He's in recovery right now but we'll be moving him to a private room in about twenty minutes. You'll be able to see him after that," the surgeon informed them.

William thanked him and his shoulders sagged in obvious relief. Karma watched her father as he slid back into his chair and rested his head in his hands. She couldn't remember a time she ever saw her daddy look defeated. The man was a pillar of positivity and strength. She motioned for Kenny to wheel her over to him. Karma needed to hug her father.

Austin stood huffing and puffing as he and Duke helped the firemen move beams and crumbled brick to reach their destination. Smoke filled the air but thankfully it was thinning out, making it easier to breathe. The air wasn't quite as heavy now and Austin could finally take a decent breath to fill his aching lungs. A commotion ahead caught his attention. Austin scrambled over the remaining rubble in his path toward the other group.

Thank God.

Austin heard Harold before he spotted him. He stood with four other guys, each of them smiling. Austin watched as Harold tapped some code into a keypad and gears could be heard shifting loudly behind the panel that was miraculously still standing. They held their collective breath as the door creaked and groaned from what was probably years of non-use. Grinding gears clinked loudly with every notch as they ground together, pulling unseen levers meant to coax the door open. The wait was torturous. Austin wanted to hold onto hope but as the seconds ticked painfully by, he felt a sense of dread filling him. He had already watched his big brother lose hope as the flames overtook the building and now, with each slow inch of the door, it bothered him that he didn't know how Marcus was after the ambulance had gone blaring away from him. Austin prayed he would have good news the next time he saw his brother.

"Hey, big brother," Karma spoke softly from the doorway. Marcus opened his eyes and turned his head in her direction slowly. That basic movement was all he could muster the energy for. He felt sick as his stomach threatened rebellion. Apparently, it was a potential side effect of the anesthesia. As long as he stayed mostly still, it wasn't so bad, but the second he tried to move to get more comfortable, his stomach would churn. He was waiting for the nurse to come back with the promise of anti-nausea meds. Marcus hadn't been expecting to see his baby sister rolling around in a wheelchair.

"How are you?"

"Ever felt like you were the meat on a skewer?" he responded hoarsely with a weak smile.

Marcus didn't recognize his own voice when he spoke. His throat felt sore, raw. Maybe water would help. Karma must have read his mind because she rolled the wheelchair into the room and reached for the pitcher of water on the tray table. Marcus watched as she poured the cool liquid into a cup and popped the straw in to make it easier for him to drink. Karma held the straw up to his mouth, holding it until he'd had enough. His stomach rolled as the water hit its mark. Perhaps the water hadn't been such a good idea after all. Marcus quickly reached for the tub the nurse had left for him. Karma rubbed his back awkwardly as he threw up the little amount of water and some bile. He groaned despite the morphine coursing through him to mask the pain from his injury and surgery.

"You look like shit," Kenny chimed from the doorway. Charlotte smacked him on the back of the head at his comment as she bustled into the room. Marcus watched in silence as his mom, dad and brothers filed into the room. Everyone except for Austin… and Alira.

Without a word, Charlotte crossed the room and sat gently on the edge of the bed. She was careful not to jar him at all as she softly took his hand in hers, worrying as mothers do over their children.

"Have you heard anything?"

It was Adam who asked the question. It was strange. Adam was more outgoing than his twin, Aiden, but he was also quieter in stressful situations. It was as if he didn't know what to say or how to respond so he withdrew into himself. He was more similar to Marcus in that respect. They shut out the world so it couldn't hurt them as badly. Heads shook in response to his question and a painful silence claimed the room, weighing heavily. The only sound was the beeping from the machines.

"It'll be okay. You'll get through this. We all will," Charlotte said encouragingly. Murmurs of half-hearted agreement chimed in. It did nothing to make Marcus feel any better. His future with Alira and their unborn baby had disappeared in the blink of an eye. His stomach rolled and he reached for the tub again. Thank God the nurse had left it within reach for him. He hadn't expected to need it once, let alone twice, so soon.

Just then, the nurse reappeared with the anti-nausea meds. Marcus groaned as his stomach clenched painfully trying to bring up something, anything. He had nothing left. The nurse quickly added the meds to his I.V. for quick administration and shuffled everyone out of the room stating visiting hours were over. Charlotte protested loudly until William wrapped his arm around her waist and gently pried her away. Marcus gave a silent nod of thanks. He needed to be alone. As much as he loved his family, they were too much to take right now. Not to mention he was having trouble keeping his eyes open. Another side effect he guessed. His body had been through trauma as well as his mind. He was exhausted. Was there another word for what he felt that would fit better? Drained. Bone tired. Dead tired. Whatever way one put it, it fit.

Marcus took a deep breath. Well, as deep of a breath as his body would allow. He felt like he was floating. The aches over his body were mild thanks to the morphine coursing through him from his I.V. Marcus closed his eyes and drifted off to sleep unable to fight it any longer.

Alira stood next to Zoe with a smile on her face as she scratched the horse's neck. When she turned and spotted Marcus watching her from the porch, a brilliant smile, reserved only for him, broke out across her face as she waved. Her rounded belly showed her advanced pregnancy. Marcus swore there was nothing more beautiful in the world. She was stunning. His wonderful, amazing, spectacular wife never ceased to steal his breath. Alira glowed. All it took to make him lose his train of thought was to have her walk into the room and he was a goner. Conversations disappeared around him as he gazed upon her. She was magnificent and he was hopelessly in love.

Marcus watched her give one more kiss to Zoe's soft nose before she turned to make her way back across the yard to him. Feeling like he hadn't seen her in ages, Marcus jumped down the steps and strode toward her. Alira squealed as he pulled her into his arms, peppering her with kisses before he nuzzled her neck. He inhaled deeply of her scent.

"I love you," he whispered as he nuzzled her. Alira pulled back, touching her hand to his cheek. He leaned into her hand, turning to press a kiss to her palm.

"I love you, Marcus. Forever," Alira told him lovingly as she gazed up into his eyes.

Marcus pulled her into his arms once more, closing his eyes tightly, never wanting the moment to end. His sister opened the backdoor and called out that dinner was ready. With a deep sigh, Marcus opened his eyes and turned to tell her they would be in momentarily. When he turned back around, Alira was gone. In her place was a fire. Hot burning flames and choking smoke filled the space where she had been.

"Alira!" Marcus yelled. He searched the yard frantically for her, but something told him she was in the fire. He reached into the flames, reached for her. If he could just grab her hand and pull her out, everything would be alright. She would be safe. She would be in his arms and he would never let her go.

"What are you yelling for?" Karma hollered at him from the door, clearly annoyed.

"Alira! She's in the fire! I can't reach her!"

Karma laughed and closed the door once more. Why weren't they running out to help him? Couldn't his family see that she was dying? Alira! Marcus reached into the flames once more, only they were no longer there. There was a pile of ash on the ground in its place. Marcus collapsed to his knees, reaching for it, reaching for Alira.

"Please come back to me," he begged.

Austin flopped down in the chair by the door, his body begging for sleep. Exhaustion didn't cover what he was feeling. This was deeper. Heavier. He just needed to shut his eyes for a little while and he would be right as rain. It didn't take long for him to begin snoring from his slumped position.

Marcus felt the warmth of a hand in his. Maybe his mother had snuck back into the hospital room. He almost chuckled at the thought. Marcus opened his eyes, blinking in the dim lighting. He shook his head trying to shake away the weights that seemed to have taken up residence in his eyelids. The warmth was still there so he hadn't imagined it. Someone was holding his hand. Ever so slowly, Marcus turned his head so the room wouldn't spin on him. A head of thick dark hair rested on the edge of the bed. Marcus lifted his hand and touched the soft locks. She lifted her head. Bright blue eyes met his dark ones.

"I hope I didn't wake you," she whispered. Marcus's heart raced. This was a dream. It had to be. He was still sleeping. That made sense. She felt so real though.

"You're not really here. I'm still dreaming. You died. Nobody could have survived that," Marcus stammered, emotion thickening his voice.

A soft smile graced her beautiful mouth. She gripped his hand and brought it to her lips, pressing an easy kiss to his palm.

This wasn't real! The mind could be cruel. This was his imagination playing with him. Morphine could make you hallucinate right? The pain relief was hitting extra hard and making him see things. If this was a hallucination, he never wanted it to end.

"It's real because there is no chance you would dream me up," Austin said sleepily from his chair by the door having been woken by Marcus's somewhat loud rambling about hallucinations. Marcus looked at his brother sitting in the dark across the room. Slowly he returned his gaze to meet hers. Tears slid silently down her cheeks as her eyes seemed to drink him in. Her hand gripped his tightly, almost painfully now.

"See me, Marcus. I'm here. I'm real," she told him firmly.

Alira could see the confusion clouding his eyes. She could only imagine how he felt at that moment. She had been in that confused state herself not all that long ago. It made sense that after what he had seen and thought that this would be throwing him through a loop. He was also incredibly high on morphine from his surgery. Austin had swiped his chart on the way into the room and read over it. As it was, Austin had sweet-talked the head nurse to even let them in past visiting hours. Alira had insisted on going straight to Marcus at the hospital. She had adamantly refused any treatment for herself beyond making sure her baby was alright. The bruising and scratches would heal. After all, Alira had certainly healed from worse! Quite recently in fact.

When Austin was the first face she saw once that door had opened as much as it could open, Alira knew in an instant that something had happened to Marcus. Her heart had stopped thinking that Greyson had somehow gotten to him. Maybe he had someone outside helping him. Austin had pulled her through the opening and over the rubble that was still smoking in spots. Her brother-in-law hadn't wasted any time in telling her that Marcus had been rushed to the hospital after being impaled during the secondary explosion. Alira's fear must have been more evident than she had originally thought because, in seconds, they were running through the rubble straight to Austin's car. The sun had already set by the time her rescuers had gotten that old and outdated door to open before pulling her to safety.

"Alira?"

Alira watched as Marcus struggled to process what he was seeing in front of him. He spoke her name slowly like he wasn't really sure it was what he wanted to say.

She knew his head had to be swimming. Alira remembered the feeling all too well. That pain-free floating feeling. It was like magic because you could sleep easily but the struggle to focus was almost impossible with the constant pull to close your eyes and rest. That part of it could be a tad maddening. The fog invading in your mind as your entire body relaxed forcing you to lose track no matter how badly you wanted to hold a conversation with someone or stay alert. Flashes of asking yourself if you dreamed it or if it was real once that high wears off. Alira shivered remembering Greyson showing up when she was in the hospital after her car accident.

No, Greyson is gone now. He doesn't deserve any more space in your head.

"Yes, baby, I'm here," Alira told him as a single tear slid down her cheek. Alira brushed it away quickly hoping Marcus was too out of it to notice. She couldn't have been more wrong.

"I'm sorry. I didn't mean to make you cry," Marcus whispered as he struggled to keep his eyes open. Alira sniffled, squeezing his hand tightly.

"Sleep, Marcus. I promise I'll be here when you wake up."

Marcus opened his eyes, blinking against the sunlight streaming through the window of the hospital room. It was a slow process adjusting to the bright light and chasing the haze from his mind. He shifted slightly in the bed and inhaled sharply as pain shot through him like lightning. Slow, deep breaths.

Austin watched quietly from his chair. His brother didn't seem to notice him. Hell, he probably didn't even remember he was there at all. Alira was still sitting in her chair next to his bed with her head resting on the edge. She had stayed awake for longer than necessary after Marcus had fallen back into a morphine-induced sleep. Despite his exhaustion, Austin watched over them until Alira had rested her head on the bed and drifted off herself.

When she had learned Marcus was injured and at the hospital, Austin had seen that there was nothing on earth that was going to keep her from going to him. Austin couldn't help but wonder if he would ever find someone to love him as much as Alira and Marcus loved each other. They rivaled even his parents.

"Austin? What are you doing here?" Marcus asked hoarsely. Austin shifted uncomfortably in the chair he had spent the night in and nodded toward Alira.

Marcus followed his brother's gaze. A head of dark hair rested on the edge of the bed. Her hair had fallen softly across her face, but he would have known her anywhere. Marcus's breath caught in his throat. He hadn't imagined it. She was there. Slowly, as if she would disappear before his eyes, Marcus raised his hand to her head. Gingerly, he touched her hair. Soft. So soft. When Alira stirred, Marcus pulled his hand away, suddenly nervous.

"Marcus."

Alira said his name in a breathy whisper as she lifted her head, bright blue eyes meeting his dark ones once again. Marcus released his breath. His hand lifted, seemingly on its own, to her face. Fingers traced softly along her jaw.

"You're real," Marcus said in disbelief. Alira leaned into his touch, holding his hand firmly against her cheek.

"I'm real."

The emotion Alira saw reflecting back at her in his eyes told her everything she needed to know. Cautiously, Alira allowed him to pull her into his arms. She was careful not to put her weight on him knowing the severity of his injury from his chart. Alira didn't try to hold back the tears. Wave after wave slid down her cheeks as Marcus held her tightly to his chest.

"I thought…" Marcus started but the words seemed to catch in his throat, stalling. He hugged Alira tightly despite the increasing ache in his side. Marcus feared letting her go – like she would disappear in a puff of smoke right before his eyes.

Austin stood to give them some privacy, but the door swung open just before he reached it. The entire Duvall family poured into the room, talking quietly until they spotted Marcus and the woman he was hugging tightly. Shocked silence filled the room before they all started talking at once. The noise quickly drawing attention from the hallway. Marcus barely heard the angry nurse demand they lower their voices or be escorted from the building by security.

Marcus didn't want to let Alira go. He knew he should, but when she made no attempts to move away from him, it was clear she had no intentions of leaving his embrace any time soon. His family could wait.

Chapter 22

So she searches for light, only to realize it's in her, like an ember equipped to ignite.
~Jessica Sorensen

"I am fine! How many times do I have to say it?" Marcus grumbled while his mother stuffed a pillow behind his back on the couch. The woman had insisted he put his feet up and rest while his brothers helped set up the patio for the dinner get-together that they did twice a year with their neighbors and friends.

"You have been out of the hospital for a week. Until your doctor clears you for normal activity, you will do as you're told and keep your butt planted on that couch! Do you understand me, young man?" Charlotte growled back at her surly son.

Marcus crossed his arms and pouted like a sullen teenager. Alira stood back watching her husband try to argue with his mother. The scene was incredibly amusing, and she couldn't help but laugh. Marcus turned his glare on her knowing that she would not argue with Charlotte. If anything, she encouraged it because while they were all so focused on Marcus and his recovery, nobody was asking her how she had survived the blast or what had happened once Karma had been released just a week before. She knew it was coming though. The questions that needed answers. The general public didn't know details except what had been in the papers and on all of the news channels.

Karma sat in her father's recliner watching Marcus deal with the same motherly madness she had just dealt with. As far as their family was concerned, they were invalids until the doctors said otherwise. Even Alira hadn't managed to escape the bubble despite having a clean bill of health from her doctor. The family still didn't know there would be a new Duvall coming soon and Karma couldn't wait for her mother's reaction to the news. Alira and Marcus had already told her they were telling everyone at dinner. It was going to be an event to be sure.

"I think it's time to tell us how you miraculously survived that blast," Aiden said seriously. He stared at Alira over the rim of his water glass waiting for a response. Several heads around the table nodded in agreement. Everyone had gone home, and the Duvall's were sitting around the patio table leaving cleanup for another day.

Alira sighed. Guess this was happening tonight. She had hoped it would wait or fade into a distant memory but that clearly was not going to work out in her favor. She shivered in the cool air. Marcus slid his arm around her shoulders, pulling her snugly against him.

"When I saw Karma, beaten, broken, I didn't really think about how things would go. My goal was to just get Greyson to let her leave. I couldn't worry about anything, anyone else. I don't know how I did it, but I managed to convince Greyson to let me take Karma to the doors. He stood behind one of the pillars in the lobby. He didn't notice when I came back and was slowly inching my way closer to the security office. Greyson was too busy listening to himself talk," Alira started. She paused to sip at her water suddenly feeling thirsty. Unwelcome memories of the events from that day danced through her mind. Sensing her unease, Marcus gently rubbed her arm. When Alira looked at him, he simply nodded for her to continue. She had already told him all of this, but they needed to hear it as well.

"When I bought the building, nobody knew the previous owner had been one of those ultra-paranoid apocalypse prepper types. So much so, he had a bomb shelter built inside. The security office had a hidden door that led into the shelter. The only other person who knew about it was the head of my building security, Harold. We never figured we would need something like that, so it was something we kept between us. Not even Harold's daughter knew about it," Alira continued.

Alira could feel their eyes on her. Their attention on her one hundred percent. Their intensity over listening to her story made her uneasy. As long as nobody shone a spotlight on her, she could make it through this retelling and never speak of it again as far as she was concerned. Her skin still crawled at the thought of Greyson being so close to her that day.

"The short version is that Greyson, to the end, thought he had won somehow and through all of his self-important chattering failed to see that I was getting away from him. When he finally connected the dots, I slammed the door of the security office in his face and locked it. I managed to get to the hidden door and through it before Greyson broke through the other door. The blast door had barely closed when he detonated the bomb. It was terrifying. I've never heard anything so loud in my life. I truly didn't think the shelter would hold but somehow it did. The mechanism on my side to open the escape door was damaged so I had no choice but to wait for help," Alira told them with finality.

She didn't want to re-live any of it. There was finally a future to be excited about. Greyson had died a death of his own making. All of her tenants had been cleared from the building well before anything happened. Once it was safe, rebuilding would commence. Alira had her assistants help relocate everyone who had been displaced. Anyone who wanted to move back into the apartment building once it was complete had head-of-the-line privileges to do so. Everyone had been taken care of while she and Marcus had moved into his house. Well, hers now too.

Thankfully, the section of the building Alira's apartment was in had had minimal damage. They had been allowed, with an escort, to retrieve her belongings. Marcus's brothers had all gone to pack up her apartment and deliver it to her. The only thing missing was her furniture which was not necessary at Marcus's house. Alira had been so grateful when the first box she had opened contained all of her pictures. Everything else could be replaced easily but pictures and mementos could not be. Those were all that she truly cared about getting back.

Karma whispered something to Marcus. Marcus nodded and leaned over to whisper in Alira's ear, startling her from her thoughts. Alira asked him to repeat what he said. His only response was a soft kiss to her temple before he rose from his seat beside her and disappeared into the house. It only took a second for Alira to understand what he had said. It became more obvious when he reappeared carrying the small yellow gift bag. Alira watched Austin, Karma, and William's eyes all shift quickly to Charlotte. She tried to hide her amusement.

"Here, mom. Alira and I got you a little something," Marcus told her as he plopped the bag down on the table in front of her before quickly moving back to sit beside Alira.

"You didn't have to do that! I have everything I could ever want!" Charlotte explained happily. Marcus winked at Alira as she gazed up at him. His arm slid around her waist, his fingers smoothly stroking the edge of her stomach as had become his habit recently. It was the only telling sign anything was different. That was until Charlotte opened that bag.

"Would you just open it already? Never known a woman to complain about getting a gift!" William ordered though the smile on his face said he was joking with her. Charlotte huffed and reached for the bag.

The entire Duvall clan leaned forward expectantly waiting to see what all the fuss was about. Marcus's grip tightened around Alira's waist as she leaned more heavily against him. Soaking in his warmth, she watched as Charlotte pulled a tissue paper-wrapped bundle out of the bag. Carefully she unfolded the paper. Charlotte lifted the cloth inside, the material unfolding to reveal a small soft green onesie.

Charlotte dropped the onesie in surprise. Marcus grinned.

"You're... I'm going to... Don't you dare play with my emotions!" Charlotte all but yelled at them.

"No way, dude! I'm going to be an Uncle?" Aiden and Adam said at the same time. This brought a round of laughter as the twins glared at each other. Clearly, age didn't matter. Twins would do what twins do.

Charlotte started talking faster than anyone could understand before jumping up and rushing around the table to hug them. Alira was all but squished between her husband and her mother-in-law, who was clearly so excited about becoming a grandmother that she couldn't contain herself. When the older woman jogged into the house, Alira stared after her wondering what on earth she was up to. She knew enough to know they would probably have several large packages on their doorstep by the end of the week.

"You do realize that woman is going to have everything you'll ever need for the nursery at your house in a matter of days, don't you?" William told them as though he had read her mind. Marcus nodded knowingly while his brothers patted him on the back and congratulated them enthusiastically. Alira simply smiled, said her thanks, and leaned into Marcus's side. She was worn out and more than ready to go home. They had an appointment on Monday afternoon to find out the sex of the baby as well as Alira's follow-up from the events from the previous week. Right now, Alira wanted nothing more than to curl up in bed with her wonderful husband and sleep the rest of the weekend away.

Alira rested her head against his shoulder and closed her eyes while he talked quietly with his brothers. Not a single word of their conversation slipped into her mind as her mind drifted to thoughts of the future. For the first time in forever, she absolutely couldn't wait to see it play out.

Epilogue

7 months later.

"Marcus, I love you but if you think I'm getting off this couch right now, you have absolutely lost your mind," Alira growled at her husband. Marcus laughed and sat down with her. Alira lifted her feet to rest in his lap while she leaned back with her hand resting on her rounded stomach. Gently, Marcus began massaging her feet, running his fingers along her arches working out the soreness he knew was there.

Alira groaned. His hands were like magic working on her aching feet. She felt like she was all belly and not much else. The increasing aches from the extra weight she was carrying made her cranky too. Marcus had been nothing but the loving and doting father to be. Alira really couldn't have asked for a better partner in this adventure.

As the day progressed, her back hurt more and more, but they had promised to be at the Duvall's ranch for dinner and so here they were. Planted on the couch waiting for dinner. Alira had protested loudly when Marcus suggested they cancel and stay home instead. Sure, she knew nobody would have a problem with it, but they had committed to going. Backing out last minute would have been rude. As per usual, upon their arrival, Marcus had rushed around the truck to help Alira get out and escorted her out to see her horse. Zoe, true to her personality, had pinned her ears back and attempted to bite him but she'd turned into a big mush when Alira began speaking to her. Marcus just shook his head and moved to sit in the weathered chair under the nearby tree. As soon as she was finished talking to her horse, Marcus had scooped her up to carry her into the house against her protests. Thus, how she had wound up on the couch grumbling at her husband about moving unnecessarily.

"You know that I will bring you a plate if that's what you want. I promise I will not make you get off the couch if you are comfortable,"

Marcus told her sweetly as he continued rubbing her feet in the most perfect way. Alira's head fell back against the couch as his fingers worked their magic.

Marcus couldn't help watching Alira. He was the luckiest man on the planet to be married to the most beautiful woman to ever walk the earth. Even when Alira felt miserably uncomfortable, she hid it well with a bright smile on her face.

Alira adjusted her position on the couch, hoping the shift would help the painful pulling in her lower back. She had been experiencing Braxton hicks all day and no amount of water seemed to help chase them away. As the afternoon progressed, that pulling spread out across her belly. Alira figured she was in early labor but hadn't told Marcus. He would only worry over her more. She was content to suffer in silence, well mostly, until it was definitely time to go. There was no denying that there had been conversations speculating over his reaction when it was go-time. They were about to find out.

"What is it?" Marcus asked suddenly. Alira's eyes had gone wide.

"I... think my water just broke," she said peering over her belly. Marcus's hands stilled. Alira looked up at him in time to watch the play of emotions cross his face.

"Mom! We're heading to the hospital!" he yelled through the house.

It sounded like a herd of horses was coming their way as people from various parts of the house were converging on the living room. Excited voices filled the large room as Marcus jumped to his feet.

Alira struggled to sit up before she could stand. She was amused over the panicked look her husband wore as he seemed to struggle with the next steps. Karma helped pull Alira to her feet while Marcus started pacing. It was like watching an expectant father in a movie. He patted his back pocket for his wallet and started for the door only to realize he needed his keys. Marcus backtracked to the keys bowl on the kitchen counter before starting for the door again. When he turned back a third time, Alira stepped in front of him. She stopped his forward movement with a hand against his chest. Marcus's hand covered hers and he smiled down at her.

"There you are," Alira said softly when she saw his focus shift and his panic ease away.

"I'm sorry. I got lost there for a minute," he apologized quietly.

Alira shook her head and lifted up on her tiptoes to press her lips against his. He relaxed instantly. It was an easy kiss. Undemanding in its message but it was enough. It also helped to distract her from a contraction that was presently tightening her belly with increasing discomfort.

"We'll meet you there," William, Marcus's father told them from his post near the stairs. Marcus nodded. They already had a plan. Austin and Karma would stop at the house to pick up the bag that sat just inside the front door. It had been packed for a few weeks, waiting and ready to go.

"You ready to have a baby?" Marcus asked her excitedly.

"Let's go meet our son," Alira said with a smile and her hand still on his chest. Marcus smiled and Alira swore she could hear hearts breaking all over the world because the devastatingly handsome man standing before her was all hers. Her whole world held her heart protectively in his hands and she couldn't imagine anything more amazing.

Well, maybe there was one person more amazing, and she couldn't wait to meet him!

A note from Krystal

When I began writing Unchained Embers, I had just finished Caged Jewel and had tentatively published that to amazon to get my feet wet. I had no idea when I started Unchained Embers where it would go. Honestly, I knew the basics because it was one of those stories running wild in my head, but I didn't expect Alira to come out as this amazing kick butt chick after everything I put her through.

As I brought these characters to life, I realized there was a fire in Alira waiting for the right conditions to ignite it and burn bright as it always should have done. I wanted to free her from those chains she had been born into and feed the embers inside her until this amazing Phoenix-like character could burst forth and claim what was rightfully hers.

I sincerely hope you enjoyed Unchained Embers!

Krystal Zoppa

Norfolk, VA

www.Facebook.com/KrystalZoppaAuthor

About the Author

Krystal is a wife and mother who writes in her spare time. When she isn't writing, you can usually find her out training with her dogs, binge watching a favorite TV show, curled up with a good book and refusing to take life too seriously because it wouldn't be any fun otherwise. She currently lives in Norfolk, VA with her husband, kids and their zoo of dogs, cats and fish.

www.Facebook.com/KrystalZoppaAuthor

Goodreads: KrystalZoppa

Acknowledgments

I want to take a quick moment to thank my family for supporting me in my literary adventures be it reading or writing them. I also want to acknowledge and thank YOU, my readers for taking the leap into a story I've written. I hope I can continue to write more and that you continue to enjoy them. THANK YOU!

Thanks for reading!

Please add a review on Amazon and let me know what you thought! *Or the avenue in which you purchased this book!*

Amazon reviews are extremely helpful for authors. Thank you for taking the time to support me and my work. Don't forget to share your review on social media with the hashtag #UnchainedEmbers and encourage others to read the story too!

You can also find me on Goodreads!